A
Little
in Love

ABOUT THE AUTHOR

Florence Keeling LOVES weddings. She married the man she met when she was four months old, and twenty-one years of married bliss later, they are still VERY much in love. Her love of stories started with *Mr Men* and *Topsy and Tim*; she longed to attend Cackle's Academy and spend days sharing adventures with the *Famous Five*. As an adult, she wrangles two grown-up kids, two mad huskies and three day jobs. *A Little in Love* is her third work of fiction. Follow her on Twitter at @KeelingFlorence.

www.SimonandSchuster.co.uk/Authors/
Florence-Keeling

FLORENCE KEELING

A Little in Love

**SIMON &
SCHUSTER**

London · New York · Sydney · Toronto · New Delhi

First published in Great Britain by Simon & Schuster UK Ltd, 2021
This paperback edition published in 2023

1 3 5 7 9 10 8 6 4 2

Simon & Schuster UK Ltd
1st Floor
222 Gray's Inn Road
London WC1X 8HB

Simon & Schuster Australia, Sydney
Simon & Schuster India, New Delhi

www.simonandschuster.co.uk
www.simonandschuster.com.au
www.simonandschuster.co.in

A CIP catalogue record for this book
is available from the British Library

Paperback ISBN: 978-1-3985-1782-0
eBook ISBN: 978-1-3985-0381-6

Typeset in Bembo by M Rules
Printed and Bound in the UK using 100% Renewable
Electricity at CPI Group (UK) Ltd

To Anna and Kim,
for their never-ending faith,
support and encouragement

CHAPTER ONE

For what felt like the hundredth time that morning, and the millionth time that week, Rose went through her written and mental checklists.

'Are you sure you don't want me to drive you?' Her dad stepped out of the back door and into the garden, shielding his eyes from the bright glare. After what felt like months of rainfall, the sun Rose had been praying for had finally arrived. 'We can take the minibus – no one's using it today. The bike will fit perfectly between the seats.'

'Honestly, Dad, it's fine.' She kissed him on the cheek. 'It kind of defeats the object of being environmentally friendly if I arrive in a diesel-guzzling minibus.'

'I see your point.' He fiddled with the dog collar around his neck. 'You'd think after thirty years I'd be used to this by now.' Her father smiled. 'Those first five minutes of wearing it, I always feel like it's choking me.'

Rose's father, the Reverend John Pedal, was the minister at St Michael's church, which served the small population of Tointon, the tiny village where Rose and her family lived. It was a beautifully quaint old church: grey stone and a spectacular pointed steeple with a clock on each of its four faces. The steeple still held a bell and rope, but this was only used on special occasions such as weddings or Christmas; a recording was used for 'less important times' as her father had told her when she'd asked at the age of five.

'Don't forget this.' Rose's mum Janet came rushing out of the door, waving a crocheted cream bag decorated with yellow roses. The bag had been handmade by Rose's grandmother on her mother's side, and Rose was currently using it to carry her new business cards. 'I took the liberty of bringing these down as well.' She handed Rose a small cardboard box.

'Thanks, Mum, I'd forget my head if it wasn't screwed on.' Opening the box, Rose pulled out the pale pink business cards. She'd spent hours designing these a few weeks ago and smiled with pride at them. It was only right they looked this good considering the cost – but she pushed that thought to one side.

They proudly displayed the name of her new business – Pedals and Prosecco – in a sweeping arch over an old-fashioned bike with a bottle of fizz in the wicker basket, its cork bursting open and heart-shaped bubbles spraying onto the card.

'Your dad and I are so happy for you,' her mum said, placing an affectionate arm around her husband and slapping his hand away from his dog collar. 'We always told you that you'd find your way, and here you are with your very own business.'

'Not quite a business yet.' Rose knew her parents were a little disappointed in the decisions she'd made but they would never say it or even imply it. Dropping out of university at the age of twenty had never exactly been the plan – she blamed Meghan Markle and the impeccably dressed cast of *Suits* for her misguided interest in pursuing a law degree. Oh, she did love a man in a suit. There was just something about a tailored jacket and clean crisp lines that turned her insides to jelly.

Rose had spent many, many hours agonizing over her decision to leave. Was it just the course or the whole university thing that she hadn't got on with? In the end, she'd realized that a university life just wasn't for her. She missed her family. Her whole life, she'd only been apart from them on the odd occasion, and she knew that her future plans would never take her far away from them again.

She'd told her parents she wanted to leave over Christmas break of her second year. Her mum had tried to persuade her to stay – 'But you were so excited to start. Isn't there another degree you could do instead?' – but after a while, although they were a little sad, her parents had agreed that if she wasn't happy then of course she shouldn't stay.

Although finally making a decision had come as a relief, it left her with a huge student debt. Eventually she would need to repay the loan she'd taken out for her tuition fees, plus the money her mum and dad had given her over those eighteen months to help supplement the small maintenance grant she'd received from the government to help pay for her rent and food. She knew her parents didn't want it back, but she also knew that they weren't the wealthiest of people and that every penny counted.

Within weeks of leaving university, Rose had found herself a part-time job with Mr Booth, who owned the small off-licence next to the chip shop in Tointon. The shop was never busy and Mr Booth often complained about the big supermarkets taking his business with their bulk-buy deals. But his knowledge of wine was impeccable, and Rose soon learned the difference between a cheap bottle of red and an expensive claret.

'If you're going to sell wine then you need to know what you're talking about,' Mr Booth had said to her on her very first day. 'It's all well and good picking up a bottle for a fiver, but for a tenner you get so much more depth and flavour. You need to be able to sell the customer the best wine they can afford with their budget.'

This had given Rose the idea of a monthly wine tasting event and loyalty card. These had taken off instantly and by the end of that year she'd been working full-time allowing Mr Booth to semi-retire, content to leave the business in her hands. They'd even talked about the possibility of taking on another employee in the spring.

Then, one rainy April morning, Rose had arrived for work to find a sign stuck to the outside of the shutters saying 'Closed due to family bereavement' and a brand-new shiny padlock in place of the rusty old one she used. Eventually, Mr Booth's son had called her to explain they'd lost his mother, and that his father had taken it very badly and would not be returning to the shop. Rose had offered to manage the business on their behalf, but two weeks later a 'for sale' sign had gone up, and by the autumn the off-licence was a Subway store.

Rose hadn't known how to tell her parents at first. Mrs Booth had been a valued member of the congregation, so they were aware of her passing, but they hadn't realized it had cost their daughter her job, and Rose quickly set about looking for another. Luckily, the supermarket a few miles away was hiring, but this meant getting a car and insurance, and half of her savings were gone in an instant. It was part-time hours only though, which meant she was able to help her mum and dad out around the church and vicarage.

It was as she was helping her dad change the posters on the church notice board in January the following year that she'd had the idea for Pedals and Prosecco. A new poster had come in, announcing the launch of a new wedding fayre to be held on the first Saturday of every month from May to September in the nearby village of Weddington. Rose loved weddings. Since she was a small child, she'd attended every wedding she could at St Michael's.

She loved watching the grooms arrive first, seeing if they were nervous or playing it cool. Watching their mothers or sisters straightening ties or flattening stray curls with spit-wet hands. The array of bridesmaid's dresses she had seen over the years was countless; her very favourite was a delightful lilac colour, off one shoulder, falling to the ground in a little puddle, with a dark purple ribbon around the waist.

But the best bit for Rose was always the arrival of the bride. From horse-drawn carriages to Rolls-Royces, and even a moped once, the brides always arrived in style. She had never seen the same dress twice, and marvelled at how designers came up with such an array of different looks.

So it suddenly seemed blindingly obvious to Rose, as she pinned the flyer to the green felt of the notice board, that she should do something with her life that involved weddings.

That evening, before tea, she sat in her bedroom at the front of the vicarage with a pen and notebook and jotted down a few ideas before FaceTiming her best friend Megan.

'Cakes?' Rose suggested first, to which Megan immediately burst into laughter.

'Slight problem with that,' she'd replied. 'You burn everything.'

'Flowers?'

'You need to train for that.'

'Wedding planner?' Megan laughed even harder and shook her head. Rose couldn't help but be a little hurt. 'I'll have you know I planned all the events at the off-licence.'

'Planning a wedding is a little different to a piss-up in a wine shop.' Megan paused, taking a sip of wine, then asked, 'What are you good at?'

'Absolutely nothing by the look of it.' Rose watched as

Megan took another sip. 'Wine!' she screamed. 'That's what I'm good at.'

She'd ended the chat with Megan, excited that she'd finally managed to find the perfect idea, but how to make it stand out? There was nothing original about serving wine at a wedding; she needed something different, something fresh and new.

It was only after dinner, when Janet brought out a tub of ice cream and placed it on the table next to a steaming hot apple pie, that Rose landed on an idea. Nibbling pensively at her dessert, she was reminded of a summer event at university, at which ice cream cones had been served from a vintage bike.

'That's it!' she'd screamed, much to her parents' amusement.

And Pedals and Prosecco was born.

She'd scoured the internet looking for an old-fashioned bike and suitable trailer. Her dad had helped her paint it and fashion a trailer out of a rather large wicker basket with a smaller basket at the front. She'd bought a folding parasol and attached straps to the inside of the basket to allow her to safely store a few glass bottles for transit, but she would have to rely on the venues for glasses and extra storage if the event was a larger one. There just wasn't the room to transport hundreds of glasses safely. And anyway, Megan had said, it's the gimmick they're buying, not the actual product. The top of the trailer then became the serving table.

'Explain to me how it all works again?' John asked, as

Rose was just about to head out of the garden gate and travel the mile or so to her first wedding fayre.

'The couple rent me, so to speak.' This was the only way she could think of to describe it. 'I park the bike inside, or outside, wherever they want, and then serve the welcoming drink of Prosecco to the guests as they arrive for the wedding breakfast.'

'I think it's such a lovely idea.' Janet clapped her hands together. 'You could have a whole fleet of bikes, even become international.'

'Let's not get carried away, Mum.' Rose unlocked the bolt on the gate. 'This is my first fayre – I haven't even got a booking yet.'

'Oh, you will,' her mum said knowingly. 'Pedals and Prosecco is going to be huge.' Rose smiled at her mum's enthusiasm, and hoped she would be proved right. Rose's savings had now been almost entirely depleted, and she'd even had to dip into the money her grandparents had saved for her since she was born.

They'd proudly handed her a bank book on her twenty-first birthday with the express wish that it be put towards buying a property in the future. Even though Rose had no desire to leave her parents' house any time soon – she loved living at home – the guilt she felt at dipping into this fund was immense, and she knew she'd be putting it back as soon as she could.

But it wasn't just for financial reasons that Rose needed Pedals and Prosecco to succeed. Thanks to nerves she'd barely passed her GCSEs, and had only got on to her university degree through clearing, since she hadn't obtained the grades she'd needed for her first and second choices. It was a running joke that she'd failed her theory test three times and her practical driving test four times. She just didn't cope well under pressure – another reason that university hadn't been for her.

She just couldn't have another failure on her hands.

As Rose made her way into Weddington, she started to regret turning down the offer of a lift. She'd completely forgotten how many hills there were on this road, and they all seemed to be much steeper going up than coming down. She was becoming acutely aware that her painstakingly straightened hair, which she'd spent over an hour on this morning, was beginning to revert back to its usual frizz.

She breathed a sigh of relief when she finally saw the sign for Weddington Hall: the stately home where the wedding fayre was taking place was only three hundred yards away, and she decided to take five minutes on the side of the road to catch her breath and try to smooth her hair again. Pulling her phone out of the front basket, she gave herself a quick appraisal in the screen.

Not too bad, she judged, and reapplied her pale pink lipstick, wiping a stray blob of mascara from under her eye. Making sure everything was still firmly attached to the bike, she stepped back into the road.

The sound of a frantic horn startled her, and she swore

profusely in a rather unladylike manner as a dark green van with gold porthole windows swerved past, splashing a huge puddle of water all over her in what could only be described as a *Bridget Jones* moment.

'You have got to be kidding me!' she screamed after the van, which had already disappeared, and she stuck two fingers up as well for good measure. She climbed back onto the seat of the bike with a squelch and prayed she'd be able to dry herself off with one of the hand dryers in the toilets, thanking her lucky stars that the apron she was using as part of her uniform was rather large and tucked safely away in the basket.

She cycled along the road and turned left onto the long sweeping drive of Weddington Hall. She'd visited the house many times over the years, but it had only recently started to be used as a wedding venue after it featured in last summer's big blockbuster romance movie, *A Little in Love*, starring Jenny Golding and Mitch Maddens. Rose had even been lucky enough to get their autographs and a selfie when they'd been filming one day.

The hall stood in the distance, its red-brick walls glowing in the sun. Elegance and wealth oozed from the leaded windows and Rose wished, not for the first time, that she had been born in a different era, when balls were the norm and gentlemen politely requested a dance or a turn around the garden. When people rode on horses and bid each other good day as they passed by.

Cars and vans of every shape and size were having their

wares unloaded, and people were carrying tables, manne-quins and boxes in through the double oak doors. Rose loved the ornate hall through those doors, but she had asked whether, as long as the day was dry, she could set up by the entrance, as she would at an actual wedding.

She parked the bike on the beautiful green lawn that lay to the right of the house and headed inside with her bag to change into her shoes and apron, and sort her hair and dress out as best she could.

Luckily the ladies' toilets still had the older style of dryer with a funnel that turned, rather than one of the newfangled things that you put your hands into, so she was able to dry her dress a little, which, once her apron was on, looked at least presentable. Her hair on the other hand, was another matter, and all she could do was scrape it into a high ponytail.

Nodding at her reflection, she headed back out into the sunshine and stood by her bike, waiting for everyone else to head inside before she started to set up. It was almost eleven o'clock and the fayre was due to start at half past. She knew she only needed about fifteen minutes to get everything ready and smiled in anticipation when she realized no one had come in or out for the past five minutes and all the vehicles had now been moved into the car park at the rear. This meant she could get set up without being in anybody else's way.

'Here we go then.' She kicked the stand from the bike and wheeled it into position, stepping away a few times and look-ing at it from different perspectives to ensure it was looking its absolute best. The hand-painted 'Pedals & Prosecco' sign fitted between the frame of the bike as if it had been made for it, and the parasol matched the colours to perfection. Even her apron was the same pale pink, with the company name embroidered across her chest.

She tutted to herself as she heard a van approaching, knowing that visitors had been instructed to park in the front car park and walk up the drive so as not to obscure the view of the hall.

'Is this where the wedding fayre is?' a male voice shouted. 'I went to the castle by accident.' Rose turned to assure the driver that he was indeed in the correct place, but her pleasant smile quickly soured as a dark green van with gold porthole windows started reversing towards her.

CHAPTER TWO

Rose could feel the anger bubbling up inside her. Hadn't he recognized her? Did he make a habit of soaking people with puddles and just driving on as if nothing had happened? She was more than ready to give him an earful – but then she realized that the van wasn't stopping. It came closer and closer with no sign of slowing down.

'Stop!' she screamed at the top of her voice. It was only a few feet away now. 'Please stop!' she screamed again, and banged frantically on the doors, seeing visions of her bike lying crushed under the wheels of the van.

But the van carried on and Rose stepped out of the way, turning her face and waiting for the crunching sound of her bike being smashed. But it didn't come. In fact, there was suddenly no sound. The engine was off.

She risked a peek and released the breath she hadn't realized she'd been holding, thanking the heavens that her bike was still intact. It had a green van right in front of it – in fact, it was so close the front basket was actually touching the doors – but it was intact. She heard the van door open and her relief turned to anger once more.

'What the hell do you think you're doing?' She marched towards the open door, the gravel crunching angrily beneath her feet. 'You need to take your test again, mate.'

'Calm down, love.' A tall man, smartly dressed in a dark green suit, stepped out. 'What's all the fuss?'

'All the fuss?' Rose gaped. 'All the fuss?' She stood in front of him, kinking her neck to the side so she could actually see his face instead of talking to his chin. She wasn't small – five foot eight inches in her heels – but this man stood a good six inches above her. 'You almost ran me over a few minutes ago on the road and bloody soaked me from head to toe and then—'

'Was that you?' His calm demeanour suddenly changed. 'You stepped out into the road! What was I meant to do?' He turned away, closed the van door and walked past her towards the back.

'Don't you dare walk away from me!' Rose marched past him, fully intending to get in front of him. 'Not only did you drive on without a bloody care, didn't even check to see I was okay, but then you swan in here, late I might add, and nearly drive over my bike.'

'Who the hell parks a bike there?' He tutted, grabbed her bike by the handlebars and started to push it out of the way.

'What do you think you're doing?' She grabbed the saddle and stood firm against him. 'You just leave that right where it is.' She dug her heels into the gravel.

'I need to unload.' He shoved the bike, not harshly but enough that she had to step back a little. 'I'm already late and I need to get set up.'

'Well, you should have been on time then.' She pushed the bike back.

'I would have been' – he pushed again – 'if I hadn't been distracted by some silly girl stepping into the road and missed my turning.'

'Don't blame me!' She looked at him with what she hoped was a fierce stare and couldn't help but notice how incredibly green his eyes were, almost emerald in fact. She shook her head, telling herself off. She shouldn't be thinking about his eyes, even if they were perfectly set in his face with a remarkably straight nose and delicately tinted pink lips.

'Is something the matter?' A smartly dressed lady was watching them from the doorway of the hall, clutching a clipboard in concern.

'Yes!' Rose said, turning back to the man. 'This buffoon here thinks it's okay to run people off the road and then reverse into their stand.'

'Buffoon?' he scoffed. 'What century are you living in?'

'I happen to believe that swearing shows a poor vocabulary.' She decided not to mention that she lived with her father, the vicar, and that swearing was banned in their house.

'Hark at little Miss Prim and Proper here.' He looked down at the bike. 'What do you mean by stand?'

'Well ... er ... if you could both just ... er ...' It was clear the lady with the clipboard wasn't used to confrontation. She pushed her half-moon spectacles back up her nose. 'If you could just move away from the doors a little, sir, and unpack before the public start to arrive, then that would be most helpful.' She turned to Rose. 'Is the bike okay?'

'It's fine, thank you.' Rose jerked her bike out of the man's hands. 'No thanks to some people.'

'Why are you out here anyway?' he asked, as the clipboard lady hurried back inside.

'I'm allowed to be out here.' Rose didn't feel like she had to explain, but did anyway. 'It's my business: Pedals and Prosecco. I serve welcome drinks to the guests as they arrive.'

'So, you'll be the first business anyone sees?' She could hear the cogs in his brain working, and didn't like the sound. 'Well, if you can be out here, then so can I.'

And with that he jumped back into his van, started the engine, and in a flash had parked it on the opposite side to Rose's bike. Now she could see the word 'Blume's' on the side of the van, written in exquisite gold calligraphy. She watched with anger – and just a touch of jealousy – as he slid half of the van's side panel away to reveal what could only be described as a garden. Flowers in every colour and arrangement she could think of appeared to be on display inside.

Within minutes, there was a table set up outside, covered with a green and gold tablecloth, to which the man swiftly added centrepieces, vases, bouquets and even buttonholes. A sandwich board had also magically appeared proclaiming: 'Blume's Florist – from the city to your heart'.

'Bloody city boy!' she mumbled under her breath,

mentally apologizing to her dad as she did. 'You can't set up there!' she called to the man.

'Why not?' he shot back. 'You have.'

'I have special permission.' She was about to head into the hall and find someone official, but hearing approaching footsteps, she turned and saw that people were starting to arrive.

She took one last look at the bike, rearranged her apron and stood to the side of the front wheel, plastering a smile on her face and trying to ignore the fact that, even though her stand was closer to the path, most people headed straight over to the green van and its handsome owner.

After three hours, Rose's face was aching from smiling and talking. The numbers of people arriving had dwindled as closing time approached. She felt quite proud of herself: she'd chatted enthusiastically, handed out business cards and had even managed to provisionally book two weddings for September.

'Well, I wasn't expecting that many people.' The flower man was standing in front of her. 'First time fayres are normally a bit rubbish, if I'm honest with you.'

'It's because of the film,' she said shortly. She really didn't feel like being friendly with him.

'We got off to a bit of a shit start.' He held out a hand towards her. 'James Blume.'

She paused for the briefest of seconds before shaking his hand. 'Rose.'

'Explain this to me a bit more then.' He seemed genuinely interested as he picked up a business card and listened to Rose chatter on about the ins and outs of her business.

'All amazingly simple to be honest,' she finished. Perhaps she'd had him all wrong. Maybe it hadn't been his fault at all; perhaps she really had just stepped into the road. Come to think of it, she didn't remember looking – she'd been too preoccupied with getting to the fayre.

'I think it's really good.' He smiled at her. She tried to ignore the feeling she got in her knees at the sight of that smile. 'Really original, should take off.' He ran a hand through his dark hair, and it sprang straight back into its quiffed position.

'How long have you been in the flower business then?' she asked. Suddenly, he seemed a lot more interesting than he had five minutes ago.

'Blume's has been going for years and years,' he said with pride. 'My dad's dad started the business, and now it's passed on to me.'

'Ah, here she is.' Rose and James both turned to see a short man, dressed in the same uniform as the lady with the clipboard, coming towards them from the hall, accompanied by a young woman and an older lady. 'I knew she'd still be here. Miss Pedal will be happy to help you with any information you need.'

'I didn't know you were out here,' the younger of the two ladies said. 'I heard someone talking about you inside and I said to Mum that it sounded perfect for the garden party we're having later next month.'

'Well, I hadn't thought about doing parties, but yes, that would be absolutely fine.' Rose handed her a business card and price list, briefly discussed their requirements and told them she would be in touch with a full quote, all the while trying not to notice the giggle that James was clearly trying to hold in.

After the two ladies were out of earshot, he could contain it no longer and burst out laughing.

'And what, may I ask, is so funny?' She knew exactly what it was: everyone who heard her name for the first time thought it was hilarious.

'Pedal,' he said through his laughter. 'Rose Pedal. Your name is Rose Pedal.'

'Yes, I know my name.' She started to pack the things back into the bike.

'I thought it was Pedals and Prosecco because of the bike.' He was still laughing.

'It's both.' She angrily undid her apron, pulling at the knot, which unfortunately made it tighten even more. 'Bastard thing.'

'I thought you didn't swear,' he said, the laughter subsiding slightly.

'Let's just say you bring out the worst in me.' She pulled again at the knot before giving up completely and just pulling it over her head.

'I'm sorry.' He smiled. 'But you have to admit, it's a funny name.'

'It is not a funny name,' she retorted. 'It's just a name.'

'Hey, I've had a thought.' She paused in her packing for a moment. 'If we got married, you'd be Rose Blume.' The laughter returned, this time worse than before. Rose ignored him and continued with her packing.

By the time she'd finished, he was still laughing and had had to sit himself down on the floor.

'I'd like to say it's been a pleasure meeting you,' she said, kicking the bike's stand up and wheeling it a little way, 'but it really hasn't.' She placed one foot on the pedal and hooked her other leg over the saddle in what she hoped was an elegant and dismissive manner. 'Do enjoy the rest of your day, won't you?' And with that, she cycled down the drive, swerving to miss the vans that were now reappearing and beeping angrily at her. 'And you can fuck off too.'

CHAPTER THREE

'Honestly, I have never met such a rude man in all my life.' Rose was marching round her bedroom. Megan had come over that evening for tea and to hear all about how the fayre had gone. 'He was so up himself. Setting up his pitch right next to mine with his perfect bloody van and perfect bloody sign and perfect bloody flowers.'

'Lots of bloodies in there,' Megan remarked. 'Sure you don't fancy him just a little?'

'I certainly do not,' Rose protested rather too quickly, and Megan smiled knowingly. 'And you can wipe that smirk off your face, missus.'

'Oh, come off it, Rose,' Megan laughed. 'I've known you since you were four years old. I know every look that beautiful face can produce and I certainly know when you fancy someone.'

'He has nice eyes,' Rose admitted. 'And his hair suits him.' She looked over at Megan, who was trying hard to hide that she was currently searching Facebook.

'What did you say his name was? James Blume was it?'

'Don't you dare!' It was only now that Rose realized it was her phone in Megan's hand, her Facebook that she was using.

'Yes, he is a bit of a dish, isn't he?' Megan clicked 'add friend'. 'Let's see how long it is before he accepts.'

'I can't believe you just did that.' Rose snatched back her phone and went to undo the request. 'Shit me!' She put her hand to her mouth, hoping her dad wasn't in his office next door. She really was doing a lot of swearing today.

'What?' Megan was behind her, looking over her shoulder. 'Ha ha!' She slapped Rose gently on the back. 'Already accepted it. You made an impression on him, that's for sure.'

'He's messaged me.' She threw the phone onto the bed as if it was hot.

'Right, got to play it cool.' Megan picked up the phone and placed it in her pocket. 'We're not reading it yet, and we are certainly not replying yet.'

'Rose! Megan! Dinner's on the table,' Janet called up the stairs.

'And that's a perfect excuse.' She opened the bedroom door and ushered Rose out, who suddenly seemed to have lost all ability to speak and function normally.

'I think using the bike at parties is an excellent idea,' John said after he'd asked her to explain everything that had happened that day for the fifth time. She had of course omitted any mention of James. 'It opens up a whole world of possibilities.'

'Summer parties, engagements, hen parties,' her mum piped in. 'It's just endless.'

'You're forgetting one thing though.' Rose loved that her parents were so enthusiastic, but they didn't see the whole picture. 'I'd need another bike, which means more money and another person to serve from it. I've got two provisional bookings only, haven't even done a party or a wedding yet.'

'I can help if you want.' Megan reached for another slice of homemade fruit cake. 'Mrs P, your fruit cake is just divine. No wonder you win first prize every year at the fete.'

'Thank you, dear.' Janet smiled. 'And what about that party? You said the young lady seemed very keen.'

'She was.' Rose didn't know why she wasn't happy. Her first fayre had gone well; she'd 'networked', as Megan put it, and at the very least had spread the word about her business. 'I need to work on her quote this evening so I can email her tomorrow.'

'Did anyone actually hear me?' Megan spoke through mouthfuls of cake. 'I said I can help.'

'What do you mean you can help?' Rose turned to her. 'With what?'

'With the business.' She picked up a stray sultana and popped it in her mouth. 'I don't work weekends; we get another bike sorted and Bob's your uncle.'

'You? Help with the business?' Rose tried not to laugh.

'And why not?' Megan's smile disappeared.

'Remember our lemonade stand?'

'We were five.'

'The flower shop?'

'How was I to know that lily pollen stained?' Megan complained. 'Silly woman made my mum pay for a new dress.'

'When we sold cakes?'

'The recipe should have been clearer,' Megan protested. 'How was I to know a "tsp" of salt was a teaspoon and not a tablespoon?'

'Oh goodness me, I remember those cakes,' John said. 'They were so salty I drank nothing but water for a week.'

'Yes, well,' Megan mumbled, 'we were very young.'

'And who could forget the charity kissing booth at sixth form?'

'Yes, okay, I understand the whole point was for people to pay to kiss us and not for me to use the money to get Johnny Castle to kiss me but ... I'm an adult now with a job,' Megan reminded them. 'And it's not like I'd be doing any of the business stuff – you'd do the quotes and all that malarkey – I'm just offering to help out with the serving. Even I can pour drinks.'

'I return to the lemonade stand,' Rose remarked.

'This is the problem with knowing someone since you were little.' Megan stuck her tongue out playfully. 'They remember all your indiscretions.'

'Anyway, I think we're running before we can walk here.' It wasn't that Rose didn't appreciate Megan's offer, but she wanted to do it herself, at least to start with. She just needed to prove to the world, her parents, but mostly to herself that she was good at something. That finally she could be a success and actually have a career. 'I haven't even got two parties booked at the same time or even on the same day.'

'But if you do, at least you'll be prepared.' She shrugged her shoulders. 'I don't mind either way, but I'm just saying, you don't want to have to turn down business.'

'Megan has a point.' Her dad waved a butter knife as he spoke. 'You know it took a while to find the right bike and get it ready. You were still working at the supermarket then but we're heading into wedding season now and I won't have as much time on my hands to help out.'

So, without even saying yes, Rose found herself sitting at the table while her parents and Megan searched the internet for a suitable bike. The expansion of Pedals and Prosecco had begun.

It was almost ten thirty before Megan left, handing Rose her phone back as she did, the message from James completely forgotten after hours of chatting. Not one of them had realized that Rose had hardly said a word since dinner. With her parents and Megan discussing plans to expand her business, Rose couldn't help but feel pushed aside, and she'd made the decision to tell them all kindly in the morning that, for now, she just wanted to be a one-woman show.

Grabbing her calculator, price list, diary and pen, she headed into her room, put Tori Amos on the Alexa and sat at her desk. She jotted down the number of guests for the party she was quoting for, and worked out a costing with and without the supply of glasses, although where she'd store all the champagne flutes was yet to be discovered.

As she was working, her phone pinged. The notification from James was still there but she swiped past it and read her new email, smiling when she saw it was a request for a wedding in August from a couple who had picked up her card at the fayre. She pencilled the date into her diary and immediately replied with a yes, she was free that day and please could she have numbers and a location to provide a full quote.

Rose drafted her email about the party to the young lady, who, judging by her email address, was called Ruth. Then she got washed and ready for bed, saying goodnight to her dad who was, as usual, working on his Sunday sermon in his office. Rose knew he would be there till the early hours and that her mum would finally make him go to bed around 3am.

Grabbing the paperback by her bed, she snuggled down, eager to find out what was coming next for the characters, but before she could dive in, her phone lit up. Glancing over, she quickly wished she hadn't, because there was another message from James.

She mentally told herself to ignore it and went back to the book, but she couldn't concentrate and found she was reading and rereading the same paragraph over and over without actually taking in a word.

'Damn and blast it.' *Stop with the swearing,* she told herself, before picking up the phone and clicking on the message.

Hi, the first one began. *I'm really sorry for today. I shouldn't have laughed at your name. After all, my family has made a living from our name being like bloom. Hope to see you at the next fayre. James.*

Perhaps she had got him wrong. He needn't have messaged her to apologize, didn't even have to accept the friend request. Maybe she could just message back and say thank you, would be nice to see you. Is that how she should respond, or did it sound too eager? She hadn't dated since university (not that James was asking her on a date!). There'd been plenty of offers, but she really struggled to believe that any of them were looking for something genuine. The same old corny chat-up lines just reminded her over and over of her previous boyfriend, and she really didn't need reminding of him.

The relationship hadn't ended well at all. She'd met Bryan at university; he was studying physiotherapy and worked in the student union to top up his grant. Rose and her friends ... well, they weren't really friends. She hadn't kept in touch with any of them since she'd dropped out and not one had ever messaged to ask how she was. They were connected on Facebook and she could see they'd all graduated with honours and were starting high-flying careers, and Rose was happy for them, but it wasn't what she'd wanted.

One night, not long after fresher's week, Rose and her so-called 'friends' had headed into the student union after a long day of lectures to celebrate a birthday, and when it was Rose's round, she'd found herself chatting with Bryan at the bar rather than heading back to the group. He was gorgeous and he knew it. Tanned, taut muscles under a tight white

T-shirt, and she could only assume his legs and butt were just as toned underneath his jeans. He had a smile that could melt the frostiest of hearts, and his eyes were like chocolate: dark and rich.

Being a vicar's daughter, Rose really wasn't used to drinking heavily and was already slightly squiffy as Bryan poured her yet another shot of Apple Sourz.

'Are you trying to get me drunk?' she'd slurred in her most alluring way.

'Is it working?' He poured her another, which she downed in a second.

'It is.'

The next morning, she'd found herself naked in his bed, her clothes mixed with his on the floor and his arm draped possessively over her breasts.

'Morning, sweetheart,' he'd said with a smile, kissing her with morning breath that made her gag. She'd leapt out of the bed, hand over her mouth and then realized that not only did he share a dorm with another chap but she was completely and utterly naked and, more importantly, had no idea where the bathroom was.

After throwing up in the nearest thing she could lay her hands on, which turned out to be a baseball cap belonging to Bryan's roommate, she apologized, grabbed her clothes, flung on her dress and exited the room as quickly, and with as much dignity, as she possibly could.

Amazingly, Bryan sought her out later that day and they dated for almost six months. Well, Rose dated Bryan for six months while, she discovered one wintery morning, Bryan had also been dating Rosemary, Tasha and Michael.

Shaking her head free of the memories, she looked down at the second message from James.

Would you like to meet for a drink next week? That was it. Just those words, staring up at her from her phone. Now, she really hadn't been expecting that. What should she say? Did she want to meet him for a drink? A little voice inside her head told her that she did, and without thinking, she fired off an answer: yes.

Panic set in as soon as she realized what she'd done, and she went to close the Messenger app, hesitating when she saw the bubble that indicated the other person was typing. Not for the first time, she wished she had Megan's confidence and ease with men. It wasn't that she hadn't had experience with the other sex – she'd had the odd boyfriend in senior school, and had dated her lovely childhood friend Josh through sixth form – but being a vicar's daughter, she found it hard to bring boys home.

She'd never fully understood why that was; her mum and dad had never said she couldn't bring her boyfriends home. In fact, on the rare occasion she did invite a boyfriend over, they would then become a regular visitor to the vicarage. She supposed she just felt stereotyped by other people and let that affect her behaviour. Being an only child didn't help matters either. She'd often wished for an older sister to lead the way, or an older brother to tease but ultimately protect her. But she had neither, and Megan was the closest she would ever get to a sibling.

The bubble was still flickering.

Bloody hell, is he writing an essay or something? she thought to herself, desperate to know what his next message would be, but also desperate not to know.

Sorry, squash that. Rose's heart died a little. *I'm out of town next week, big flower thing.*

Now she wished she hadn't read either of the messages, and certainly that she hadn't replied so quickly. This was exactly why she didn't get herself involved: men were unreliable and men lied. Internally squirming, she realized that, if they ever met again, James would have the advantage over her, knowing she'd said yes to a date. She threw her phone down angrily, knowing sleep would elude her, but she snuggled under the covers anyway, and stared at the ceiling for the rest of the night.

CHAPTER FOUR

Rose managed to push the messages from James to the back of her mind as the week passed and, luckily, Megan seemed to have forgotten about him too.

'Any fayres this weekend?' Janet asked late that Friday evening.

'There's one on Sunday morning at St Agatha's church. It's only a small one, though, so I'm not sure it's worth all the hassle, to be honest. They have such a tiny church hall – they can only fit about ten stalls.' It was further away than Weddington Hall, on the opposite side of the town, and after the disastrous journey last Saturday, Rose had decided against being environmentally friendly in favour of actually arriving at her destination alive.

'So what if it's only small!' her mum scolded. 'You need to be going to all of the fayres possible at the moment.'

'I'd need Dad to drive me in the minibus, and he can't do that on a Sunday morning.' Rose knew there were many ways around this, but she honestly didn't think it was worth attending this one. St Agatha's was an extremely pretty little church, but the emphasis was definitely on the *little*.

Then her mum said the exact words Rose had been dreading. 'I'll drive you.'

Rose plastered a fake smile of thanks on her face. 'Only if you're sure, Mum.'

''Course I'm sure.' She patted her hand. 'I know Mrs Montague and Jean and Joe won't mind arriving a little early to church if I tell them it's for you. Then I'll come straight back to take them home after service and then come and get you at the end.'

'That's brilliant, Mum.' Rose's smile never faltered. 'I'm heading off to bed.' She kissed her mum on the cheek. 'See you in the morning.'

'Night, love.'

'Ready?' It was Sunday morning. The bike had been loaded into the aisle of the minibus the previous evening, much to the annoyance of Mrs Montague, who liked to sit by the window in the front row. But this was now taken up by the handlebars of the bike, and Mrs Montague had had to squash onto the back seat with Jean and Joe.

'It's like being back at school, isn't it, Joe?' Jean had laughed, tucking her floral headscarf around her ears and placing her overly large handbag on her lap.

Rose didn't normally accompany her mum on the Sunday morning trip to collect parishioners who needed a lift to church – in fact, Rose usually avoided getting into any vehicle her mum was driving, especially when that vehicle was the church minibus – but Janet had insisted.

They'd narrowly avoided a group of cyclists out for a Sunday ride, and it was definitely a case of luck rather than judgement that had left Mr Young's wing mirror still attached to his car and not dangling off the side when they'd driven into the church car park to drop off their passengers.

'As I'll ever be,' Rose muttered quietly.

'Pardon, dear?' Her mum turned the Cliff Richard CD down.

'All set, Mum.' Rose pulled the seat belt even tighter.

'Off we go then.' Rose winced as her mum crunched into first gear and bunny-hopped down the drive of the church.

Why didn't I let Dad put me on the insurance? Rose asked herself for the third time that morning as the minibus lurched into second gear when her mum should have been going into fourth.

'Oh, this stupid thing.' Janet pushed the gear stick into fourth, but by now they'd lost speed and the engine protested at the high gear when doing twenty up a hill. 'I've told your dad over and over again these gears need looking at, but he won't have it.'

Rose resisted the urge to reply with 'because it's not the gears, it's you' and instead turned the CD back up to drown out the sound of the poor old engine.

Her mum's off-key singing to 'Summer Holiday' was the straw that broke the donkey's back, and Rose pulled out her headphones and tried to lose herself in the dulcet tones of Charlie Puth.

'Jesus Christ, Mum!' Rose's head almost crashed into the dashboard as Janet braked harshly and took a turning rather too sharply.

'I forgot we had to turn there.' She grinned sheepishly. 'And don't blaspheme.'

'Sorry, Mum.' Taking the Lord's name in vain was the least of her worries – Rose instinctively tried to make herself smaller while her mum navigated the narrow drive up to St Agatha's.

'Here we are then.' Rose threw a silent 'thank you' to the heavens as Janet pulled on the handbrake and turned off the engine, sending a prayer that her dad would be the one to pick her up later. In fact, she thought, she'd send him a quick text now asking him. 'Well, that's new.'

Rose looked up from her phone and followed her mum's line of sight to a huge marquee in the grounds of the church.

'The fayre has always been in the church hall before now.' Rose stepped out of the minibus, not taking her eyes off the hustle and bustle that was coming and going. 'Reverend Timms never mentioned this when I booked a place.'

'Rose, Mrs Pedal, how lovely to see you both.' As if he'd heard his name, Reverend Timms came rushing over. He wore tiny gold spectacles on an overly large nose, which always made Rose laugh. 'Isn't it just fabulous?' He threw his hands out towards the marquee. 'It's been loaned to us by one of our stallholders. It means we can have so many more stalls, which means more money for the coffers and the church roof.'

34

Why is it always the church roof that needs fixing? Rose asked herself as she made her excuses and headed to the back of the minibus to start gently edging her bike out.

'Need a hand?' The hairs on the back of her neck prickled instantly at the sound of James's voice.

'I'm fine, thank you.' The bike chose this exact moment to wedge itself in between the seats. 'Oh, for fuck's sake!' James's laughter did little to ease her frustration as she pushed and pulled at the crossbar angrily. When she turned around, he was standing leaning against the back door, looking gorgeous once again in his green suit, his arms folded nonchalantly across his chest. Rose reminded herself that she was *not* attracted to this man. 'Well,' she said, 'don't just stand there.'

James threw his hands up and walked towards her. Rose wished she'd left her hair down; then at least she wouldn't be able to feel his breath on the back of her neck. He threaded his arms through hers to reach the handlebars and gently twisted them, instantly freeing the bike from the clutches of the seat. She felt suddenly cold as he stepped back and helped steady the trailer so she could wheel it backwards and onto the wheelchair ramp her dad had installed early the previous year.

Rose hovered awkwardly by her bike, while James stood and looked at her. 'Want me to wheel it inside for you?' he asked.

'No, I can manage now.' She realized her tone was rather harsh, and quickly added, 'Thank you.' He smiled, heading off towards the marquee.

'I'll be getting off now, love.' Her mum had appeared behind her. 'Service will be over soon, and you know how Mrs Montague gets if she's not back home on time.'

'Thanks, Mum.' A quick kiss and Janet was back in the minibus, crunching the gears once again and knocking over one of the flowerpots as she tried to reverse. 'Sorry, Reverend,' she shouted out of the window. 'I'll replace it for you.' And then, with a sigh of relief from Rose, she was gone.

'This is all very wonderful,' Rose told the reverend as he accompanied her towards the marquee.

'We were just astounded when Mr Blume offered it to us.' Rose raised her eyebrows; she could have guessed James would be the one behind something so over the top. 'And they've said we can hire it out as a wedding venue whenever we want.'

'That's brilliant, Reverend.' Rose smiled with gritted teeth, not really knowing why she felt such animosity. After all, he was only trying to help a community – but she had a nagging doubt that just wouldn't go away.

'Here we are then.' As Rose stepped into the marquee, her doubts were confirmed. Blume's Florist seemed to take over the entire tent. A six-foot table stood at the entrance where James was busy making little adjustments to his display. To the left and right, there were slightly smaller tables set up in the instantly recognizable green and gold. Two younger males stood nervously behind these. Then at the back, taking up the whole length of the marquee, was another table, beautifully laden with various table decorations and flower arrangements. An older, grey-haired version of James was checking the table display from various angles, and Rose assumed this must be his father.

'Now, I've put you right here at the front next to . . . Oh.' Reverend Timms stopped suddenly. 'I'm sure I left this spot free for you when I was setting up.' Rose looked at the table that was in her place.

A tall red-haired woman, immaculately dressed in a tight-fitting business suit and with impeccable make-up, sat tapping on an iPad. Her table proclaimed her as 'Madison Michaels . . . wedding planner!'

'Er . . . Miss Michaels . . . I'm terribly sorry . . .' Reverend Timms stuttered. 'There seems to have been a little mistake . . . I'm sure this spot was reserved for Rose here.'

'Well, my name was on the table when I came in.' Madison stood up and smiled at the reverend. 'I mean, I can move if you want me to. I really wouldn't want to be in anyone's spot.'

'No, no,' Reverend Timms answered far too quickly. 'You're all set up now. I'll just pop Rose . . .' He looked around. 'Oh look, there's a lovely space for you down there.' He indicated a corner at the back of the room that didn't look big enough for her to stand in, let alone set the bike and trailer up.

'Thank you.' Rose headed off.

'I'm ever so sorry if I've put you out at all,' Madison called after her.

'Not at all.' Rose smiled her cheeriest of smiles, while praying for a stray bee to fly in and sting Madison Michaels on the nose. Or for the reverend's British bulldog to escape from the vicarage and wipe that sickly sweet smile off her perfectly formed rosebud mouth.

'Do you need a hand?' Rose turned to see Natalie, one of Weddington's local cake makers, standing behind her. Natalie had made many birthday and anniversary cakes for the Pedal family over the years.

'Would you mind?'

Natalie shook her head.

'If I squidge my table over a little this way, then we'll be able to angle the trailer and give you a bit more room.' Together the two of them managed to carefully manoeuvre Natalie's table without damaging any of the beautifully decorated cakes, and Rose declared that the bike looked pretty darn good in the small space they had managed to create.

'Thanks.'

'You're more than welcome.' Natalie stepped back behind her table and swept a stray strand of black hair from her face and behind her ear. 'That Madison Michaels is a bitch,' she said a little too loudly, but if Madison heard her, she showed no sign. 'I've been at these wedding fayres for ten years now and she's a nasty piece of work.'

'Reverend Timms did leave that space for you,' the older lady on the table opposite selling wedding favours under the name of Fanny's Favours piped in. 'Saw her myself. I was the only one here. Always get here early I do, like to get myself settled. She moved all the tables up so there was no gap and placed her name card on the table next to the florist.'

'What did I tell you?' Natalie shot an angry look at Madison's back.

'And I think I know why.' The lady Rose assumed was called Fanny – although, she really must check that at some point – nodded towards the front of the marquee.

Madison Michaels was talking to James, and from the way she was running her hand down his arm, it was obvious to everyone in the room that they were on more than first name terms with each other.

'I'm sure they dated for a while, you know.' Natalie directed her statement to the other lady, who nodded her agreement. 'Looks like she wants another bite of the cherry.'

James chose this exact moment to look over at Rose. Catching her eye, he smiled at her before Madison reclaimed his attention by placing her perfectly manicured fingers on his chin and placing a kiss on his lips. Rose looked away instantly and prepared her bike for the visitors.

CHAPTER FIVE

'It's not what you think.' It was the end of the fayre and everyone was packing away, remarking on how busy it had been and what their sales or bookings had been like.

'I don't believe it really matters what I think.' Rose had been pushing the bike towards the entrance when James had seen her and left his stand to intercept her.

'It does to me.' He spoke with a sincerity that threw Rose off balance for a second. Then she remembered the kiss he'd shared with Madison Michaels and her composure returned instantly, her guard back up.

'I really don't see why it should.' She tried to steer the bike past him, but every way she turned, he stepped in front of the wheel. 'If you wouldn't mind, Mr Blume, my father is outside waiting for me.'

'Mr Blume, is it?' He raised his eyebrows. 'Surely you can call me James.'

'But that would imply that we are friends, Mr Blume.' Rose released her grip on the bike and stood back, plastering what she hoped was a bored expression on her face.

'Oh, I think we could be a little more than friends.' He stepped towards her. 'After all, you did accept my invitation for a drink.'

Rose flushed red instantly. She *knew* he'd use that to score points!

'James! Will you stop chatting up the local skirt and get those flowers away? They need to be back in the van cooling off if we stand any chance of selling them tomorrow.' The older version of James was now standing behind Rose's bike, seemingly completely oblivious to her presence. 'Uncle Tony is waiting back at the shop and your grandma is expecting us for tea at four, and you know how your grandpa gets if we're not all sitting round that table when the clock chimes. And remind me never to use agency staff again – those two wet blankets were useless.'

'Yes, Dad.' Rose took an instant dislike to James's father, but had to admit that she enjoyed seeing James squirm all the same.

'Good afternoon, *Mr* Blume,' Rose said, emphasizing the 'mister', and headed out into the May sunshine.

'Still here then?' Rose turned to find 'Fanny' wheeling a trolley laden with boxes towards the car park.

'Waiting for my dad – the minibus is playing up a bit.' Rose thought it was probably protesting after being driven by her mum for longer than usual.

'Never introduced myself.' She parked her trolley next to Rose and sat down on the grass verge beside her. 'Fanny Longbottom.'

Rose couldn't hide her giggle and was mortified. 'I'm so sorry!'

'Don't you worry yourself.' Fanny smiled. 'It's Frances really, after my dad, so I was Fanny and he was Frank.' She burst out laughing. 'Not bloody one of us was actually called Frances.' She laughed again and Rose joined in.

'Rose Pedal, pleased to meet you.' She held out her hand and Fanny shook it warmly.

'I'd say you didn't do too well in the name stakes either.' Rose shook her head. 'Just makes us more memorable.'

'How long have you been making wedding favours then?' Rose knew she was going to like Fanny.

'Since I retired last year.' She handed Rose a business card. 'I was a seamstress up until then, and I knit and crochet as well.'

'Wow.' Rose was genuinely in awe of anyone with sewing skills. She couldn't even sew on a button without pricking her finger several times.

'I keep my hand in with the dressmaking too.' Fanny pulled out her mobile phone and clicked through a few photos before showing Rose one of a bride and three brides-maids. 'That's my granddaughter,' she said proudly. 'I made her dress, the bridesmaids' dresses and the waistcoats and cravats for the boys.'

'They are amazing. So professional-looking.' Rose paused. 'Oh lord ... no ... I didn't mean—'

'Don't worry yourself, little love.' Fanny patted her knee. 'I know exactly what you mean.'

Rose wanted the ground to open up and swallow her whole, but her dad turning up at that exact moment was the next best thing.

'It's been so lovely to meet you.' Rose smiled her most apologetic smile. 'Are you booked in for any other fayres?'

'I've got a few, so I'm sure we'll meet again soon.' Fanny picked herself up off the grass. 'Actually, now you're part of the scene, so to speak, a few of us got together the other year and made a sort of directory of wedding people. We have meetings when we can. You should come!'

'Thanks.' Rose tapped the business card. 'I'll message you.'

'We have a little WhatsApp group I could add you to it if you like?' Fanny pulled out her phone again. 'Let me have your number and I'll add you when I get home.'

'That would be lovely, thank you.' Rose read out her number, and Fanny punched it in, then waved and pulled her trolley towards a small red van, the only vehicle left in the car park.

'Hey, Dad.' Rose kissed him on the cheek. 'Thank you so much for coming to get me.'

'When your mum told me about the reverend's flowerpot, and then what you said in your text about the gears again . . . well, I couldn't let poor old Bessie here take any more abuse today.' Her dad was the only one who called the bus Bessie. 'Good day?'

'Yeah, it was great, actually.' Rose had received even more

enquiries this time and wondered whether it had helped being next to Natalie's cake stall, a wedding essential.

'Next week is Haggerston Hall, isn't it?' Rose nodded. 'Now that's a big event every year. You booked in for both days?'

'No, just the Saturday.' Rose had been late booking and had taken the last spot left for the Saturday. The lady organizing had said she would put her on the waiting list for the Sunday, but with it being the biggest wedding event in the area, Rose wasn't holding out much hope. 'Are you still okay to take me?'

''Course I am.' They loaded the bike into the back of the minibus, then jumped into the seats, clicking their seat belts on. 'Your mum is coming with me and we're going to make a day of it. Have a look round the house. If it's nice we'll take a picnic and eat it in the grounds.'

'Sounds perfect, Dad.' Rose switched on the radio and she and her dad sang along to Radio 2 as Bessie delivered them safely home.

Rolling off the sofa after her mum's huge roast dinner followed by raspberry pavlova, Rose headed to her room and pulled out her contacts and enquiry list from that day's event. She smiled at the long list before her, and was sending emails and sorting quotes when her phone buzzed.

> **Megan**: How was today?
> **Rose**: Really good, lots of enquires, just
> working through them now.

Megan: And?

Rose: And what?

Megan: Was HE there?

Rose: Who?

Megan: James!!!!!

Rose: Yes.

Megan: And?

Rose: And what?

It was after this message that the phone rang. Unsurprisingly, it was Megan.

'Do I need to come round there and beat you with a stick?' she said before Rose had even said hello.

'Honestly, there is absolutely nothing to tell.' Rose knew this tactic wouldn't wash with Megan, but she tried it anyway.

'I can tell you're lying, you know.' Rose sighed. 'I can always tell when you're lying.'

'I don't know why he asked me out only to say he couldn't come a few seconds later, and then he's kissing someone else at the fayre anyway.'

'Whoa there, Nellie!' Rose cringed – she'd forgotten she hadn't told Megan this vital piece of information. 'Kissing someone else I'm coming back to, but what do you mean he asked you out?'

'That message he sent me last week.' Rose could almost hear Megan's eager nodding. 'First he apologized for making fun of my name, and then he asked if I fancied meeting him for a drink in the week.'

'You never said yes?'

'Uh-huh.'

'Have I taught you nothing?' Rose could hear the tut in her voice. 'You've played right into his hands. Always act hard to get.'

'It just sort of happened,' Rose said. 'Doesn't matter anyway because within five seconds of me saying yes, he'd messaged back to say he was out of town.'

'What an arsehole!' That was mild for Megan. 'And this bit about kissing someone else?'

Rose explained all about Madison, how she'd taken Rose's spot next to James and 'the kiss'.

'I don't think he's into her at all.'

'Well, he looked pretty into her from where I was standing.'

'You said you looked away,' Megan reminded her.

'Well, yes . . . I did . . . but—'

'Then how do you know?' Megan asked.

This was true. There had been no further kisses exchanged. In fact, James had practically ignored Madison for the entire fayre, despite her best efforts to engage him in conversation whenever there was a lull in visitors. At one point, Madison had even taken clients over to introduce them to him, but although James had smiled warmly at the guests, his reaction to Madison had appeared cold. Not that Rose had been watching at all.

'You could be right,' Rose agreed somewhat unwillingly.

'Trust me, I am.'

As she was saying goodbye to Megan, her phone lit up with a WhatsApp notification, telling her she'd been added to the WOW's group. Rose had no idea what WOW stood for, but after seeing that it was Fanny who'd added her, she figured it was the little group of wedding folk they'd talked about earlier that day. She saw that Natalie was part of the group, her number already being in Rose's contacts, but the other members only appeared as anonymous contact numbers. A few of them said hello after Fanny explained who Rose was, and as the chat turned to previous fayres that Rose hadn't attended, she closed down the chat and took herself off to bed.

Monday morning found Rose enjoying a lie-in. Her mum and dad were doing the weekly shop as they had done every Monday morning for as long as Rose could remember. It was already ten o'clock, but she was so comfortable she just couldn't face getting out of bed.

A knock on the door made her groan, but she knew she had to answer it. You always had to answer the vicarage door if you were at home, and her dad was pretty darn good at making sure someone was always at home.

She didn't bother putting a dressing gown on over her Mickey Mouse nightshirt; after all, everyone in the parish had known her since she was born. She walked wearily downstairs, rubbing her eyes and running her hands through what felt like extreme bed hair.

'Morning.' She opened the door yawning and rubbing the

sleep out of her eyes. 'Dad's out at the moment. Can I tell him you called round?'

'Well, you could, but it's you I've come to see.' Her head snapped up at the familiar voice.

'James!' Why was he here? How had he found her? But more importantly, why the hell hadn't she got up this morning and got washed and dressed at the very least?

'See, you can use my first name,' he said, smiling. He was dressed in his usual green suit, so Rose guessed he was on work time, and her suspicion was proved correct when she saw the van parked on the drive. 'These are for you.' He pulled a huge bunch of flowers from behind his back. Sunflowers, yellow roses and orange chrysanthemums, mixed with the green leafy stuff Rose could never remember the name of. 'I really, really need to apologize to you.'

'How did you know where I live?' She looked outside as though there might be some stalker hanging around telling everyone all her secrets.

'Not awfully hard to find people by the name of Pedal.' He shrugged his shoulders and shook the bunch of flowers. 'Are you going to take these off me?'

'Oh ... yes ... thank you so much.' She found herself smiling back at him. *Goodness me, but he's got a nice smile*, she thought. 'You really shouldn't have.'

'I really should have.' He leaned one hand on the door frame. Her stomach flipped a little – she liked it when he leaned on things. 'I was out of order that first time and my dad was extremely rude to you on Sunday. And about Madison—'

She felt herself prickle at Madison's name. 'Honestly, your love life is none of my business.'

'She isn't part of my love life.' He shook his head gently. 'She wants to be.'

'So, you haven't dated her?' Rose remembered what Natalie had told her, and then cursed herself for sounding too interested. Megan would have her guts for garters.

'Three years ago.' He laughed. 'Absolute disaster. Far too high-maintenance for me.' He looked her up and down. 'Give me a normal girl any day.'

'Yes, well . . .' Rose wasn't quite sure she liked being called normal in this instance. It felt like a bit of a dig that she was standing there with messy hair, no make-up and dressed in her nightshirt. Madison Michaels, on the other hand, would never be seen in such a state of undress.

'How does Wednesday grab you?' Her stomach lurched.

'For what?'

'For that drink?'

'Erm . . .'

'Let me buy you dinner?' He looked at her with puppy-dog eyes.

'I'm not sure . . .' she started to say, while her whole body was screaming yes, yes, yes! But then a plan started to formulate – a little revenge maybe. 'Actually, meet me in the Pig and Whistle.'

'Is that the little pub on the outskirts of Weddington?' he asked.

'That's the one.' She smiled. 'About seven?'

'See you there about seven then.' And with that, he turned and headed off to his van, giving her a quick wave from the open window.

'The Pig and Whistle! This Wednesday!' she said to herself, closing the door and chuckling. Thank goodness he wasn't a local lad.

CHAPTER SIX

Megan: I don't know why I bother with you sometimes. You may as well have stripped naked and shagged him on the vicarage steps.
Rose: That's a little extreme.
Megan: Well, not really. First you ask him if he's dating this Madison woman and then you say yes to a date, just like that.
Rose: I'm not like you, Megan. I get flustered. Anyway . . . it's Wednesday in the Pig!
Megan: 😕😕😕😕 THIS Wednesday night in the Pig? You have to change it, Rose. Big city boy won't know what's hit him.
Rose: Maybe it will knock him down a peg or too, I get the impression he has rather a large ego.
Megan: I'd love to see his face. Better make sure you've got a good seat. Better go, boss on the prowl xx

Rose spent the rest of Monday and all of Tuesday answering a sudden influx of enquiries for Pedals and Prosecco to attend various parties, weddings and events, and she now considered Sunday's fayre to have been an out-and-out success. She'd even had to turn down one enquiry because it was on the same day as another booking, and she was now seriously considering taking Megan and her parents up on the offer of helping get another bike up and running. She hated the idea of leaning on her friends and family, but maybe, down the line, when Pedals was properly off the ground, she could hire an assistant to take out the second bike on days she was double-booked.

Flicking on eBay, she scoured the ads, liking a few that were close or would deliver. There was one ending that evening at eight o'clock, just a few miles away, and she set a reminder to start watching it ten minutes before.

There was always something exciting about bidding on eBay. She'd never been to a real auction, something she hoped to remedy one day. The auction was currently at one bid of fifty pounds; Rose had paid almost two hundred pounds for the first bike, and then had to pay twenty pounds delivery as well. With just ten seconds to spare, she placed her bid, delighted to be the highest bidder. Then, just as the auction was ending, she was outbid by one pound.

'Bugger,' she muttered. 'A bloody pound!'

She closed down the app and headed downstairs to help her mum bake scones for tomorrow morning's parish meeting. Although, what she really meant by helping was snatching one or two as soon as they came out of the oven and running off to her dad's office, where she and John would devour them like naughty schoolchildren.

Wednesday evening came, and Megan still hadn't persuaded Rose to change the venue for her date with James. Even her mum and dad were a little shocked.

'The Pig? Tonight?' John quizzed.

'Is he not from round here then?' Janet looked puzzled. 'I mean it's a lovely pub but ... tonight?' She left her sentence hanging; they all knew what happened in the Pig in Weddington on the second Wednesday in May.

'Have you warned him?' her dad asked as Rose smoothed her hair in front of the antique mirror that hung above the fireplace in the living room while she waited for her Uber to arrive.

She shook her head. 'Nope.'

'Do you think you should?' her mum asked, concerned.

'Nah!' Rose replied. 'He's a city boy – I'm sure he's seen worse.' Her phone flashed to say Mohammed in his black Toyota had arrived and was waiting outside. 'Best go.' She kissed her mum and dad on the cheek, before racing out of the door to the waiting car.

She arrived in Weddington with plenty of time to spare. The Tudor timbers and stone tiles of the pub were illuminated by lamp posts and fairy lights strewn around its wooden door. Although the pub could be seen from the main road, it could only be reached via a winding country lane.

The Uber dropped her in the car park, and she noticed a brand-new Audi parked up towards the back. She couldn't help but roll her eyes when she saw that its registration read BL19 UME.

As she headed towards the door, a familiar voice called her name.

'Oh, I didn't realize you were behind me,' Rose said, turning to address James as he made his way across the car park. She was caught off guard by how handsome he looked. He was dressed in a crisp white shirt with an embroidered motif she didn't recognize – she made a mental note to ask Megan or Google when she got home which designer used a bee as its logo. The shirt was tucked into black jeans, and a black belt and shiny black boots completed the outfit. She could have bet that his belt alone cost more than the red gypsy dress she'd picked up from Primark last summer. But she felt comfortable in it. It showed off her boobs and complimented her brown hair and eyes.

As he fell into step beside her, she was glad she'd thought to wear heels. He was still a good few inches taller than her, but she liked that. Bryan had been the same height, and Josh was actually a little smaller than her. She knew it was very traditional thinking on her part but it felt right for the man to be taller, or maybe it just felt right walking beside such a sexy man as James.

All eyes turned to watch them as James held the door open for her. Rose recognized many of the faces and some nodded in acknowledgement or shouted hello.

'Well known round here, are you?' James asked as they headed towards the heavy oak bar.

'You could say that,' she said, wondering whether to tell him she was the vicar's daughter. He'd made no comment of the fact that she lived in a vicarage when he'd showed up the other day, but then these days not all vicarages belonged to the church; many had been sold to raise funds or in some cases the church had closed or one vicar was shared between two parishes.

In the end, the decision was taken out of her hands. 'Well, hello there, young Rose.' Alan, the bartender and owner, walked over to them, drying a pint glass on a blue and white tea towel. 'How's your dad? Apologize to him for me for missing the Easter service, will you? I got a little ... shall we say ... pissed on Good Friday.' He chuckled heartily. 'I'm never giving up beer for Lent again.'

James made no comment as he paid for their drinks – lemonade for him and Parma Violet gin for Rose – and ushered her towards an empty table at the back of the pub.

'Go on, say it.' Rose took a sip of the ice-cold gin. 'I know you're dying to.'

'I don't know what you mean.' She could see the beginnings of a smirk on the corner of his lips. 'At least I know why you don't like to swear now.' And that was the only comment he made.

They chatted easily, talking about his business for a while, but then the conversation moved on to Pedals and Prosecco. He bombarded her with questions and suggestions for possible improvements and expansion, and different markets she could look into. He only stopped when he was interrupted by Alan ringing the bell on the bar.

'This is your five-minute warning!' People started faffing about with their bags, grabbing pens or trying to attract the attention of Alan's wife, Mary, who had suddenly appeared carrying little booklets.

'What's going on?' James leaned in towards her. She could smell his aftershave: cool and sharp with a hint of sandalwood. Certainly not the Lynx body spray or Millionaire that most of her boyfriends had worn.

'It's bingo night.' She shot her hand up in the air and Mary, who was close by, came over and handed them two booklets in exchange for £15. 'There you go.' The look on James's face made her laugh. It was a mixture of disbelief and interest, if that were possible. 'You have played bingo before, haven't you?'

'Can't say that I have.' She watched him flick through the booklet.

'You know how to play though?' *How could he never have played bingo?* she thought to herself. Hadn't everyone played bingo at some point, even if it was at primary school?

'I think so.'

She handed him a felt-tip pen and opened up the first page for him.

'The idea is to cross off a line of numbers, then two lines and then all three lines for a full house.' She pointed to the rectangular tables of three lines, each with five numbers in. 'Alan will call out the numbers and you mark them off as they come out.' She pretended to cross off one of the numbers. 'If you get them all in a row, then shout "house" and you win.'

'Seems easy enough.' He looked around at the suddenly silent room. 'What do we win?'

But Alan was speaking again, and Rose put a finger to her lips.

'Now, as usual, we'll play the first three houses, have a break, then play the second lot of three.' Mary was setting up a wire ball with different-coloured balls inside. 'As always, one line wins five pounds, two lines a tenner and it's fifty quid for a full house.' He started turning the little handle on the wire ball. 'Now, as it's our special bingo night, we all know that means an incredibly special grand prize.' There were oohs of excitement. 'You all remember Mr Wong's sweet-and-sour balls back in 2015, and who could forget Mr Brown's pair of plums last year.' Laughter erupted around the room and Rose stole a peek at James, who was taking all this in with a puzzled expression on his face. 'Well, this year, ladies and gent,' – Rose realized James had missed the singular use of the word gent and smiled inwardly – 'it's the turn of Mr Tucker and his award-winning sausage.'

There was a round of applause and screams of excitement at this announcement, followed suddenly by deathly silence as Alan turned the handle and the first coloured ball rolled out.

*

'I can't believe I won.' James was grinning from ear to ear. 'Here, this is yours really.' He handed her the crisp fifty-pound note, but she shook her head.

'You won it fair and square.' She couldn't believe how excited he was. 'I tell you what . . .' *I can't believe I'm going to say this*, she thought. The gin must really have gone to her head. 'You can take me to dinner next Saturday if you like.'

'It's a date.' He chinked his glass against hers.

'Let's call it a promise, shall we?' She'd had enough cancelled dates in her time.

'A promise it is.' He nodded. 'So, what's this grand prize thing? Is it like a meat raffle or something?'

'You could say that.' Rose gulped the last of her gin. 'Another drink?' She stood up and headed to the bar.

'Time for the grand prize draw.' Alan was ringing the bell once again. 'I've got the names of the six full house winners here and my lovely wife is going to pick one.' A hush fell around the room as Mary picked a piece of paper from Alan's hand.

'And the winner is,' she called, ' . . . James Blume!' Rose put her hand to her mouth to hold in her laughter. There were sighs of disappointment. 'Now, now, ladies, we all get to enjoy some of it, but James here gets the full sausage.' Rose was almost on the floor at these words and had to turn away when James turned to her with two thumbs up.

There wasn't time to get another drink, so she just watched from the bar as the lights began to dim and the opening bars of 'You Can Leave Your Hat On' started to play through the speakers. She watched James's face look more and more confused as he and everyone else turned towards the door at the back of the room.

Standing illuminated in the doorway was a middle-aged man who Rose recognized as Weddington's butcher, Mr Tucker. He was dressed in his usual green and white suit, green and white apron and green and white hat. There were claps and shouts of encouragement as he started to wiggle his hips and walk into the bar, stopping at the front.

'What! The! Fuck!' James mouthed and she just shrugged her shoulders innocently.

The apron came off first, followed by the shirt and jacket. Mr Tucker was really getting into the spirit of things and everyone except for James appeared to be enjoying it. Rose watched him squirm in his seat as Mr Tucker, now down to just his trousers and hat, started to move around the tables. The trousers were ripped off to reveal boxer shorts with sausages on as the song neared its end.

The big finale was almost upon them and Rose knew exactly what was coming. Mr Tucker sashayed towards James, took his hat off, placed it in front of his groin and peeled off the boxer shorts. James had his eyes covered and, as the last line of the song rang out, Mr Tucker threw his hat at him.

CHAPTER SEVEN

The room filled with wolf whistles and claps, and Rose could see James peeking through his fingers, then visibly relaxing when he realized that Mr Tucker wasn't entirely naked and was wearing a gold glittery thong. However, when Mr Tucker turned around to bow to the crowd, the view that he gave James must have been eye-watering, because the poor man put his hand to his mouth and swallowed heavily as if stopping himself from throwing up.

Rose made her way back to the table with their drinks after Mr Tucker had departed.

'Did you know about this?'

'I did.' She couldn't help laughing. 'Your face was a picture.'

'Are stripping shopkeepers a regular occurrence around here?' He took a rather large gulp of lemonade.

'Thankfully not.' She smiled. 'It took me three months before I could buy plums from Mr Brown last year. I just couldn't look him in the eye.'

'Come every year, do you?' He took another gulp.

'Good God, no!' She shivered involuntarily. 'My friend Megan tricked me.'

'A little bit like you did to me then.' He smiled at her as he said this, and her stomach flipped.

'Guilty.' She smiled back.

'You're forgiven.' He was still smiling, his gaze locked with hers. Rose resisted the urge to fan herself.

'Here are your sausages.' Mr Tucker had re-emerged, fully dressed in jeans and a jumper. He placed a tray of chipolatas on the table, and Rose and James burst out laughing.

Rose couldn't sleep that night. She kept going over and over the night's events in her head. The lingering look before they were interrupted by Mr Tucker and his sausages. How James had accidentally brushed her thigh when putting the car into gear after offering to drive her home. The laughter they'd shared as they recalled the night's events, and then the soft kiss he'd planted on her cheek as he said goodnight. The WhatsApp chat hadn't helped matters either.

> **Millie**: I see our resident hot house bloom is back on the dating scene.
> **Lucy**: Is he indeed? Who's the lucky lady?
> **Millie**: No idea, but they looked very loved up in the Pig earlier.

Rose had groaned when she'd seen the notifications. She hadn't realized they'd been spotted, but she should have known that nothing went unnoticed in these little villages. She just thanked her lucky stars that Millie didn't know what she looked like.

> **Millie**: Even Mr Tucker's sausages couldn't distract them.
> **Lucy**: Mr Tucker . . . bleurgh.
> **Fanny**: Nothing wrong with Mr Tucker.
> **Millie**: Fanny's in love.

And to Rose's relief, the chat had moved away from her and James. But it had made her think. She hadn't intended to have a good time – just wanted to play a little joke on the city boy – but she'd found herself enjoying his company; the way his eyes crinkled at the corners when he smiled, how she could still feel the touch of his lips on her cheek.

In the end, she crept out of bed and down the stairs as quietly as she could, and flicked on the kettle to make herself a hot chocolate. That was her go-to when she couldn't sleep, always had been. She could remember the first time she'd tasted hot chocolate. She'd been five and was stopping overnight at her grandparents' house for the very first time.

She'd never been so excited and had worn herself and her grandparents out playing in the garden, and then playing card games. Eventually, her grandad had admitted defeat and whisked her off to bed. She'd fallen asleep before he'd even read the first page of her favourite *Little Miss Naughty* story, but a loud bang a few hours later had woken her up and she'd gone to her grandparents' room.

They'd both taken her downstairs, her grandmother wrapping a hand-knitted blanket made of different coloured squares around her while her grandad made frothy hot chocolate with squirty cream and little pink marshmallows on the top.

She smiled at the memory, reminding herself to make sure she rang her grandparents later that day for a catch-up. It had been a while and she missed them.

Taking the hot chocolate back upstairs, she sat in the chair at her desk rather than getting back into bed. She noticed her phone flash; an eBay reminder about an auction that was ending in fifteen minutes. She clicked on it and double-checked the details and pictures of the bike. Again, she waited until the last minute, and yet again, she was beaten by a pound.

'Bugger!' She threw her phone onto the bed. What on earth was going on? Why was there such an interest in vintage bikes all of a sudden?

The hot chocolate was beginning to work its magic and she felt her eyelids start to droop so she got back into bed. Just as she was drifting off, a loud clunk startled her, and she realized her phone had fallen to the floor. Picking it up, she noticed a new message from James.

Leave it till the morning, a little voice in her head that sounded distinctively like Megan said, but she couldn't resist.

James: Are you awake?

That was all it said. Should she reply?

Rose: Yes.

Her fingers had already answered for her.

James: I can't sleep.
Rose: Nor me.
James: I had a really good time tonight.
Rose: I did too.
James: Let's not wait till next week? Are you free Friday night?
Rose: Yes, but have an early start the next morning for a wedding fayre.
James: Is that the one at Haggerston Hall?
Rose: Yes. Are you going?
James: It's one of my favourites. You're not pedalling all the way there are you? Must be thirty miles from you.
Rose: Dad's driving me in the church minibus.
James: I could take you.

There was a pause.

James: I've got a larger van I can take; your bike would fit in the back no problem.

Rose: I couldn't ask you to do that.

She desperately wanted to accept the offer, but could feel herself pulling back. They may have had a nice time at the Pig and Whistle, but this was still the same man who'd asked her on a date, instantly cancelled on her and then kissed another woman the next day. Did she really trust all of his assurances that it had meant nothing?

Then again, maybe she was getting ahead of herself. After all, it was just a lift, and it would mean she didn't have to put her dad out. She knew her parents were probably only making a day of it so she didn't feel like a burden.

> **James**: Honestly, it would be a pleasure. I'll
> pick you up at seven and we'll grab breakfast
> on the way. I know a lovely little café called
> The Copper Kettle. Betty makes the best
> bacon and eggs in the Midlands.
> **Rose**: Only if you're sure.
> **James**: I wouldn't have offered otherwise.
> **Rose**: See you on Saturday then.
> **James**: See you Saturday.

Rose hugged her phone to her chest before remembering that she would now have to tell her dad she wouldn't be needing a lift – and why. Her dad would also insist on meeting James before he allowed him to drive her anywhere. Maybe she could tell her dad that Megan was driving. Then shook her head; she had never lied to her parents and wasn't about to start now.

Snuggling under her quilt, she knew sleep was going to be even more elusive now. Butterflies were already flipping around in her stomach. She felt sick with nerves and excitement, but at least she didn't have to worry about what to wear; that was already taken care of. She flung back the quilt in exasperation and sat at her desk. *Might as well make use of the hours*, she told herself as she turned on her laptop and began drafting emails and quotes to send to clients in the morning.

'I don't believe it!' Rose threw her hands up in exasperation. 'That's the fourth one this week.'

'What's the fourth one, dear?' her mum asked, walking into the garden with white chocolate milkshakes for them both. They had decided to take advantage of an exceptionally warm May afternoon, while Rose's poor dad was presiding over a last-minute wedding rehearsal. The bride had called up last night in a panic, worrying that people would forget where to stand or what to say.

'I've been beaten on another blooming bike,' Rose said. Even in front of her mum, she tried not to swear.

'I didn't think you were buying another bike, dear?' Janet sat next to her and tried to push the lounge chair into a reclining position. 'Why can't I ever do this? It was so easy when I was a child – you lifted the handles up and the chair went back, and the handles locked where you wanted them.'

'You just push back with your feet, Mum.' Rose tried

not to giggle at the sight of her mum pushing and getting nowhere. 'Here, let me.' Rose stood up and pushed down on the back of her mum's chair, which had the desired effect and her mum sighed contentedly.

'So ... bikes.' She looked at Rose, shielding her eyes from the sun.

'Yes, bikes.' She showed her mum the eBay app on her phone. 'I know I said I wasn't going to get a second bike, but the response from the previous two fayres has been so positive and I've already had to turn someone down because I was already booked for that day. So I started looking for another bike that we could do up and get ready for Megan.' She clicked on the last auction, which showed she'd been unlucky. 'I've bid on four auctions this week and lost all of them by one pound.'

'That's a little strange, isn't it?' Janet took the phone and started flicking through listings. 'There are lots and lots for sale. What's wrong with this one?' She pointed the phone towards Rose.

'It's in Edinburgh, Mum.' Rose rolled her eyes. 'A little too far I'm afraid.'

'Oh, yes.' She looked at the phone again. 'Your dad would drive you, though, I'm sure.'

'I am driving her tomorrow, aren't I? We both are.' John walked into the garden, taking off his dog collar as he went.

'About tomorrow ...' Rose started. She wished she'd plucked up the courage to tell her parents sooner. 'It's just ... well ... I've kind of made other arrangements.' There, she'd said it.

'Really?' Her dad raised his eyebrows. 'And *who* might these other arrangements involve?'

He knew her so well. 'James.'

'Oh, well, now.' Rose could see her mum was getting excited about the possibility of a new man in Rose's life. 'Do tell.'

Rose explained in as little detail as possible, hoping that if she neglected to tell them a pick-up time, she could sneak her bike into the back of James's van without them knowing.

She was wrong.

Her alarm went off at 6am and she jumped quietly into the shower, got dressed and came downstairs to find both her parents sitting in the kitchen, fully dressed and drinking tea. It even looked like her mum had done her hair and had make-up on.

'Really, you two.' Rose shook her head in disbelief and poured herself a cup of tea from the pot. No matter what time of day it was, there always seemed to be tea in the pot, kept warm by one of her nan's hand-knitted tea cosies. The current one in use was designed like a strawberry, red with black stitches for seeds, complete with green leaves and a stalk on the top. Her nan had even knitted matching egg cosies and little covers for the sugar bowl and milk jug.

'What sort of parents would we be if we didn't introduce ourselves?' Rose could tell her dad was enjoying himself.

'The sort of parents that realize this is only the fourth time I've met him, and it is not the time for you to be meeting him.' Rose started checking she had everything in her bag: diary, pen, business cards, hairbrush – all there. She'd thoroughly examined the bike and baskets the night before. 'In fact, it's not even a date. He's just taking me to the fayre because we happen to be going there at the same time.'

Her mum and dad looked at each other knowingly and Rose shook her head again.

'I think I hear an engine.' Her dad was out of the back door and through the gate before Rose had even put her cup down. 'He's here!' he shouted at the top of his voice, and Rose wished the ground would open up and swallow her whole.

CHAPTER EIGHT

'I'm so sorry about my dad.' Rose was sitting in the passenger seat of the van, James in the driving seat. It was an exact replica of the green and gold van he had driven to the fayre at Weddington Hall, just on a slightly larger scale.

'He was cool,' James said with a little laugh. 'And your mum's biscuits are to die for.'

John had explained to James all about her bike and how they'd made the trailer into the wicker basket and all the finer details of the design as they'd both wheeled and lifted the bike into the back of the van. James had secured it with a couple of tow ropes, so it wouldn't slip and slide around too much during the journey.

Upon seeing all the flowers in the van, John had proceeded to quiz James about the latest trends and prices, and made him promise to come to tea one day to discuss a possible contract for supplying the church.

Then Janet had insisted on them having a cup of tea before they left, but James had graciously declined, claiming they didn't have the time, and had instead been plied with home-made shortbread biscuits and given a box to take home.

'As soon as Dad heard the engine, he was out before I could stop him.' She smiled, slightly embarrassed by her parents' behaviour and by what this city boy would think.

'They're only looking out for you.' And she knew this was true. 'My mum would be the same.' He paused for a second. 'Not my dad though.' Rose sensed he wanted to say more but didn't push him. 'Here we are then.'

After signalling right and checking his blind spot, James pulled into a layby on the opposite side of the road. A hand-painted sandwich board announced the presence of The Copper Kettle, but so far Rose couldn't actually see the café.

James opened the door and helped her step down out of the van, holding on to her hand for slightly longer than was necessary. She followed him in the direction that the sign was pointing, even though it seemed to lead through a hedge.

'Are you sure it's even here?' Rose asked, detangling her-self from a stray branch.

'Don't worry, it's here.'

And there it was.

Nestled between hedges sat a dark blue and red static caravan. The front opened onto decking that spread around one side, and neatly laid tables and chairs sat evenly placed under parasols. 'The Copper Kettle' was written in elegant red script and a chalkboard menu displayed the day's dishes.

'Well, I wasn't expecting that.' The dirty, hand-painted

sign on the road bore no resemblance to the exceptionally clean, upmarket café that stood in front of her.

'Betty likes to keep her regulars – new customers rarely stop when they see the sign outside, especially as there's no sign of an actual café.' He laughed. 'There she is now.' He waved as a middle-aged woman stepped out of the caravan, precariously balancing plates in her hands and on her arms. Once these were deposited on their respective tables, she turned to James and ushered him over with a smile.

'Where have you been, my lad?' She pulled him in for a hug. 'It's been ages since you've been to see old Betty.' She pushed an escaping wisp of grey hair back under her cap. 'Now then,' – she turned to Rose – 'who's this little beauty with you?'

'Betty, this is Rose,' James said. 'Rose, this is Betty.'

'Well, it's an absolute pleasure to meet you.' Betty grabbed one of James's hands and one of Rose's, clasped them together in hers and pulled them along the decking towards the very back. 'This is my best table, away from all the hustle and bustle.'

Rose looked around and had to agree. The table was situated right in the back corner, against the wooden spindle railings that ran around the entire length of the decking. But because it was in a corner, it felt much more secluded than the other tables, and it had a lovely view over the farmland.

'I'll give you both a minute to have a look at the menu, but can I get you a drink? Tea? Coffee?' Betty pulled a pencil from behind her ear and a notepad from out of her apron pocket.

'Tea for me, please,' Rose said, and James asked for a latte.

'I'll send my Sam out with them in a minute and then come and get your orders.' She bustled away, making sure her other guests were happy as she did. James explained that Sam was her grandson.

'She doesn't look old enough to have a grandson,' Rose remarked.

'He's only fifteen but helps his nan out at weekends and holidays.' James handed her a menu. 'I know exactly what I'm having.' He pointed to the first thing.

'Betty's Belly Buster!' Rose read.

'Oh, yes.' He leaned back in his chair and patted his non-existent stomach. 'You don't get a physique like mine eating salad, you know.'

'One tea, one latte.' A gangly lad interrupted Rose's thoughts about James's physique and placed a tall glass mug in front of James and a tea tray in front of Rose, complete with a second teapot.

'I do love it when you get a second pot.' Rose tapped the taller of the two pots as Sam walked away. 'You always need a little more water to make that third cup, you know?'

'Is that other pot just filled with water then?' He lifted the lid. 'Never knew that.'

'How can you not know that?' She was busy pouring a small amount of milk from the tiny white jug into her cup.

'I don't really drink tea.' He added three heaped teaspoons of sugar to his mug and stirred it vigorously, the coffee and hot milk mixing instantly.

'Surely you've been out with someone who does, though?' Didn't everyone know about the hot water pot?

'My mum drinks tea.' He took a sip of his latte. 'But she doesn't really go out a lot.'

Again, Rose had the impression that there was more to this than James was saying, but she didn't press him and was glad when Betty came back to take their order.

'You know what I'll be ordering, Betty,' James said with a cheesy grin. 'I could eat a horse, and we've got a busy day ahead of us.'

'One Betty's Belly Buster.' Rose saw her write BBB on her pad. 'You off to the fayre at Haggerston then? Looks like it's going to be a good weekend for it too. Lots of sunshine, so it will be busy. I'll make you up some sandwiches to take with you. You'll probably be rushed off your feet.' She turned to Rose, her pencil poised. 'And what can I get you, my sweet?'

'I'll have the same, please.' She ignored the look of approving surprise on James's face.

'A girl after my own heart.' Betty smiled at her. 'I'll go pop that little lot on the griddle for you.'

'You'll never eat it all,' James said when Betty had gone.

'You have an incredibly low opinion of me, don't you?' She poured tea into her cup, slowly and deliberately.

'Actually' – he picked up his mug again and looked over the rim at her – 'I have a rather high opinion of you.'

Rose tried hard not to blush. 'What do you bet me?'

'A kiss.' He spoke matter-of-factly. 'If you don't finish it all, then I can kiss you.' This statement was accompanied by raised eyebrows. 'But if you do finish it all, then you can kiss me.'

She laughed. 'That's the same thing.'

'Oh, but it isn't.' He put down his mug and leaned over towards her. 'If you kiss me, I suspect it will be a peck on the cheek, perhaps the lips if I'm lucky.' He stroked the back of one of her hands gently. 'But if I kiss you . . .' He paused. 'Then I would most definitely kiss you on the lips. Softly at first, like butterfly's wings, then ever so slightly increasing the pressure until . . .'

Rose wasn't aware when he stopped talking. She also wasn't aware that her mouth was wide open in anticipation, her whole body tingling.

'Yes . . . well.' She tried to compose herself. 'We'll leave the kissing for another time, shall we?'

'Oh, we will.' He sat back in his seat. 'We definitely will.'

'I don't think I'll get my apron around my stomach.' They were back in the van and almost at Haggerston Hall. 'I've never eaten so much in my entire life.'

'I swear it was bigger than I remember.' James had had to undo his belt when he got in the van, claiming the buckle had always been too tight, but Rose knew it was because he was as stuffed as she was. 'Betty definitely put more on it. Five of everything! Who can eat five of everything?'

'I'm sure the picture was of three.' Rose pulled a bottle of water out of her bag and took a sip. 'And fried bread and toast definitely weren't in the description.'

Rose's eyes had widened when Sam delivered platters of food, accompanied by five rounds of toast, with each and every flavour of jam and marmalade imaginable.

'Did you see the looks we were getting from those three workmen?' James laughed. 'They kept glancing at ours then looking at theirs and counting.'

'I don't think we'll be needing these sandwiches either.' Rose patted the neatly packed brown paper bags. 'In fact, I don't think I'll be eating for a week.' She rubbed her tummy and groaned. 'Oh, it hurts so much.'

'You'll be okay when you're up and about.' He started to slow down. 'Nearly there, look.' He pointed in front. 'Always a queue to get in.'

They stopped behind a longish line of assorted vehicles, moving slowly but steadily towards the entrance. Rose could see Haggerston Hall in the distance and was once again thankful to live in an area with such wonderful history and historical houses. It was obviously what had drawn the Hollywood filmmakers here. Although the film wasn't strictly historical, it had time-slip elements to it with the main character travelling between various points in history where she met the male lead each time until, eventually, they fell in love in the present day.

Rose sent a quick text to her parents to tell them that they had arrived and were just waiting to get in. Even now, they worried about her. In fact, her mum had told her one day that it wouldn't matter how old she was, she would always worry about her.

Have a lovely day with James xx, was her mum's reply, which Rose ignored completely. She put her phone away and vowed not to tell her mum and dad anything about her life ever again.

'You have got to be kidding me.' They were driving towards the hall now, and Rose felt James stiffen. 'I told him I didn't need any help. When will he ever listen to me?'

She couldn't work out what, or whom, James was talking about. Clearly, he had spotted something she hadn't. All she could see was the Georgian hall on the left and the rumps of two white horses inside a horse trailer in front of them.

James parked the van on the left-hand side of the horse trailer and got out without a word, slamming the van door. Rose grabbed her bag, stepped gingerly out onto the gravel and felt her stomach shift downwards slightly, just like James had said it would.

She headed to the back of the van and was starting to unload her bike when she heard raised voices.

'When are you going to accept that Grandpa has given the business to me, not you?' It was James.

'Don't raise your voice with me,' came the reply.

Rose judged that the voices were just on the other side of the van.

'I'll bloody well raise my voice whenever I bloody well want to. It's been six months since Grandpa retired, and he made it perfectly clear you weren't to have anything to do with the business.'

'Well, Dad has said otherwise.' The other voice sounded cocky. 'And as he owns thirty percent now, he overrules you.'

'He may overrule me,' James said, 'but I overrule you.'

The sound of angry footsteps made Rose jump and she quickly climbed into the van so James wouldn't know she'd been eavesdropping. In her hurry, she tripped over some rather long boxes, which toppled and spilled lilies onto the floor of the van.

'You'll need to undo those first, you know?' Rose was trying to move the bike and its trailer, completely forgetting the ropes that were tying it down.

'Well, you put them there,' she retorted, annoyed that she always seemed to make herself look stupid in front of James. 'I'm afraid some of the flowers have got a little damaged.'

'Oh, I'm sure James and his magic fingers will sort those.' Rose's head snapped around.

'What do you mean?' And there in the doorway was James – except it wasn't James. 'Who on earth are you?'

CHAPTER NINE

'Peter Blume.' He held out a hand. 'An absolute pleasure to meet you.'

'Rose.' She shook his hand, somewhat in shock.

'Oh, I know who you are.' He winked.

'Well, you have me at a disadvantage then, because apart from the obvious fact that you're related to James, I have absolutely no idea who you are.' Peter was the spitting image of James, except his hair was quiffed to the other side and he had a slightly cruel twist to his mouth.

'Let's just say James has told me all about you and your quaint little business.' Rose hadn't particularly liked James when she'd first met him, but with Peter, she felt an instant hatred.

'I see you've met my brother.' James had appeared at the back of the van. Rose noticed he looked rather flustered.

'Come now, James.' Peter threw an arm around his brother's shoulders. 'We are much more than just brothers.' He placed his face right next to James's. 'We're identical twins!'

'I think Rose has probably worked that out for herself.'

He gently dislodged himself from his brother's grasp. 'No!' He let out a cry. 'What happened to the lilies?' He started picking them up one by one and examining each one to see what could be saved.

'My fault, I'm afraid,' Rose confessed. 'I'll pay for any damage.'

'I'm not worried about that.' James had so far salvaged about five and thrown ten. 'I'm just not sure I'll have enough to make the bouquets.'

'Stop fretting, James.' Peter started looking through the other boxes. 'Just use the carnations.'

'This is why Grandpa doesn't want you anywhere near the business.' He closed the lid on the box Peter had opened. 'You have absolutely no bloody idea about flowers and arrangements.'

'Just because you have fancy floristry qualifications and go on courses doesn't mean you know everything.' Peter made a face at James as though he was five years old.

'I don't claim to know everything.' James had started to undo the ropes on Rose's bike, but he'd not taken his eyes off Peter for even a second. 'But I know a hell of a lot more than you with your degree in dropping out.'

Rose swallowed, hoping that James didn't share the same animosity for *all* university drop-outs.

'Well, I'll just go and register,' Rose said, making a quick exit as soon as her bike was free and out on the ground. She left it parked next to the van, but out of the way of anyone else, and headed off to the entrance.

'Oh wow.' Rose had forgotten how magnificent the hall was. It had been years since she'd visited. She walked along the marble floor, today covered with a deep red carpet. She passed the marble staircase, roped off for the day, and symmetrical, pillar-framed doors until she came to the double doors she knew led to the ballroom.

It was a hive of activity. The original floor was protected by modern-day floorboards lain over the top, and tables sat in between alabaster pillars that ran from floor to ceiling. *My goodness the ceiling.* Rose had no idea if it was typical of the Georgian period, or whether the original Lord Haggerston had just liked it, but the ceiling was painted with clouds and cherubs and beautiful angels.

Rose was so busy looking up that she walked straight into the back of a gentleman dressed in a dark grey suit. 'I am so sorry!' When he turned around, she noticed he was carrying a rather large folder and a pen and had Haggerston Hall embroidered on his blazer.

'No worries,' he said, waving her apology away. 'I quite often do that myself, you know. Been here fifteen years and I'm still in awe of the place.'

'I used to come here with my parents all the time, but I'd forgotten how beautiful it is.'

'Thank you.' The man seemed to take the compliment personally, and Rose could tell he took great pride in his place of work. 'I presume you're a stallholder?' He opened up his folder. 'What's the name of your business?'

'Pedals and Prosecco.'

'Pedals and Prosecco,' he repeated slowly, dragging a finger down the list. 'Here you are. Right at the bottom.' Rose resisted the urge to raise her eyebrows. 'We've put you outside under the pavilion. There are a few others out there with you, so you won't be lonely.' He took her to the large sash windows that ran along one side of the room and pointed to the large metal gazebo festooned with ivy and honeysuckle. 'Just head back outside and round to the left.'

'Thank you.' Rose did exactly as she was told, passing James laden with boxes on the way. She smiled at him. 'They've put me outside.' He still looked extremely flustered and out of sorts, and she even noticed that his usually immaculate hair had started to flop into his eyes a little. 'Do you need any help with anything?' It was over an hour until visitors would start arriving, and she knew it would only take a few minutes to set the bike up. Plus, she had damaged some of his flowers.

'We're fine, thank you.' Peter was behind him, wheeling a trolley. In complete contrast to James, he looked cool and composed.

'That would be great,' James contradicted, ignoring Peter completely.

'I'll just park the bike up and I'll be right back.'

Rose knew absolutely nothing about flowers except a few of their names, and she knew even less about how to arrange them. James talked about teardrops, posies and baskets, buttonholes, crowns and centrepieces, and all sorts of things that meant nothing to her.

A Little in Love

Peter was even less help than Rose. James had asked him to arrange some flowers in vases for simple yet elegant centre-pieces. When he'd shown them to James, Rose thought even she would have done a much better job. The tall roses and lilies that should have been adding elegance to the pieces had been cut so short that they just balanced on the rim of the vase, and the gypsophila seemed to be taking centre stage rather than adding depth and helping to accentuate the other blooms.

'Dear God, Peter.' James pulled each flower out and cut them even shorter. 'These roses are only good for button-holes now, and the poor lilies.' He sighed. There had been hardly any lilies left after Rose's disaster with the boxes, and now there were even fewer.

'Why can't you use the lilies for buttonholes?' Rose asked.

'People like roses and carnations,' James answered. 'Plus, lily pollen stains so we have to remove the anther part of the stamen as soon as it opens. It would be quite time-consuming for a buttonhole. Although ...' He took one of the short-stemmed lilies and attached it to what looked like a hair band. 'Voila! A corsage.' He held it out to Rose. 'May I?'

'You may.' She held out her hand and James slipped the band onto her wrist. She stroked the pink petals gently. 'It goes with my uniform.' She held it up against her chest; it matched the embroidered writing perfectly. Looking up at James, she found he was looking right back at her and her stomach did that flip-flop thing again.

'Can I throw up now please?' Peter's voice interrupted the moment.

83

'Goodness me, is that the time?' Rose looked at her other wrist, even though she wasn't actually wearing a watch. 'I'd better be getting back to the bike. Won't look particularly good if I'm not there when the guests arrive now, will it?'

She hurried out of the ballroom, rushing past the last flurry of people setting up.

The garden was almost as busy as the ballroom. There was a pen with alpacas, a lady with a rather large cage containing two pure white doves, and there, right next to Rose's stall, were the two white horses they'd followed up the drive. They were now fully kitted out in their tack, chomping on their shiny bits. Behind them stood a regal-looking white carriage, currently with its top down. A gloriously painted metal sign proclaimed that they belonged to Lucy Greenfield and were 'as seen in the Hollywood blockbuster *A Little in Love*'.

'These two are gorgeous.' Rose had always loved horses and had no hesitation in heading over to them and stroking their noses. They nuzzled their heads against her hands.

'They are indeed. Meet Topsy and Tim.' A lady dressed resplendently in red and black, and looking like she'd stepped right out of the Cinderella fairytale, introduced them. 'Named them after my favourite kids' books.'

'I've never seen a white shire horse, let alone two.' Rose held out a hand in greeting. 'I'm Rose Pedal.'

'So, *you're* Rose,' the woman said, taking Rose's hand. Rose stared blankly. 'I'm Lucy, from the WhatsApp group.'

Rose recognized the name. 'Oh, of course! It's nice to meet you.'

'Technically they're greys,' Lucy continued, turning back to the horses. 'They'd need to have pink skin to be officially classed as white.' She came to the front and started combing the mane of the slightly larger one; Rose assumed this was Tim. 'Took me years to find them and hours of training but it's been worth it. The brides love them. And the film didn't hurt business either.' She winked cheekily at this.

'I remember them in the film,' Rose said. 'When Jenny Golding stepped out of the carriage in that amazing wedding dress outside the castle . . .' She clasped her hands over her heart. 'Oh, it was just pure heart-melting stuff.'

'Took five days to get that scene,' Lucy said conspiratorially. 'There was always something wrong with the lighting, or one of the horses' manes wasn't right, or the dress didn't look right. Honestly, never work with film directors.' She scoffed. 'I'm just jesting. It was fabulous fun.'

'Well, these two are just delightful.' Rose gave them both another pet and headed off to her bike.

'Is that yours?' Lucy called over as Rose pulled everything out and started setting up. 'What a fantastic idea. Ever thought of using a horse and cart?'

'I can just about manage one bike.' Rose laughed, shaking her head. 'But it's an idea I'll keep in mind for the future.'

'Here we go,' Lucy said, and Rose turned around to see the first visitors coming into the garden. She straightened her apron, smoothed her hair and put on her best smile.

'There she is.' Rose searched for the owner of the voice.

'See, John, I told you she'd be out here. Just look how wonderful she looks. Like a proper businesswoman.'

'Mum, Dad, what on earth are you doing here?' Rose wished she could crawl under the nearest rock.

'It's such a nice day we decided not to waste it, so your dad gave the car a quick wash while I packed up a picnic and here we are.'

'There's my girl.' Rose looked behind her parents and saw her grandparents walking towards her, arms outstretched.

'What are you two doing here?' She almost ran into their arms, hugging them both tightly. Parents were embarrassing, but grandparents were a different matter.

'Your mum rang us up and asked if we wanted to join them for a picnic.' Her nan was beaming.

'And when she mentioned that we'd get to see you, well, that was just a bonus.' Her grandad hugged her again.

'Where is he, then?' Her mum looked around covertly.

'Who?' Rose decided to play dumb.

'James, of course,' her mum said. 'He seems lovely, Rose, he really does.' And not for the first time, Rose found herself thinking the same.

'He's in the ballroom,' she said. 'With his twin brother.'

'Twin? Wow!' her dad piped in. 'Must be nice to have such a supportive family.'

'I get the feeling they're not very close.' Just as Rose spoke these words, there was an almighty smash, and an unidentified Blume brother came crashing through one of the sash windows, glass and flowers flying everywhere.

CHAPTER TEN

The horses had been spooked by the noise and sudden rush of activity, and were now stamping at the ground and whinnying. Lucy had them settled again within a few seconds and Rose, closely followed by her parents, grandparents and everyone else it seemed, rushed over to help.

Rose breathed a sigh of relief when she realized it was Peter lying on the ground and not James.

'Quickly, he's bleeding. Someone call an ambulance.' The staff from the hall were on the situation in seconds. One removed their jacket and held it firmly on Peter's arm, where a surprising amount of blood was starting to ooze. Another was on the phone ringing 999, and a third, fourth and fifth had immediately run off, returning moments later with more staff all armed with dustpans and brooms. Seconds after that, two gentlemen dressed in overalls appeared carrying a large piece of wood and proceeded to cover up the damaged window.

Once Peter had been taken away in the ambulance, Rose

looked for James in the crowd of people who had come out of the hall. 'What on earth happened?' she asked him. 'Don't you want to go with him?'

'Not particularly,' James said. 'He'll just be stitched up and sent home, nothing major.' Rose couldn't believe how cold he sounded. It was his brother, after all – his twin, come to mention it.

'What happened then?' Rose asked again. The crowd was starting to disperse. People headed back to their stalls, and the guests started milling about once more.

'Let's just say a fiancé didn't take too kindly to his flirting with the bride.' James shrugged. 'I told him to stay by me and the stall but no ... as per usual, Peter knows best. Next thing I know he's through the window and on the floor.'

'Blimey! Was he a big chap?' Although James and Peter were quite slender, their height gave them an advantage, and it would have taken some strength to propel Peter through a window with that much force.

'*She*,' James said, 'is an amateur body builder.' He shoved his hands in his pockets and looked around. 'We could get thrown out for this. I'd best find the manager and apologize, and of course pay for my brother's damage.'

'Let me know what happens.' He gave her a despondent wave as he headed back inside, and Rose went back to the bike, which was being admired by three young women.

'What a fabulous idea,' Rose overheard one say as she came within earshot. 'I'm definitely booking it for my reception.'

'Well, I'm booking it for mine and I'm getting married first.'

'My engagement party is before any of your weddings, so I'm booking it.'

Rose felt like she'd stepped back in time and was about to referee a screaming match between debutantes.

'How can I help you, ladies?' She came up behind them and stifled a giggle as the three women vied to be the first to speak.

The one with short brown hair spoke first. 'I want you at my wedding.'

'Petunia!' the other two said in unison.

'I'm the eldest and I've got the biggest wedding, so there.' She stuck her tongue out at the other two.

'It's not fair!' The one with long blonde hair stormed off.

'Now then.' Petunia turned her attention back to Rose. 'June 12th next year. Mark me down please. Five hundred guests at Coombe Castle.'

'I'll just check my diary.' Rose already knew she was free that day. She so wanted to say no to this spoilt brat, but five hundred guests? There was no way she could turn that down.

'I want the finest crystal goblets, please, one for each guest, engraved with Petunia and Edward.' Rose hadn't even agreed and already she was scribbling down this woman's requirements. 'You'll be in the entrance hall, of course, right by the grand staircase. I think ten servers should be enough. And I want everyone to be able to take their glasses home with them, so they'll need boxes. And I want champagne not Prosecco please. The name is quaint, but only the best at my wedding.'

'Petunia, you are such a spoilt ass,' the third sister said, and Rose admired her spunk. 'Let the woman get a word in. She hasn't even said she can do that day – you've just assumed she can.'

'Well? Can you?' Petunia turned to Rose, who almost jumped to attention.

'Yes, I can, but . . .'

'Fantastic!' She handed Rose a white card with gold lettering. 'Here are my deets. Ring me tomorrow about four, and you can speak to Daddy about prices and things.' And with that, she was gone, heading towards Topsy and Tim with a squeal of delight. 'Well, I simply must arrive in this carriage if it was used by Hollywood stars.'

'Sorry about her.' The third young woman was still loitering. 'I try to reign in her in, but it's no good.' She held out a hand. 'I'm Daisy.'

'Rose.' They shook hands.

'We're all a little spoilt, I'm afraid, used to getting what we want, but Petunia takes the gold medal. It's our father's fault. Apple of his eye – we all are, but there's just something about Petunia that makes him give in so easily.' She sighed. 'We hoped Edward, her fiancé, would be able to . . . tame her a little, shall we say, but he's absolutely spineless and like a big wet blanket.' She giggled. 'Really shouldn't say that about my future brother-in-law, should I?'

'I won't tell if you won't,' Rose assured her.

'I like you, Rose,' Daisy said. 'You're a breath of fresh air.' She turned to go. 'Make sure you get full payment, non-refundable, up front. Petunia has a habit of changing her mind.' With a wave, she was gone.

'What a horrid young woman.' Janet said, making Rose realize that she had completely forgotten about her parents and grandparents. 'And what an absolutely awful thing to happen to James. I hope he doesn't get in trouble for his brother's behaviour.'

'I'm sure he won't.' Rose knew James would somehow manage to charm the manager. After all, Blume's was a big-city florist, well known in the area, and she was sure they'd been regular stallholders at Haggerston's fayre for years.

'We're going to head off and leave you to it.' Her dad was pulling her mum's arm. 'Janet, will you accompany me for a turn around the gardens?' Rose could see her mum was reluctant to move, and mouthed a silent thank you to her dad.

'We'll join you.' Her grandad offered his arm to her nan, blew Rose a kiss and followed her parents.

> **Lucy**: Well you lot missed a treat. Did anyone see what happened inside? Alice? Millie?
>
> **Millie**: I'd bloody well nipped to the loo, when I came back it was all over.
>
> **Fanny**: What's happened? I knew I should have booked a stall.
>
> **Alice**: Peter Blume was on the receiving end of a right hook, he went flying through the window.

Natalie: Why does all the gossip happen when I'm not there?
Lucy: Been taken off in an ambulance, blood everywhere.
Alice: Poor James is with the manager now, never seen him so downcast.
Natalie: He'll be ok, the Blumes can charm the backside off a donkey.
Millie: And don't forget, money talks.

The rest of the day passed without further incident. James had been allowed to stay on the proviso that his brother never returned and they paid in full for the window to be replaced. If anything, the furore had only increased the amount of traffic heading to James's stall, and he told Rose later over Betty's sandwiches that he'd been absolutely rushed off his feet.

The visitors had long since departed, the hall locked up with most of the stalls still inside for Sunday's event, but the gardens were staying open until eight. They'd found a lovely spot under an oak tree by the lake and sat down wearily.

'I can't believe these are still okay.' Rose waggled a ham sandwich in front of him. 'I expected the crusts to be curly at least.'

'The bonus of a having a chilled van for the flowers.' They had already parked the bike and placed some of the arrangements inside to keep them chilled overnight. Anything that stood in water or an oasis had been left on the table. 'Shame you haven't got a place for tomorrow. We've not really seen each other much today.'

'We're seeing each other now.' She felt suddenly shy under his gaze. 'There's no room for me tomorrow. They're using outside for a fashion show and need the space to set up a catwalk.'

'Why don't you help me tomorrow then?' he said quickly, as if the idea had just hit him. 'We'll leave the big van here and take back the one Peter brought. You could stay over at ours, if you like. Plenty of spare rooms. We only live five miles away.'

'I haven't got anything with me.' She paused, taking in what he'd just said. 'What do you mean you only live five miles from here? I thought you lived in the city.'

'The business is based in the city, but Grandpa and Grandma moved out of the flat above the shop when Dad and Uncle Tony were toddlers.'

'You drove all the way to Tointon to pick me up?' She was flattered.

'Guilty as charged.' He held his hands up. 'Now, you're not going to make me drive all the way back again are you?'

'Yes, I am.' His smile faded into instant disappointment, and she laughed. 'You promised me a lift and that involves a return journey home.'

'Very well, then.' She could see he was hurt.

'It will give us more time alone together on the way home.' This seemed to abate him a little and he leaned over and hugged her like an enthusiastic puppy. As he drew back, she realized how close his lips were to hers. How if she just reached up the smallest, tiniest amount then they would touch. Her eyes flickered to his, then back to his mouth. Time seemed to stand still, frozen around that perfect moment.

'We're closing, you know.' A gruff voice interrupted them, and they turned guiltily to see the park keeper swinging keys impatiently. 'Good job I took a walk down this way otherwise you'd have been locked in all night.'

'Sorry.'

'So sorry.' They both spoke at the same time, hastily gathering their belongings and following the park keeper out into the car park.

'I'll lock the gate as soon as you're gone.'

'But there are loads of vehicles still here,' Rose pointed out.

'Well, if they're not staying local then they'll be walking home.' He seemed to be ushering Rose and James along.

'Darn it.' James patted his pockets. 'Peter's got the keys.'

'We'll just take the big one then.' Rose walked towards the other van.

'Both sets.' He looked at her helplessly. 'I'll have to call Dad.'

'I'm not waiting another bloomin' minute,' the park keeper said. 'You either move one of them vans right now or they're both staying in here for the night.'

'But—' James started.

'No buts.' He pushed them to the gate. 'Out you go.' And despite further protests, James and Rose found themselves on the opposite side of the huge iron gates while the park keeper rattled the padlock in front of them to make sure it was locked.

'That's that then.' Rose leaned on the wall. 'You'd best ring your dad.' It was looking increasingly like she was going to have to stay the night at his after all. James driving her home was one thing, but expecting his dad to drive thirty miles there and then thirty miles back was a little extreme.

'We could both get an Uber?' James said. Rose got the impression he didn't want to ring his dad and tell him he'd got the vans locked up for the night, even if it was technically Peter's fault.

'That sounds fine.' She smiled, relieved that she could just call an Uber later to take her home. It wasn't that she didn't want to stay at his house, she just didn't want things moving so quickly. 'What about a drink first? I'm sure there's a pub just down the road.'

'As long as it's not bingo night.' He laughed and took her hand in his.

'No promises.' She smiled back, enjoying the feel of his fingers on the back of her hand. It felt right, comfortable even and, despite herself, her heart smiled inside.

CHAPTER ELEVEN

'I honestly don't believe how someone as clever as you can be so bloody stupid.' Rose felt totally uneasy in the back of the Jaguar as James's dad shouted at him like he was a five-year-old. 'Your brother comes home covered in blood without so much as a phone call from you to warn us. Your mum's had one of her attacks and taken to her bed again, and now this . . .' Rose wasn't sure if 'this' referred to the vans being locked up or her staying the night.

'It wasn't my fault, Dad,' James argued.

'It never is, son, it never is.' He tutted. 'And I suppose you'll be needing a bloody lift in the morning?'

'You've got to come and pick up Peter's van anyway, so I don't see why—' James was cut off in mid-sentence.

'You never do see,' his father said angrily. 'That's your problem. Always off doing something else instead of concentrating on the matter in hand, never stopping to think about the consequences of your actions.' He beeped his horn and swore loudly as a fox ran across the road in front of the car.

'Now your uncle and I have to get up early in the morning to drive the pair of you back to Haggerston Hall.'

'I couldn't help that Peter took the keys with him.'

'Peter had just been thrown through a window and carted off in an ambulance.' James went to speak again, but his father put up his hand, signalling the end of the conversation. 'I should think the last thing he was thinking about was bloody van keys.'

The rest of the journey passed in silence and Rose wished they hadn't left it so late to call an Uber. Thanks to the remote location, the app had said it was going to be over two hours' waiting time, and as all of James's keys were on one keyring, it turned out he didn't have his house keys either. When James rang home to ask if someone could wait up for them, his dad had said he may as well pick them up; then at least he could be in bed this side of midnight. And somehow Rose had found herself agreeing to stay the night. If she'd known how this day was going to end, she'd have walked the thirty miles back home.

Rose had rung her mum to say she wouldn't be home that night and that she was helping James out the next day.

'But where will you sleep?' Rose could tell her mum was worrying about her virtue. Surely they knew she wasn't a virgin?

'In a spare room,' Rose reassured her. 'It's okay, Mum. He still lives with his mum and dad.'

'Your dad and I will come pick you up.'

'We've had a bottle of wine, Janet,' Rose heard her dad say in the background. 'We're not going anywhere.'

'Honestly, Mum, it's fine. Like I said, he still lives at home with his parents.'

In fact when they arrived at the Blume family home – which reminded Rose of a ten-bedroom bed and breakfast she had stayed in with her parents in the New Forest, complete with a lounge, breakfast room and separate accommodation for the owners – she discovered that it wasn't only his parents he lived with.

When they entered the lounge, which was the same size as the vicarage's entire downstairs – and Rose knew the vicarage wasn't small, by any means – the room was already full of people.

'I didn't think you'd all still be up.' James ran an agitated hand through his hair. 'Everyone, this is Rose. Rose, this is everyone.'

Rose smiled and said hello.

'We weren't until your father starting banging about and slamming doors.' The elderly gentleman in the far corner, who Rose assumed was James's grandfather, stood up and helped the elderly lady next to him to her feet. 'Now, we'll be off back to bed. Show Rose to the guest room at the back of the house next to ours.' With a curt nod to Rose, he ushered the lady along, but she gave Rose a friendly wink as she passed by.

'Oliver, William, come along.' The other older man in the room, who by means of elimination had to be Uncle Tony, urged twin boys, around the age of four, up off the sofa.

'Night, Gramps,' they said in unison, kissing everyone in the room including Rose and heading out the door.

'I'll go tuck them in,' said a woman, who must have been James's cousin. She left the room, followed by her husband a few seconds later.

The room now seemed almost empty. James's father was pouring himself what looked like whisky, while Peter was looking very pale in one of the chairs, a crisp white bandage wrapped round his arm, and Uncle Tony and his wife were cradling steaming mugs in their hands.

'Would you like a cup of tea?' The aunt stood up. 'I'm Maureen by the way. Absolute pleasure to meet you.'

'I'm fine, thank you.' Rose desperately wanted to get out of the room. Everyone seemed so stiff and on edge. Nothing like the welcome you could expect at the vicarage. 'I'm really tired.' She pretended to yawn and stretched her arms above her head.

'I'll show you to your room,' James said. Rose felt his hand reach for hers but then it was gone.

'Does everyone live here?' She'd assumed they did, what with all of them being here so late at night, but thought she'd check.

'Yep.' James didn't sound too pleased. 'Grandpa just adds more rooms on. When Elizabeth, my cousin, got married he added a whole new wing. They've got three bedrooms, their own sitting room, dining room and kitchen. It's just like a house within a house.'

'Must have been nice growing up with all your family around you?' Rose envisioned dinners around the table each night, playing hide-and-seek in all the rooms and sliding down banisters. 'Christmas must have been wonderful!' Both her parents were only children, and her dad's parents had died when Rose was just a baby, so Christmas had always been a small affair with just her mum and dad and her maternal grandparents, but it had been magical every year and still was even now.

She'd bounce onto her mum and dad's bed around 5am; the bonus of having a vicar for a father, he allowed it as he had to be up and off to church for the Christmas Day service at eleven.

A cooked breakfast would follow the present opening and then they would all get washed and dressed for church. This was the only time Rose was ever made to go and she always said she would have gone anyway because she loved Christmas and singing the hymns. Everyone was always so happy on Christmas Day.

Her nan and grandad would arrive around two with more presents and dinner was always served at quarter past three after the Queen's speech. Then, with full bellies, the five of them would take a walk around the village before heading home for board games and nibbles in front of the fire.

'Not so much.' He shrugged, bringing Rose back to the present. 'I don't think my father really wanted children, and certainly not two of us.'

'That's not true, surely?' Although part of her could believe it. On the two occasions she'd met James's father so far, she hadn't got a fatherly vibe from him in the slightest. In fact, the only vibe she got from him was one of constant annoyance.

'Geoffrey Blume doesn't do mess, noise or anything that upsets his routine.' They had come up a beautifully carved staircase, smooth as silk to the touch, and were now standing outside a wooden door; one of many, Rose noticed. 'Mum tried her best, but she gets ill a lot.' Before Rose could ask any more, James had opened the door and switched on the light. 'Here we are then. En suite bathroom just there.' He pointed to a door by the window. 'There'll be toiletries and stuff in there, and I'll grab you one of my T-shirts to wear to bed.'

He headed off down the landing while Rose went into the room. It was decorated with flowery blue wallpaper and a deep blue carpet. The covers on the soft-looking double bed matched the wallpaper perfectly, and Rose noticed that the cushions on the bed and the rocking chair that sat in one corner matched the border that ran around the top of the walls just under the coving.

'This is a lovely room,' she said to James when he came back a few minutes later. He'd changed out of his suit and now wore long black pyjama bottoms and a plain white T-shirt. She'd only ever seen him in formal attire before, but the casual clothes suited him just as well.

'It was my grandma's before she married my grandpa.' He looked around. 'Mum used to read to me in that chair.' He nodded towards the rocking chair that Rose had noticed earlier. 'We'd sit there for hours on rainy afternoons while Dad was at work and Peter was off causing mischief somewhere. It gets the best light and has a gorgeous view of the roses in the summer.'

'This isn't the Blume family's ancestral home then?' She chuckled. If it had been his nan's room before she married, then it couldn't have been in the Blume family for more than a few decades.

'Grandma and Grandpa caused a bit of a scandal back in the day.' He laughed. 'Grandpa didn't have a penny to his name – his family were miners – but he loved the fresh air and flowers. Great-Grandma used to tell us how he was always making bouquets from the wildflowers and sometimes weeds he found growing in their village. Apparently, he used to say it's only a weed because it wasn't meant to be there, but that doesn't mean it isn't beautiful.'

Rose had to agree. Weeds weren't necessarily ugly. She loved the buttercups and daisies that grew on the vicarage lawn, and who hadn't blown a dandelion clock or two on a summer's day?

'How did they meet?' Rose enjoyed a good love story.

'It was at a Christmas dance in the early Sixties,' he began. 'Grandpa had escorted his sister there and Grandma was there because her family were hosting it as a charity event for the local orphanage. By the following New Year, my dad had been born. Even though it was the Sixties, it was still quite frowned upon to have a baby out of wedlock and to marry out of your class, but Grandpa proved them all wrong. He worked night and day to build up Blume's. Luckily my great-grandparents allowed them to marry but Grandpa swore he wanted to stand on his own two feet and he bought the shop and he and Grandma lived in the flat above until my grandma persuaded him to move back here a few years later, when Dad and Uncle Tony were ready for school.'

'That's like something from a romance novel,' Rose said, taking the T-shirt James had suddenly remembered he was holding. 'Thank you.'

An awkward silence hung above them. Rose didn't want him to leave but couldn't think of anything to say to keep him there, and she got the impression that James was feeling exactly the same way.

'I suppose I should get to bed,' he said. A distant chime signalled it was now one o'clock. 'I'll set my alarm for seven and knock you up on the way.' She raised her eyebrows at this, and he laughed. 'You know what I mean, Miss Pedal.'

'Now look who's being all formal.'

'It's the only way I can stop myself from kissing you.'

She stepped closer to him, feeling suddenly brave and reckless. 'Why are you stopping yourself?'

'Because once I start kissing you, I won't want to stop.' He reached out a hand and caressed her cheek. She leaned into his palm.

'Who said you have to stop?' She couldn't believe how forward she was being.

'You two had best be getting to bed.' Grandpa Blume was standing outside his door. 'And by that, I mean your own beds.'

CHAPTER TWELVE

Breakfast was a stilted affair. The Blume senior brothers were both already up when Rose and James came into the kitchen. Tony tried to make conversation, asking Rose about her family and seemed genuinely interested in the business.

'What's new about using a bike to serve and sell from?' Geoffrey 'don't call me Geoff' – as he would always now be known in Rose's head after she'd addressed him as such earlier that morning – scoffed as she told them about her bike. 'People have been selling from bikes for years. Look at the ice cream sellers and bakers back in the day. Honestly, when James told us about it the other week, I couldn't believe what a stupid idea it was.'

'Dad!' James shouted.

'Geoff!' Tony said at the exact same time (clearly, his brother was allowed to call him that).

'It's a bloody brilliant idea if you ask me,' James said, to which Tony nodded in agreement.

'I thought it was too when you were telling me,' Tony continued. 'And your Aunt Maureen agreed with me.'

'You two wouldn't know a good business idea if it slapped you in the face,' Geoffrey said. 'That's why Dad gave the business to me when he retired and not you.'

'Actually, he gave it to James,' was Tony's reply.

'He only gave his shares to James so I wouldn't have more than you because he knew you'd moan about it.' Rose squirmed uncomfortably in her seat. Was this how rich families treated each other?

'You own twenty-five percent and I own twenty-five percent so that makes us equal in my eyes.' Tony slammed his cup down on the marbled counter. 'Although why he gave ten percent to that useless son of yours, I'll never know.'

'He gave ten percent to your daughter who wouldn't know a chrysanthemum from a carnation.' Geoffrey slammed his cup down too, except his was almost full and coffee spilled over the edge. 'Now look what you made me do!' He got up and grabbed a cloth from the sink.

'Morning, Gramps.' One of the twins came bounding in, dinosaur slippers flopping on the kitchen tiles, and clambered up onto one of the bar stools beside the breakfast bar.

'Morning, Oliver.' Tony ruffled his hair. 'Where's your brother?'

'Still asleep.' Oliver threw his hands up in the air in despair. 'He always sleeps longerer than me.'

'What do we want for breakfast, then?' James grabbed a couple of cereal bars from one of the cupboards, two small bottles of orange juice from the gigantic American-style fridge and a few pieces of fruit, before indicating for Rose to follow him.

'Is breakfast always such a quiet affair?' Rose asked, biting into an apple. They were sitting side by side, a small distance apart, at the bottom of the garden under a canopy of late-spring blossoms, their breakfast picnic laid out between them on three tissues James had found in his pocket. (He had assured her they were clean before opening them out and emptying his pockets of his mini feast.)

'I'm afraid there's usually some kind of argument or disagreement going on.' He was currently munching on a cereal bar, one elbow resting on a bent knee. He wasn't yet dressed in his suit – jeans and a T-shirt were his current attire, and Rose, who was luckily a similar size to Elizabeth, had borrowed a beautiful pale yellow summer dress and yellow Converse trainers. What borrowed actually meant was James pinching from the clean washing pile in the laundry room. But the day was already hot, and Rose was glad of the cool clothes. 'It's a bit like that Madness song, "Our House". There's always something going on and it's very rarely quiet.'

'So different to my house,' Rose said. 'There's only me, Mum and Dad, and some days it's just me if Mum and Dad are out and about doing church stuff. I can go a whole day sometimes without actually speaking to anyone.'

Her phone beeped, and Rose smiled to herself as she glanced at the lock screen, before putting the phone back in her bag.

'And who is making you smile like that at this time of the morning?' Rose detected a hint of jealousy in James's voice.

'It's my best friend, Megan.' She picked up one of the orange juices. 'She wants to know if I'm playing hard to get.'

'I don't believe I've had the pleasure of meeting Megan,' he said with a smile.

'You'd like her.' Rose took a sip of juice. It was cold and tart and she drew her lips in and shuddered at its sharpness. 'She's been looking out for me since the first day of primary school.'

'Then I look forward to meeting her one day.' He looked down at the remaining bits of food. 'Sorry it's not as good as yesterday.'

'To be honest with you' – she patted her stomach – 'I don't think I could have managed even a bacon butty let alone another one of Betty's Belly Busters.' She laughed.

'I'll take you for afternoon tea there one day,' he said, grabbing a banana and peeling it. 'Betty makes amazing cherry scones and homemade jam.' He wagged the banana at her. 'And she doesn't scrimp on the clotted cream either.'

'It's a date,' she said.

'It's a promise.' He caught her eye and smiled. Her stomach did that flippy thing again and she looked away, pretending to have a sudden intense interest in a butterfly that was flitting slowly around. 'You can't keep looking away from me you know,' he said.

She turned her gaze back to him. When had he got so close to her? She was sure he'd been at least two feet from her when they'd first sat down. In fact, she'd made bloody well sure he was at least a small distance away. But now he was right beside her, his leg touching her leg, his hip touching her hip, his hand stretched out behind him, his fingers reaching out to touch the tips of hers.

Then, with speedy grace, he was on his knees facing her, his hand touching her chin, his fingers cupping it gently as he drew her face closer to his. His eyes never left hers as slowly, desperately slowly, his lips inched ever nearer. Then, just as she was sure he would kiss her, he stopped. His lips hovered above hers, so close she could feel the soft breath. *What is he waiting for?* She watched his gaze flick from her eyes to her lips and back again. Was he waiting for permission? Well, she wasn't going to wait any longer.

She turned her head slightly to one side and this was all the movement required to bring their lips together. Softly at first, like the wings of the butterfly she had watched a few moments ago. Electricity seemed to flow from his lips into hers, and coursed through her veins. Then they broke apart as quickly as they had come together, each composing themselves.

She felt alive, tingling, and also strangely bereft. She was already missing his touch, his kiss, after those briefest of seconds.

This time it was James who leaned in first. The hand that had been cupping her chin now found its way around the back of her head and into her hair. He pulled her against him, every part of his body now touching hers. His other hand circled her waist as she moved hers around his back.

After what felt like forever, they moved away, each breathing heavily. It had been so long since she'd let a man under her skin, and she had to admit, she liked the way it made her feel.

'We'd best be getting back inside.' James's voice sounded much higher to her than it usually did.

'Yes, very good idea.' She stood up, smoothing the dress down and running her fingers through her tousled hair in a bid to straighten it again.

Holding hands, they wandered slowly into the house where James's grandma was busy making tea.

'You'd best get your suit on, my boy – your dad's ready to go.'

'Thanks, Grandma.' He kissed her on the cheek and headed off. 'Look after Rose for me,' he said over his shoulder as he disappeared through the door.

'Don't you worry about Rose here.' She patted Rose's hand. 'I've got a feeling we'll get on just fine.' She smiled up at Rose, a genuine, warm smile, and for the first time, Rose actually felt welcome in the house.

'Your grandma is amazing,' Rose said to James as they packed more flowers into yet another green and gold van. This one was the same size as the one Peter had driven to the fayre yesterday. The one James had almost reversed into Rose's bike was parked in front of the huge garage that Rose now found herself standing in.

'She really is.' He grinned. 'I'm so glad you like her. It means so much to me that you do.'

'How could I not?' Rose recalled their conversation. 'She's so easy to talk to and so down to earth. She told me her three cardinal rules.'

'I bet she did.' James nodded. 'I know exactly what she said to you.'

'Go on then, smarty-pants.' Rose folded her arms and looked at him expectantly.

'Number one, play hard to get,' James said, and Rose nodded. 'You kind of played hard to get but I knew you'd agree to go out with me in the end.' Rose slapped him playfully, and he continued. 'Number two, don't kiss on the first date.' Rose nodded again.

'And the third?' she asked.

'The third is not to have sex without protection.'

Rose burst out laughing. 'It was so strange to hear that from someone of her age.' She shook her head in disbelief.

'I bet she didn't tell you that she broke every single one of those rules.' James was checking that the boxes of lilies were secure. 'It was because of Grandpa's hair.'

'His hair?' Rose screwed her face up.

'In those days, Grandpa had a fine head of hair on him.' James pulled out his phone and scrolled through the photos. 'There you go – a quiff to rival even mine.' A black-and-white version of James in drainpipe trousers and winkle-picker shoes was smiling out of the photo. 'Spit of him, aren't I?'

Rose had to agree. 'You are indeed. But what has his hair got to do with anything?'

'He bet Grandma that his hair would stay in place while they did the twist.' James put his phone back in his pocket.

'The twist?' She'd seen the dance moves many times; who hadn't? 'Not very vigorous, the twist?'

'It was in those days,' he assured her. 'They mixed all sorts of flips and goodness knows what else in there.' He started wiggling his hips. 'Of course, he won. He wasn't a Brylcreem boy for nothing.'

'And what did he ask for as a prize?' Rose had already guessed the answer. 'A kiss?'

'He did indeed.' James chuckled. 'So that was rule one and two broken, and the fact that Dad was born thirteen months later shows that rule three wasn't far behind.'

'At least I know where you get it from,' Rose said. James looked at her, confused. 'Breakfast at Betty's?'

'Oh yes.' His eyes lit up suddenly. 'I never did get my reward.' He placed a hand round her waist and pulled her gently towards him.

'That's because I never took the bet.' She loved and hated the feeling of him being so close to her.

'I'm still claiming my prize though.' His lips found hers within seconds, and without protest. Rose had never known a kiss to feel so good, like she could just stay that way forever.

'Come on, you two.' Tony's voice broke them apart and they stared guiltily at each other. 'Don't look like that. I think it's brilliant you've found each other, but don't let your dad catch you. You know what he's like.'

'Speak of the devil,' James muttered as his dad appeared, seemingly out of nowhere. 'Shall I drive, Dad?'

'Have we stepped into a parallel universe?' Geoffrey put some more boxes into the back of the van. 'I'll be driving, as I always do.' James went to shut the back doors, but his father stopped him. 'You need to get in first.'

'What do you mean?' Rose watched the confusion on James's face and was pretty sure hers held the same expression. 'You said you were driving us?'

'Egad!' Geoffrey shook his head. 'I am, but as there are only three seats at the front, you'll have to perch in the back somehow.' He smiled nastily. 'Unless, of course, you want Rose to travel in the back? I'm not fussed either way.'

'I'll go in the back.' Tony was already stepping up.

'Don't be silly, Uncle Tony.' James put a hand on his shoulder. 'It's only a few miles. I'll be fine.' James leapt into the back of the van.

'I'll travel with you.' And before James could protest, Rose was in the back of the van with him.

'Have it your way,' Geoffrey said, and slammed the doors shut.

CHAPTER THIRTEEN

'I don't think there's a part of me that isn't bruised.' Rose rubbed her arms and legs. 'Does he always drive like that?' The van had finally slowed to a snail's pace, and Rose assumed they were now in the queue to get into Haggerston Hall.

'No.' James was rubbing his neck. 'I swear it took longer than it should have done as well. Probably took the long way just to be difficult.'

'He really isn't a very nice man, is he?' Rose observed.

'You've noticed, have you?' James raised his eyebrows. 'Grandpa can be a bit like that, but his is more a generation thing. Dad's just plain rude and annoying.'

'Here we are then!' Thankfully it was Tony's cheerful face and voice that greeted them as the van doors opened. 'Oh dear.' He helped them out. 'You two don't look so good.'

'We don't feel so good, either.' Rose rubbed her stomach; she felt sick all of a sudden.

'Have some water.' Tony handed her a bottle and she sipped softly.

'Thanks.' She handed him the bottle back, but he waved her hand away and told her to keep it.

'Right, let's get the vans emptied and the stall set up,' Geoffrey ordered as he came around the side. 'Then you can get this one home, Tony, and I'll take the other one.'

It was all hands on deck to empty both vans, but after an hour, the table looked even better than it had the previous day, and Rose begrudgingly had to admit that Geoffrey certainly had an eye for floristry. His bouquets were perfect. He knew just what to put where, which shade of flower to use and what complemented what. And although Tony's efforts were as good as anything that Rose had seen at any wedding, there was just something about Geoffrey's that made them a cut above.

'Your dad's flowers are stunning,' she said to James, in a whisper so Geoffrey wouldn't hear. Rose had been given the very simple task of topping up the vases with water and re-wetting the oases in the table decorations.

'I know, sickening, isn't it?' James tutted. 'I can't even say it's years of practice because Uncle Tony has been doing it almost as long. Just natural flair I think.'

'Yours are good too,' Rose said, a little too hastily.

'You don't need to compliment me.' He smiled wryly.

'But they are.' She was being totally honest. 'I think you've got natural flair too.'

'Trust me,' he said, 'there's nothing natural about what I do. Years of training and long nights of practice.'

'Well, I wouldn't be able to tell the difference between

one of yours and one of your dad's.' She nodded as if to end the conversation.

'You are very sweet.' He gave her a quick kiss on the cheek. 'I know you're lying, but thank you anyway.' She smiled sheepishly. 'Fancy grabbing us a coffee?' He picked a twenty-pound note out of the inside pocket of his jacket.

'We'll be off then, you two,' Tony said, placing a set of keys on the table in front of James.

'These are for van one, aren't they, Uncle Tony?' James said. 'The one with Rose's bike inside?'

'Course they are,' his dad interrupted. 'Have a good day and no smashing windows this time. I dread to think what the bill will be.'

'I didn't smash any . . . oh, I give up.' He threw his hands up in the air. 'I'll see you back at home tonight after I've dropped Rose back. Remind Grandpa that I won't be there for dinner, will you?' This question was directed to his uncle; Rose was quickly getting the impression that James trusted and respected Tony far more than anyone else in his family. His uncle nodded and then they were gone.

'Latte, three sugars for you.' She placed two cups on the table, one in front of him.

'You remembered.' He sounded surprised.

'It wasn't hard.'

'Put it this way . . .' He took a sip and pulled a face. 'Bleurgh.'

'Oops.' Rose took the cup back off him. 'Helps if I stir

it.' She took the lid off and whisked a wooden stick around before tapping it on the side, replacing the lid and handing it back to him, before wrapping the stick in a serviette.

He took another sip and sighed. 'Much better. Anyway, as I was saying . . . my own mother can never remember how many sugars I have.'

'That's appalling!'

'Don't make fun,' he teased. 'What's in your bag?'

'Nothing.' Rose pushed her bulging bag behind her back.

'Rose?' He made to step out from behind the table.

'Don't you leave your stall, Mr Blume.' She indicated behind her. 'There are customers coming.' She stepped away to leave.

'Rose Pedal, you come back here this instance.' She pulled out a brown paper bag. 'You're meant to be helping me.'

'I think I'll enjoy this in the garden.' Opening the bag, she took out a delicately iced white cupcake, waving it teasingly in front of him. She had no appetite for it after the van journey, but she knew James would be hungry.

'That's so unfair,' he called after her before plastering a smile on his face and greeting his first customer.

Rose placed the cupcake back in her bag and wandered around the stalls. It was so lovely to be on the other side. She'd dragged Megan to many a wedding fayre; they would each take it in turns to be the bride that day. The cupcakes – of course she'd bought one for James – were on sale at a stand right by the entrance, which she'd seen on her way out to fetch the drinks from the little café in the converted barn.

'These look amazing,' Rose had said, admiring the array of cupcakes. 'They must take you hours.'

'I haven't been to bed since Thursday.' Rose knew the lady wasn't lying. 'I wouldn't normally make so many, but I wanted to make sure I had enough for both days. And people have to taste them.' She pointed to a four-tiered tower of pink and purple cupcakes, decorated with tiny flowers. 'Two hundred on there.' She pointed to a heart shaped display at the other end. 'Fifty on there.' She stepped to one side, revealing boxes and boxes of neatly stacked cupcakes. 'Five hundred in here.'

'May I have two, please?' Rose felt a little ashamed only asking for two, but the lady smiled.

'Eight pounds, please.' Rose handed over the ten-pound note from James's change. She wished she'd asked the price first, but then when she thought about it, four pounds for a cupcake that had taken that amount of work wasn't bad at all.

She recognized a few of the faces from the fayres at St Agatha's and Weddington Hall, but was disappointed to see that Natalie and Fanny weren't amongst them, before remembering what she'd seen on the WhatsApp chat the day before. It was a gentleman under the name of Jake's Bakes that was representing the wedding cakes this time. Rose knew the fayre here was so popular that, in order to get the largest range of people selling the biggest variety of goods and services, the organizers limited the stalls to one of each type of supplier. Only one flower stall, one cake stall, et cetera.

The only exception to this rule was made for wedding dress suppliers. There were two stalls at the fayre that day, and Rose couldn't resist visiting them both. She was acutely aware of James's eyes on her as she flicked through the rack directly in front of his stall and chatted with one of the ladies manning it.

'I've always wanted a fishtail dress,' Rose said, admiring one on a mannequin. 'Lots of sequins so it sparkles.'

'Oh no,' the lady disagreed. 'A figure and complexion like yours don't need adornment.' She swished quickly through the ivory and white dresses. 'This would be perfect on you.' She held it up for Rose to see, sweeping her hand under it to keep it from the floor. 'A-line, fitted round the bust, slightly off the shoulder but not too much that you're hitching it up all the time – although if it's fitted properly you should never have to do that. Shaped at the waist in an inverted V to emphasize your curves. This one has a ribbon-tied corset and flows out from the V giving a lovely silhouette and a small puddle train.'

'Puddle train?' How did she know Rose loved a puddle train?

'Would you like try it on?' Rose longed to say yes, but how could she? She wasn't getting married any time soon, and she really should be getting back to James. After all, she was meant to be helping him, and perhaps he'd let her hand out some of her business cards, or at least put them on the table.

'I wish I could.' She *desperately* wished she could. 'But I should be getting back to my friend.'

'We're having a fashion show at the end; it will be on the catwalk so you can see exactly how it looks.' She handed Rose a card. 'Buttercup Bridals. That's me – Alice Buttercup.' Rose thanked her and popped the card in her bag.

'You took your time.' James feigned annoyance as she returned to the stall. 'Nice cake?' She pulled the bag out and showed him the now slightly squished pair of cupcakes. 'I knew you wouldn't forget me.' He playfully nudged her with his arm. 'Saw you looking at the wedding dresses.'

'Were you spying on me, Mr Blume?'

He nodded. 'I was. Your bum looks delightful in that dress.' She slapped him.

'How's business been?' She looked around the hall. 'Busier than yesterday?' It was hard for her to tell; she'd been outside for most of it.

'I'd say about the same, to be fair.' He handed her his diary and pen. 'Can you jot these down in here for me please? Haven't had chance yet.' He shoved some scrappy bits of paper on top of the diary.

'Miss Gobbledegook, fifty-first of Nay 5055,' she said, attempting to read the scrawl that was pretending to be writing. 'And I'm not even going to try and read the phone number.'

'Miss Western, twenty-first of May 2022.' He took the papers back off her and rewrote them. 'Better?'

'Much.' She sat down and started adding the various names and dates to his diary.

'Honestly, James.' Rose stopped writing at the sound of

the familiar voice, but she forced herself not to look up. 'Are you the only florist in this area?' Madison Michaels' voice was just a few metres away. Rose sneaked a peek. She was dressed today in a dark green suit with gold accessories, almost the exact shade of James's suit. Her hair was swept up and lacquered within an inch of its life, and her heels, Rose noticed, were Christian Louboutin. And she only knew this because of the red undersole.

'Madison!' Rose was surprised by the warmth in James's welcome.

'Oh, have you got yourself a little assistant?' Rose took the opportunity to stand up and, feeling suddenly brave, took hold of James's hand. 'What are *you* doing here?'

'Helping,' Rose said.

'Your little business gone down the pan already?' Madison's fake laugh was infuriating, but Rose stayed calm.

'On the contrary.' She took out a business card. 'I got so many bookings yesterday that I didn't need to work today.' Rose hoped God wouldn't mind that little white lie.

'Well, I've come to ask a favour.' It was then that Rose noticed the gentleman who'd shown her to her stall yesterday standing awkwardly behind Madison. 'Samuel here has been telling me what happened yesterday – well I missed a show there, didn't I?' She didn't give anyone a chance to reply and carried on. 'Anyway, I'm organizing the fashion show and I'm afraid two of our models haven't turned up. Well, of course, I've offered, and as soon as I heard what happened yesterday, I told Samuel you'd be more than happy to help.'

'I'm not a model, Madison,' James said. 'I'm a florist.'

'Nonsense, James.' She waved his protest away. 'With your height and looks.' She pretended to fan herself. 'I mean just look how you wear that suit. Effortless, isn't it, Samuel?'

'It would really help us out, Mr Blume,' Samuel stuttered. 'And you did say if there was anything you could do . . .?'

'Of course,' James agreed, and Rose felt his hand tense. 'What time do you need me?'

'I'll come back and give you the details in a few minutes; I just need to tell the suit and dress people they've got their full quota of models.' She almost dragged Samuel away with her.

'Will that woman ever leave me alone?' He rolled his eyes. 'I don't know how many times I have to tell her I'm not interested anymore.'

'It's just a fashion show, James,' Rose said in her most soothing voice. 'It could be fun.'

'It could be, I suppose.' He looked over at Rose with a smile. 'Bloody Peter. I'm still clearing up after him at the age of twenty-eight.'

'What do you mean I'm not the right size?' Rose and James looked over to Buttercup Bridals where Madison was currently holding up the very dress that Alice had shown Rose earlier. 'I'm a perfect size zero.'

'Exactly.' Alice didn't look flustered in the slightest at Madison's shrill attack. 'My dresses are all twelve and fourteen. You need curves to be able to carry them off. These would just dangle off you and look like bits of rag. I need more boobs and a bum.' Alice scanned the room. 'I need her.'

CHAPTER FOURTEEN

'Her?' Madison screeched.

'Me?' Rose pointed to herself in disbelief.

'But she's—' Madison started.

'Perfect,' James said, cutting her off.

'Absolutely perfect,' Alice agreed.

'Splendid.' Samuel clapped his hands and scurried away quickly, with Madison screaming after him about how unfair the whole situation was.

'I can't model wedding dresses,' Rose said to James. 'I've never worn a wedding dress in my life.'

'What's that got to do with anything?' He laughed. 'Didn't you have a school prom?'

'Yes, of course.' She remembered it fondly. She and Megan had arrived together in a pale blue Cadillac, giggling and laughing. 'I had a princess dress, sequined corset and a flowing skirt with different coloured layers that showed blue, pink and white when I twirled.'

'Sounds beautiful.'

'It was.'

'So, you know how to handle a dress.' He looked at her feet in the Converse. 'And I've seen you in heels so I know you can handle those.'

'But wedding dresses are a completely different matter,' she explained. 'They have petticoats and veils or are so tightly fitted to your legs that you can only take tiny steps. Why do you think people practise walking before their big day?'

'I didn't realize they did.' James looked at her as if she had told him something fascinating.

'Of course they do.' Rose had even read an article about it in a magazine once. 'You have to break your shoes in and practise your walk down the aisle. Nothing worse than blisters from new shoes, or tripping over your train on the way to greet the groom.'

'If I can do it, you can do it.' This signalled the end of the conversation as another group of future brides arrived to inspect the Blume bridal bouquets.

'We'll have to start packing up soon,' James said, looking at his watch. 'It's almost three, and the fashion show starts at four. I need to get everything away in the van so we can head off straight after.'

'But there are still people coming in.' It had amazed Rose how many people seemed to leave visiting these events till the very last minute. There was a definite divide throughout the day. You had your first buzz of people: the early birds. Then came the late-morning surge for those who'd wanted a lie-in. There was always a lull in the middle of the day when people were at home having lunch, and this was then followed by another surge before the stragglers arrived with barely an hour to spare.

'I don't really want to leave anything out though.' He looked at the arrangements and boxes of flowers. 'It was okay yesterday – we were the last to leave and then they locked the room – but today everyone will still be milling about for the fashion show.'

'I'll watch your stall for you,' the man on the next table said. 'Takes me and the missus a fair while to get all these balloons away and she said she wants to watch the show, so I'll have a nice sit down and a cup of tea while she does.'

'Are you sure, Ron?' Rose had seen James and the couple chatting throughout the day. 'Can't believe I've been dragged into it, to be honest.'

'With your Hollywood looks, James?' Ron laughed. 'I'm surprised you haven't been asked before, all the years you've been coming to these things.' He pushed out his stomach and turned to the side. 'Do you think they need an overweight, slightly balding middle-aged man at all?' Everyone laughed. 'I could be father of the bride.' He joined in with the laughter as James pinned a rose buttonhole to Ron's shirt. 'Perfect.' He sniffed the yellow bloom. 'Gorgeous.'

'Can I borrow Rose?' Alice interrupted. She was armed with a ferocious-looking hairbrush, pins and hairspray. 'You're Rose from the WhatsApp group, aren't you?' she said, tapping one of the business cards James had let Rose put out on his stall. 'As lovely as your hair is, it won't cut it as bridal, I'm afraid.'

'How about me?' Ron ran his fingers through his thinning locks. 'Will I pass?'

'It'll be tough, I'm not going to lie.' Alice ruffled his hair. 'A bit of backcombing maybe, give it some lift.'

'Do you need any bouquets or anything?' James offered.

'Are you sure?' Alice looked at the table.

'Take what you like,' he said. 'But make sure you get Blume's mentioned in the commentary.'

'Of course.' She grabbed a couple of bouquets, head wreaths and some small white daisies, handing them to Rose as she went. 'It will be lovely to have fresh flowers instead of the tired old fabric ones we normally use.'

Rose was beginning to notice how helpful and friendly everyone was. There was always someone willing to do someone else a favour; sometimes it was a completely selfless act, but other times it was mutually beneficial to both businesses. Rose remembered her initial reluctance to let Megan help out with Pedals; perhaps it was time for her to start letting more people in, and set aside this bull-headed notion of doing it all on her own.

'Always happy for you to borrow anything you want in the future.' James grinned. 'We attend most of the fayres around the area, and some a little further afield if they're big enough to warrant the travel.'

'I usually stay quite local, to be fair.' Alice picked up a couple of buttonholes and placed them on the bulging pile of flowers in Rose's arms. 'With them always being at weekends, we have to close the shop to come. There's only me and my little Saturday girl, and I can't leave her in charge of the place all day – she's brilliant, but she's only sixteen.'

'My dad and uncle cover the shop while I visit the fayres. Sometimes Dad comes too depending on how many weddings we've got on that weekend.'

'Must be nice to have such family support.' *If only she knew*, Rose thought. 'Come on then, young miss, let's get you ready to get married!'

Rose didn't recognize herself in the mirror. Alice had made her wipe off the very minimal make-up she had applied that morning, and even though she knew she was now wearing far more than usual, she looked like she had none on at all.

'That's the natural look for you,' Alice had told her when she had remarked on this. 'Most brides want to look clean and fresh as if they've just woken up after the best night's sleep they'd ever had. The irony is that most brides on the morning of their wedding have just experienced their worst night's sleep ever.'

There were three other female models and just one man milling around in what was once one of Haggerston Hall's sitting rooms. Sunlight streamed in through the windows and Alice and another lady who had been introduced to Rose as Millie of The Dress Shop (another name from the WOWs), were busy doing hair and make-up.

'I love what you've done with my hair,' Rose said to

Alice. 'It looks so simple and effective.' Alice had brushed and backcombed Rose's hair before weaving it into two plaits, attaching them around the back of her head and sticking in the little daisies she'd taken from James's stall to add definition.

'It will just go perfect with that dress I showed you.' Alice placed both hands on her shoulders. 'You're ready.'

'Why isn't anyone dressed yet?' Madison had come into the room. 'We've got ten minutes people!' She clapped her hands. 'Where the hell is James?' She stormed back out of the room, returning moments later, almost dragging James by his jacket sleeve. 'You and you.' She pointed at James and the other man. 'Take the suits on that rack into the next room. The doors open out into the garden. There are screens set up outside. Blue one first for you, Zane, and that deep red for you, James.' She ushered them away. 'Now, ladies . . .'

'We know in what order the dresses are going out, thank you,' Millie said, already helping one of the models into an off-the-shoulder white lace mermaid-style dress.

'Excuse me.' Madison straightened her shoulders, giving herself extra height. 'I am organizing this fashion show. It's my name people will associate with this if it all goes wrong, so I will tell you which dress is going on at what time.'

'She doesn't even know what bloody dresses we have,' Alice whispered in Rose's ear.

'Something to say, Alice?' Madison quipped.

'Nothing at all, Madison.' She made Rose stand up. 'Each girl has four dresses to wear. The boys have five suits each.

They'll head down first, one after the other with the boys following after that to give them more time to change. Then, at the end, Zane and Samantha will head on with Becky as chief bridesmaid and, finishing the show will be James and Rose, with Gurpreet as chief bridesmaid.'

'Everyone knows what they're doing, Madison.' Millie was now pulling the corset ties tight on Gurpreet's stunning red and cream number.

'And when is that new dress going on?' Millie and Alice looked at each other and then over at Madison. 'You know perfectly well which one I mean. I gave it to you this morning.'

'Madison,' Millie said. 'It's obscene.'

'It's designer, I'll have you know!'

'Which designer?' Alice asked, holding Rose's hand as she stepped into a tight-fitting satin dress and was extremely glad that she hadn't eaten anything but a cupcake since breakfast.

'Clearly nobody you are familiar with,' Madison huffed, storming over to the racks and pulling out the only red dress bag there. 'You haven't even got it out of the bag,' she whined.

'Trust me.' Alice took the bag from her and hung it back up. 'We got it out and put it straight back.'

'How dare you!' Madison grabbed the bag back. 'That is a one-off creation by a brand-new up-and-coming bridal designer.'

'Is everyone decent?' Samuel walked into the room, his hands covering his eyes.

'You're okay, Samuel. The girls are all dressed now.'

'We need to start – it's almost four.' He looked over at Madison before squeaking in fright and running out of the room.

'Samantha, you're up first, then you, Rose . . .' Alice reeled off the order as they headed into the other room. James and Zane wolf-whistled as they entered.

James blew Rose a kiss as he fell in at the back of the line.

'Now, remember, onto the stage, side to side, down the runway, side to side, turn round and back up with another side to side before you're off and back into the room to change,' Madison ordered.

'What on earth does that mean?' Rose whispered to Samantha.

'Like this.' She hopped out of line quickly and stepped onto her right side then onto her left, so both sides of the imaginary audience could see. 'It's all about showing the dress to everyone there and from every angle. Think like that, watch what I do, and you'll be fine.'

Rose was suddenly nervous as hell. Luckily, she only had little heels on – Alice had said she was tall enough for the dresses as she was – but what if she tripped and fell flat on her face?

'Welcome to Haggerston Hall everyone. I'm Madison Michaels and this is the event you've all been waiting for.' There was no turning back now, Rose thought.

'First up we have Samantha wearing a stunning creation from The Dress Shop owned by Millie Benson. Now all the flowers in today's show have been kindly donated by Blume's Florist, flowers from the city to your heart.' Madison went on to describe the dress as Samantha walked beautifully down the catwalk.

'And now we have Rose ...'

'Good luck,' Alice whispered before rushing off with Millie to start getting Samantha changed.

'Please God, don't let me make an arse of myself.' Rose stepped up onto the stage.

CHAPTER FIFTEEN

'Now, ladies and gentlemen.' The finale was almost upon them but, for some reason, Madison had called a halt to the proceedings, and Samuel was trying to fill time, reading from a card that she'd given him.

'Where's Madison gone?' Alice asked angrily. 'We've just got these last dresses to go and we need to hurry up. Have you seen how dark the sky has gone all of a sudden?'

Rose was swishing dreamily around in the dress Alice had shown her earlier. It was as she had said: absolutely perfect for her. Her bust was pushed up ever so slightly by the corset, the tiny capped sleeves sat perfectly just on top of her shoulders and the puddle train was just the most glorious thing Rose had ever seen. She never wanted to take it off.

'Have *you* seen Madison?' Millie asked, interrupting her thoughts, which may or may not have involved James in the gorgeous navy-blue frock coat he'd worn as his third outfit.

'I haven't seen her since she dashed in here and then dashed out again.' Rose took a look out of the window. 'Where's the sun gone?' The beautiful late May sunshine that had been streaming through the windows had now disappeared and been replaced with threatening dark grey clouds. They looked heavy and ready to burst at any minute.

'People are leaving,' Zane called into the room.

'We'll just have to do it without her.' Millie grabbed Alice's hand. 'You describe your dresses and I'll describe mine.' And with that, they all rushed outside.

'And now, ladies and gentlemen,' Samuel was saying again. 'We have a very special treat for you all. Wearing a brand new, one-of-a-kind creation by M and M, I give you Madison Michaels.'

'No!' Alice screamed, and ran onto the stage, but it was too late.

There were audible gasps of shock and wolf whistles from the audience. Rose peeked around the screens, her eyes widening in shock.

'Does she know her bum's hanging out?' The dress was so low-cut at the back that everyone could see the top of Madison's bum cheeks, and a bright pink thong showed through the sheer netting.

'It's not her bum I'm worried about. Wait till she comes back this way.' Alice was covering her eyes. 'M and M?' she said to herself. 'M and M?' she repeated. 'The silly cow has made it herself.'

'Madison Michaels.' Light dawned on Millie's face. 'Well, no wonder she was so pissed off we didn't like it – and no wonder it looks like a bag of shit!'

'Bloody hell.' Madison was now walking back towards the screens, a look of pride and triumph on her face, and Rose really couldn't tell if she didn't know her nipples were on show through the gown's heavily embroidered front, or whether she'd actually designed it that way.

'What on earth do you think you are doing?' Millie virtually pulled her off the stage as soon as she was behind the screens. 'Never mind.' She threw her hands up in the air. 'You've only made a fool of yourself, not us.' She stepped onto the stage, taking Alice with her, and grabbed the microphone from the now speechless Samuel. 'Ladies and gentlemen, now it's time for our finale.'

There was an enormous rumble of thunder overhead.

'And we're going to do it really quickly,' Alice shouted, indicating for them all to come onto the stage at the same time.

James took Rose's hand. He looked deliciously handsome in a simple black and white tuxedo.

'You look absolutely beautiful,' he whispered in her ear as they walked as quickly but serenely as they could. Just as they reached the end of the catwalk, the heavens burst open, and the largest raindrops Rose had ever seen started to fall.

Ladies screamed, men screamed, children screamed, and everyone ran for the nearest doors to the hall, or to their cars.

'This way.' James jumped off the catwalk, grabbed Rose by the waist and swung her down onto the ground. 'Under the gazebo.'

'Why don't we just go back in?' She pulled his arm in the opposite direction.

'Because everyone is doing that, and we'll get soaked.' Rose could see the small doorways to the hall were no match for the amount of people all trying to get inside at once. Ladies were shielding their hair with handbags, while men had pulled their jackets over their heads and parents were hastily pulling out pram and pushchair covers. 'Come on.'

They ran towards the gazebo; the rain was coming down fast now, and by the time they reached it, they were both dripping wet.

'They don't call it a puddle train for nothing, you know.' Rose looked at the now sodden dress. Where once it had felt light and swished with each step, it now felt heavy and dragged off her shoulders.

'You'd best take it off.' He was already slipping out of his jacket. 'Put this on instead.'

'James!' Rose was a little shocked. 'I'm not getting undressed in the middle of a garden . . . or in front of you!'

'I'll turn around.' He did just that, and Rose could see his broad back through the thin wet fabric of his shirt.

'Your jacket is just as wet as my dress, and besides, it won't even cover my arse.' He turned back around when he realized she wasn't going to change.

'Speaking of arses . . .' He chuckled heartily. 'Did you see Madison's?'

'Who didn't see Madison's?' She laughed with him. 'Do you think she designed it that way?'

'Surely not!' he said. 'She usually dresses quite classy, so I wouldn't have thought she knew her thong was on show.'

'Not just her thong.' Rose burst into laughter again, but stopped when James didn't join in. 'Don't tell me you didn't notice the front?'

'I actually thought the front was quite stunning, to be fair.'

Rose's mouth dropped open in shock. 'James! Her nipples were sticking out.'

He looked at her, then his eyes widened as he recalled the dress.

'I thought that was part of the pattern.' He covered his eyes with his hand. 'My oh my, oh my.' He shook his head in disbelief. 'I don't think she'll be selling that any time soon.'

'I just hope someone tells her, because I really feel she thinks it's a beautiful dress and that she's going to be the next big thing.' Rose looked up as a large plop of rain fell on her head. 'What was that?' Another followed it and another until both of them may as well have been standing in the open air. The gazebo roof, they'd only just realized, was actually made up of flowers, all of which were now shrivelled and dripping. 'Rather pointless standing here then,' Rose said.

'Oh, I don't know.' James pulled her towards him. 'I think there's something romantic about the rain.'

'What's romantic about being soaking wet in a wedding dress, which now weighs an absolute ton by the way, with raindrops dripping down my cleavage?' she asked, looking up at him.

'There's this for starters.' He brought his head down to hers, kissing her without pause or hesitation. The rumbling thunder overhead wasn't loud enough to drown out the beating of her heart.

'What the—' The flowers overhead finally gave way, and Rose and James found themselves drenched in a cold deluge of rainwater. 'I'm going inside,' Rose said. She turned to walk towards the house. 'I don't care how romantic it is to kiss in the rain; I'm now drenched through to my skin, with shoes that have puddles in them and I'm not even thinking about what's going on in my pants.' James raised an eyebrow, a suggestive smile on his face, earning himself a slap. Then he took her hand, and they walked back into the hall.

'Where have you two been?' Alice scolded them both as they walked in. 'Look at the bloody state of the pair of you. Do you know how much that dress costs?'

'I'll pay for the cleaning.' James looked sheepishly down to the floor.

'Cleaning?' Alice shouted. 'Cleaning? How on earth will I get it clean? It's made of silk; silk doesn't like being saturated.'

'I'll pay for the cost of it then.' Rose didn't want to think how much this weekend had ended up costing James. First the replacement cost of the window, and now a designer wedding dress . . .

'Oh, it doesn't matter.' Alice flopped down into one of the chairs. 'The other dresses are ruined as well. Everyone was clambering to get in at the same time. We can probably salvage the suits, but bloody Madison and that bloody dress. We'd have all been back in the dry if it wasn't for her.'

'Has anyone told her yet?' Rose took a towel from Millie as she approached, and began drying her hair.

'Trust me, we've tried.' Millie started to pick the flowers and pins from Rose's hair. 'The other models have already gone home, so we'll help you get changed. That room is empty, James, if you want to get out of your suit. The pair of you must be freezing.'

It wasn't until Millie mentioned it that Rose even noticed how cold she was. All of a sudden, she had goosebumps on her arms and her teeth were chattering.

'Go see if they're still serving hot drinks, Millie.' Alice started stripping the wet layers from Rose as she spoke, but this was easier said than done. 'I'll get her dry and back in some warm clothes.' Everything clung to Rose's skin like limpets on a rock.

'Rose, are you okay?' James was already back in the room, his hair a tousled mess, but at least his clothes were warm and dry.

'James!' Alice warned, turning Rose around and trying to cover her with a towel.

'She looks blue.' He stepped towards her again.

'James!' she warned again. 'I know you haven't known Rose very long, and I don't think she'll thank me for letting you see her half naked.'

'I'm fine, James,' Rose said through shivers and shakes. 'Just need to get dry.'

'I'll go and find you a hot drink or something.' He was out of the room before Alice could tell him that Millie was already doing exactly that.

'Soon be done, Rose.' The dress was halfway off now, and Alice was rubbing her arms gently. She wrapped Rose's hair in another towel to keep it away from her body, and grabbed one of the men's shirts from the fashion show to put on her, giving Rose the shirt tails to hold up while she worked on getting the skirt and petticoats off.

By the time James was back, armed with blankets, and Millie had returned with a hot chocolate from a vending machine, Rose was dressed in a frock coat and trousers that were a good few sizes too big for her, but they were warm and soft and smelled of James.

'Get her in the van, get the engine running, the heater on and wrap her up,' Millie ordered.

'I need to get the stock together,' James said desperately.

'And we need to get this lot packed up.' Alice put her hands up to her head. 'Are we the only ones left?' James nodded. 'Well then, if the three of us work together we'll have it done in no time.' She started hanging dresses up in bags, with the help of James and Millie.

'I can help.' Rose stood up and then instantly sat back down, feeling woozy.

'You sit there until we're ready.' James covered her in blankets and placed a kiss on her forehead. 'I'll pull the van right to the door, so you don't need to get wet again and I'll have you home as soon as possible.'

It really didn't take them long at all to pack everything away, and they'd even found Ron and Joyce in the hall, who, true to their word, had kept an eye on the flowers.

'You get the van, James. We'll walk her out to the door.' Millie was carrying the last few dresses over one arm and hooked Rose with the other. Ron stood on Rose's other side and together they walked her to the entrance hall.

'Here we are, then.' Ron stepped out onto the drive as James pulled up at the door.

'That's not right.' She looked at the van. 'That's not right at all.'

'What's not right, sweetheart?' Millie asked. 'Here's James now, look, getting out to help.'

'It's not the right van.' She was certain of it. 'It's too small! Where's my bike?'

CHAPTER SIXTEEN

'Don't panic,' James soothed. 'Dad took the wrong van back, that's all. Your bike will be back at mine safe and sound.' He helped her into the passenger seat and tucked her underneath five blankets. 'I'll get you home and bring the bike back tomorrow. Is that okay?'

'Okay.' She snuggled into the blankets, and with shouts of goodbyes and thank you, James headed off down the drive. 'I feel sick.' Rose put her hand to her mouth. 'Pull over.'

He stopped the van just behind the gates, and Rose threw the blankets off, leapt out and retched behind the stone wall. James held a blanket over her in a vain attempt to stop her getting wet, but after five minutes, the blanket was soaked and he gave up.

'That's better,' she said, leaning against the wall. 'But I'm a bit wet and cold again.'

'I'm just going to take you back to mine.' He helped her back into the van. 'There's no way you'll make it thirty miles. You've already caught a chill, and now we're both wet again.'

'Don't be angry with me.' She looked up at him.

'I'm not angry at you.' He cupped her cheek with his palm. 'How could I ever be angry with you?'

They had to stop three more times for Rose to be sick before they finally drew up outside the Blume country manor (as Rose had dubbed it in her head). Elizabeth was waiting for them and she immediately ushered Rose upstairs and into a bubble bath in the en suite of the bedroom she'd slept in the night before.

Rose could hear James and Elizabeth talking outside the bathroom, but she couldn't make out what they were saying, and the water was so deliciously hot that she didn't particularly care. When she finally felt warm, she dried and dressed herself in a long flannelette nightie her nan would be proud of and thick woollen socks that Elizabeth had left out to warm on the towel rail.

When she stepped out of the bathroom it was to find James sitting on the bed, a tray of tea and toast on the dressing table.

'Right, in you get, young lady.' She did exactly as she was told and snuggled into the sheets, propping herself up with a pillow. 'I've phoned your mum and told her you're stopping here another night.'

'I bet that went down well.' Rose hoped he hadn't told her she was ill.

'Told her you were a little hungover.' It was as if he'd read her mind. 'Too much wine tasting.'

'Better than being ill I suppose.' Her stomach lurched as he placed the tray of food in front of her. 'What did she say?'

141

she asked, declining the piece of toast he offered her with a shake of her head.

'She sort of tutted.' James took the piece for himself, lathering strawberry jam on top of the butter in thick globules.

'Yes, I know that tut.' Rose had heard that tut on many occasions over the years, when Megan or Josh had deposited her home after a few too many. She really wasn't good at holding her drink.

The first time she'd heard it had been after her prom. 'Whatever will the village think?' her mum had said, hurrying her inside.

'Mrs P,' Megan had slurred. Although she'd drunk far more than Rose at Daniel's after party, she was at least still able to stand. 'You live in the vicarage, it's at the back of the church, no one but Mr P and *all* the people at the after party know she's pissed.'

Rose had looked up at her mum. 'See,' she said. 'Nobody knows.' She'd held her finger to her lips with a giggle. 'Shush.'

'Shush!' Megan had copied, giggling and falling over, taking Rose with her.

Then had come the tut.

'Are you feeling better now?' James asked after his third piece of toast and her second cup of tea.

'Still a bit cold.' She wasn't cold at all. She felt warm and snug and the tea had helped to settle her stomach. Looking up at him from under her lashes, she hoped she was flirting with him.

'Do you want an extra blanket?' James got off the bed and she slammed her arms down on top of the duvet.

'They say body heat is the best way to warm someone up.' She flung back the covers. 'We could watch a film?'

James didn't need asking twice. He slipped off his shoes, grabbed the remote from the side of the bed and jumped in beside her. He placed one arm around her shoulders and she instantly snuggled into his side. It felt right. That was the only way she could describe it to herself. It just felt right.

'What shall we watch, then?' James was flicking through the channels like a mad man. 'Comedy? Action?' But Rose was already drifting off to sleep.

Rose woke up in the middle of the night, cold and sniffly. The rain was beating heavily against the window pane, and she swore she could hear thunder rumbling in the distance. She reached for James but vaguely remembered him kissing her goodnight before leaving for his own room. Heaving herself out of bed, she padded slowly to the dressing table where she knew there was a box of tissues. Grabbing one, she blew her nose loudly, just as a bolt of lightning illuminated the room. Rose screamed. A ghostly figure was sitting in the chair, rocking slightly backwards and forwards. Rushing to the light, Rose switched it on, hoping the ghost would disappear, but it remained.

'Who are you?' she asked hesitantly. She could see now that it was a real person, although with her grey straggly hair and pale complexion, you could be forgiven for thinking she was a ghost.

'They think I don't know what's going on.' The woman

wagged a finger at Rose. From afar, Rose would have put her age at nearly ninety, but when she walked closer, she saw the woman's face had a much more youthful glow. Other than a few crow's feet crinkling the corners of her eyes, it was only really her unkempt hair and dowdy nightdress that made her appear so much older. In fact, Rose would have said she was around her own parents' age.

'Are you Mrs Blume?' She had to be James and Peter's mum; it was the only explanation. 'Are you James's mum?'

'Oh, my James.' The woman's face lit up all of a sudden. 'Such a good boy.' She looked at Rose. 'We used to sit here on days like this and read stories.' She gazed out of the window and Rose knew she was thinking of days gone by.

'Shall I fetch him for you?' Rose asked, turning to go back towards the door.

'They think I don't know what's going on,' she repeated, grabbing Rose's arm and pulling her in close towards her. 'They think I can't see what's going on, but I watch.' She pointed at her eyes. 'They think I can't hear what they're saying, but I listen.' She tapped her ears.

'Who are you talking about?' Rose was worried. Was James's mum hallucinating?

There was a knock on the door. 'Rose?' James called. 'Rose, is my mum in there with you? We can't find her anywhere.'

'Yes.' Rose opened the door to find all of the adults of the family, apart from Peter, standing outside her door, but it was only James who came into the room.

'Mum,' he said gently, walking over to her and placing a blanket over her shoulders. 'What are you doing out of bed?' He helped her up. 'You'll catch a chill on a night like this.'

'I was saying hello to Rose.' She patted Rose's hand as she passed. 'Such a beautiful girl.' She smiled at her, then turned to James. 'You keep hold of her.' She tapped his cheek gently as if to make sure he paid attention. 'Don't lose her now.'

'I won't, Mum, don't worry.' He winked at Rose and mouthed 'goodnight' as he closed the door.

What a strange evening. Rose pondered on her meeting with James's mum for a while before trying to get back to sleep, but this proved impossible, for as soon as she lay down, her head pounded, her nose became blocked and she couldn't breathe.

She finally dozed off around five thirty, but was woken by her phone ringing at six. Groaning, she nearly threw it out of the window before remembering that she'd placed it on silent, as she did every night, and only had a handful of emergency contacts set up who could override the silent feature.

'Mum?' she answered, a combination of concern and slight annoyance in her voice, mixed with an extremely stuffy nose.

'Hope I didn't wake you.'

'Of course you woke me, Mum – it's six in the morning!' It was such a strange thing to say that Rose almost laughed. 'Everyone okay? Dad? Nan? Grandad?'

'Yes, yes,' her mum said hurriedly. 'Everyone is fine.'

'Then why are you ringing me so early?' Rose suddenly remembered. 'Megan? Oh no, has something happened to Megan?'

'No, no. Megan is absolutely fine, but it is because of her that we're here.'

'You're here?' Rose wasn't sure she'd heard correctly. 'What do you mean by . . . "here"?'

'We're here, outside James's house.' Her mum was suddenly whispering. 'Megan rang the vicarage because you weren't answering your phone.' Rose briefly took the phone away from her ear and saw the many notifications on the screen, most of which were from Megan and her mum. She was grateful Alice and Millie had omitted mentioning anything in the WhatsApp chat. 'She wanted to know if you were feeling any better,' her mum continued, 'after getting caught in the rain. She thought you would be at home, you see.'

'Oh.' Rose didn't really know what else to say and wished she'd thought twice before sending that text to Megan.

'Then I just couldn't rest.' Her mum's voice sounded panicked. 'Your dad wouldn't let me phone you and he wouldn't let me drive – said it would be rude to turn up on a stranger's doorstep in the middle of the night.' Rose could imagine her dad trying to calm her mum down. 'So, at five o'clock, I grabbed the car keys and here I am.'

'But how did you know where I was?' Rose knew she'd never mentioned where James lived; in fact *she* didn't even know where James lived, just that it was about five miles away from Haggerston Hall.

'Your phone tracker of course.' Rose groaned. She should have guessed.

'I can't believe you're here, Mum.' She cringed as she

spoke. 'It's six o'clock in the morning, and I've now got to go and wake up James and his family.'

'Well, if you'd rung and told us last night instead of leaving it to poor James . . .' Rose had known it would be her fault.

'Then you would have been straight here yesterday, Mum.' She almost wished they *had* come yesterday now; at least it would have saved her having to wake up the whole household.

'Don't take that tone with me, young lady,' her mum scolded. 'Oh, there's a light on, I think someone is coming.'

Rose clicked off the phone and climbed out of bed, running down the stairs as fast as her aching legs could carry her.

She reached the bottom of the stairs just as Geoffrey Blume was opening the door to find her mum standing there, sheltering under an umbrella. 'Who on earth are you?'

'I'm Rose's mum.' Rose watched her hold out a hand towards him. 'Janet Pedal, pleasure to meet you.' Rose was behind Geoffrey now.

'Mum!' she said in her happiest, most surprised voice. 'What on earth are you doing here so early in the morning?'

'I was about to ask the very same thing.' Geoffrey Blume ignored Janet's hand, and Rose watched her mum put it away, the smile fading from her face.

'Geoffrey, dear, don't leave the poor woman standing in the rain, let her in for goodness sake.' Rose hadn't noticed James's mother arrive behind them. Geoffrey moved to one side, opening the door wide.

'Thank you,' Janet said, shaking her umbrella and closing

it before stepping inside. Looking up, Janet's eyes widened. 'Tabby? Tabitha White, is that you?'

Rose followed her mum's gaze and found it directed right at James's mum.

CHAPTER SEVENTEEN

'Tabby White, it is you.' Janet was right in front of James's mum now. 'I'd know those eyes anywhere.' She turned to speak to Rose. 'Tabby and I went to secondary school together. She had the biggest pair of sapphire-blue eyes and the longest lashes I'd ever seen.'

'Janet Barton?' James's mum said. 'Janet Barton.' She said it with more certainty the second time. 'Why, I haven't seen you for ...' She paused. 'Must be over thirty years.' She grabbed Janet's hand and squeezed it tightly. 'Come into the kitchen and I'll pop the kettle on.'

No one seemed to mind that everyone except for Janet was still in their nightclothes, and just as Geoffrey was about to close the door, a scrunching of gravel and a flash of headlights heralded another arrival.

'That'll be my husband,' Janet told everyone. 'He said he'd follow me in the minibus so we could bring Rose's bike home.'

'Are we to expect any other members of the family?'

Geoffrey sneered at Rose. 'Grandparents perhaps? Aunts and uncles?'

'Dad!' James warned, his appearance startling everyone. 'Why do you have to be so rude all the time?' He stepped in beside Rose and took her hand. 'Lovely to see you both again.' Rose's dad was now inside, the minibus parked up on the driveway. 'I'm sorry I let Rose get drunk yesterday, but as you can see, she's much better now.'

'They know,' Rose whispered to James as they followed everyone else into the kitchen. 'And I'm really not feeling well at all. I'm bunged up, my head is pounding and I just want my bed.'

'Let me take you back upstairs.' He put an arm around her shoulders and started to turn back to the stairs.

'I mean my own bed.' She looked at him. 'No offence, but it's not exactly relaxing here, is it?'

'No offence taken.' He smiled. 'I know exactly what you mean though.' He looked around at the expensive furnishings. 'I sometimes wish I could move out and live on my own.'

'Why don't you?' Rose had no urgent desire to leave her parental home, but if she lived with *this* family day in and day out, she was pretty sure she'd have left years ago. Her mum could be overprotective, but Rose knew her heart was always in the right place and that she was just looking out for her daughter.

'I need money for a start,' James said.

Rose laughed. 'If *you* don't have money then there's no

hope for the rest of us, is there?' She stopped laughing when James didn't join in.

'I'm serious.' His voice matched this statement.

'How can you not have money? Look around you.' Rose spread her arms.

'This isn't my money though,' he explained. 'This is my grandparents' money, then it'll be my parents' and Uncle Tony's and Maureen's, and then at some point it will be mine and Peter's and Elizabeth's.'

'That's just the house and business though,' Rose pointed out. 'Why don't you just move out? Surely you've got some savings put by for a deposit? Or how about renting somewhere? You'd need a lot less to start with if you rented.' This reminded Rose of her own dwindling funds in the bank account her grandparents had set up for her, and guilt washed over her again.

'I don't earn any money.' Rose looked at him in disbelief. 'I don't get paid. I work in the florist and then everything I need is paid for from the family account. I have a card if I want to buy clothes or anything.'

'You don't get wages?' Rose was shocked. 'How can you not get wages? You work all those hours in the shop, weekends at wedding fayres. You must be owed thousands!'

'I've never really thought about it, to be honest.' James shrugged. 'It's not like I'm freeloading like Peter.'

'Ask for wages,' was Rose's simple answer. 'If you want a place of your own, ask for wages.'

'Dad would never agree to that.'

'Well, if you don't ask him, you'll never know.' Rose sneezed into her hand. 'Oh God, have you got a tissue?' She daren't remove her hand from her face.

'Here you go.' He handed her a tissue from his pocket and she wiped her nose and hands.

'Are you always so prepared?' she asked, tucking the tissue up her sleeve and making a note to throw it away before she left.

'Always,' he said. 'Now, let's get your stuff together and get you back home.'

'Will you get the suit back to Alice for me, please?' It had taken about half an hour to get Rose ready to leave, and still she and James were waiting for their parents to finish chatting. Well, they were actually waiting for the two mums to finish chatting; Geoffrey was sort of glaring and John was trying to make conversation and failing miserably.

'Of course I will,' James agreed. Rose had found out on Sunday that Buttercup Bridals was only a few shops away from Blume's Florist. 'Although, what she'll be able to do with the dresses and suits, I don't know.'

'I feel so bad about it.' Rose sneezed and James passed her another tissue before she even asked. 'Thank you.' She blew loudly into it. 'It was such a gorgeous dress.'

'And you looked absolutely stunning in it.' He nudged her playfully.

'Oh, stop it.' She sneezed again, and again, and again.

'I think we'd best be getting Rose home, Janet.' John stood up. 'Before everyone in the house catches her cold.'

'Lovely to meet you all. Do come again,' Geoffrey said, rather too quickly.

'Oh yes, Janet, you must come again,' Tabitha implored. 'And soon.'

'It's been so nice to catch up.' Janet gave her a hug. 'Come on, Rose, you and I will head back in the car. We'll leave James and your father to get the bike sorted.'

'Actually, Mum ...' Rose began – the thought of her mum's driving for thirty miles through country lanes was making her feel queasy, and she didn't fancy a repeat performance of yesterday evening's journey. 'I'd rather go with Dad, if that's okay. I can lie down on the back seat then.'

'Of course, darling.' Rose had known she'd get away with this if she played the sick card. 'Whatever makes you feel best.'

Rose, John and the Blumes said goodbye to Janet, who headed off in the car – they all winced as she crunched the gears – and Tabitha went back inside. The light that had shone from inside Tabitha just moments ago seemed to have dimmed as suddenly as it had appeared, and she walked slowly back up the stairs.

'Have you got the keys to the van, Dad?' James asked.

'They're where they usually are, son,' he huffed, and followed his wife up the stairs. 'I need to get ready for work, and don't be loitering yourself. Busy day ahead.'

'He's a barrel of laughs, isn't he?' John commented as he and Rose waited in the hallway for James to get the keys.

'Dad, he's horrible,' Rose admitted. 'He's the most loathsome man I've ever met, and he treats poor James like a slave rather than a son.'

'That's a little harsh, surely?' Rose shook her head. 'Every family is different Rose – it's wrong to judge without knowing the whole story.'

'Here we are then.' James was back jangling the keys, and they followed him out onto the drive again. He pressed a little fob towards the garage doors, which opened smoothly and almost silently to reveal the 'Blume' fleet of vans all parked up. James pointed the keys at the largest of the vans, the indicators flashed and an audible click could be heard as the locks opened. James swung the doors open and stepped in, John following behind.

'Why is the bike the opposite way round?' Rose asked, peeking round the doors. 'I'm sure we parked it facing forward.'

'The straps are undone, as well,' James pointed out. 'Perhaps they came loose on the way home. My dad isn't the most careful of drivers at the best of times, and he was so pissed off on Sunday.' He looked at Rose's dad. 'Sorry, sir.'

'No need to apologize.' Rose looked at her dad sceptically. 'What? I'll have you know I'm a modern man.' Rose laughed and sneezed and snotted all at once. James handed her another tissue.

'Let's get you home,' James said. It didn't take long for him and Rose's dad to get the bike out of the van and into the minibus. 'I'll ring you later.' Rose smiled and nodded, feeling sleepy all of a sudden.

'I'd like that.' She got into the passenger side of the minibus and was asleep before they'd even got off the drive.

James did phone her that night and the night after and the night after that, but Rose felt so poorly that she couldn't speak to him. Her throat was so sore she could just about manage to swallow the water and weak soup that her mum spooned down her throat every hour come day or night. She was asleep virtually non-stop for almost three days, but managed to send James a thank you text after the largest bunch of sunflowers arrived on Wednesday morning. Her mum told her he'd delivered them himself, and although he'd had a drink with Janet and John in the kitchen, he'd been insistent that they shouldn't wake her.

Rose had never felt so rotten in her life. The doctor had said it probably hadn't been caused by the soaking on Sunday, and that she'd more than likely picked up a virus a few days beforehand, a small comfort but at least she knew she couldn't have prevented it.

She'd argued with her mum several times over the past few days. Despite feeling crappy, she was still answering emails and taking bookings. She couldn't afford to miss out on work, but her mum had, eventually, taken her phone and laptop away while she was sleeping, insisting that she needed to rest properly.

Megan visited on Thursday evening after work, once she

had been informed that Rose was actually awake and starting to feel a little better. She walked into the bedroom, her shirt covering her mouth.

'Is it safe?' she asked, her voice muffled.

'You can't catch it, the doctor said,' Rose croaked.

'So how did you catch it then?' Megan asked, dropping the shirt and sitting down on the bed. Rose shrugged her shoulders and groaned. 'Does it still hurt?'

'Everything hurts.'

'You look bloody awful.' Megan never did have any tact.

'Thanks for that.'

'Anyway.' Megan waved her hand to dismiss the subject while Rose coughed. 'I can't believe I've had to wait all this time to find out the gossip.'

'What gossip?' Rose took a sip of water.

'For starters ...' She pointed at the sunflowers that her mum had lovingly arranged in a vase on her desk. 'Those beautiful flowers didn't grow in your dad's garden.' Rose couldn't stop the smile spreading across her face. 'That smile says it all.'

'What smile?' Rose tried to hide her face behind the glass of water.

'I take it there has been a kiss?' Rose's smile returned. 'More than one?' Rose nodded. 'Trust you to bloody get poorly when there's all this to tell me.'

'You'll just have to wait.' She coughed and took another sip of water.

'Perhaps I'll just ask James,' she teased.

'Ask James what?' Rose looked up and Megan looked behind her. There, standing in the doorway, was James with another bunch of flowers in his hand.

'Nothing, nothing at all.' Megan shot up. 'I'm Megan, by the way. You must be James?' He nodded, and Megan turned back to Rose. 'I'll get off home now and message you later.' She was out of the door in seconds, and James took her place on the bed. Rose burst out laughing, which only brought on another coughing fit.

'Are you okay?' James took the glass out of her hand before she spilled the water all over the bed, and placed it on the floor.

'I'm fine.' She couldn't tell him that Megan had been loitering on the landing mouthing 'phwoar' and making rude gestures. 'Just went down the wrong way.'

CHAPTER EIGHTEEN

'I'm so glad you're feeling better.' He placed the flowers on her bed; this time he had brought her yellow roses. She held them up to her nose.

She sighed. 'I wish I could smell them.'

'They smell of summer gardens and promises.' He smoothed a stray strand of hair from her face, then looked at his finger. 'Wasn't expecting that to be wet.' He laughed, pretending to wipe his hand on his shirt. He wasn't wearing his jacket, probably due to the late spring heat. Rose had been longing to go outside in the glorious sunshine, but every time she tried to go further than the bathroom, her legs failed her and she ended up crawling back into her bed.

'I've had a fever, you know.' She slapped his hand playfully.

'I know.' He touched her forehead with the back of his hand. 'You still feel a tad warm, to be honest.'

'I think it's just being cooped up in here all day.' She looked over to the window. The sun was still shining and she could feel a gentle breeze from the tiny opening. 'I so want to get out of here, but my legs just won't carry me.'

'Allow me.' He moved the flowers off the bed and pulled back the covers. 'Harry Potter?' he said, raising his eyebrows at her Mischief Managed shortie set.

'The fact that you know what "Mischief Managed" means shows a superior knowledge of Harry Potter to at least book three.' She had loved the *Harry Potter* books and films from the age of eight when her nan had given her the first four in a box set for her birthday. 'What are you doing?' she said, alarmed, as James pushed one arm under her legs and the other round her shoulders.

'Put your arms around my neck.' She did as she was told, nestling into his neck and enjoying the smell and feel of him against her skin. 'Here we go.' He pretended she was heavy to start with, lifting her legs then putting them down again, but after another playful slap from Rose, he lifted her up as if she was nothing. 'Shit! I've just knocked over your glass.'

Rose shook her head. 'It's only water, don't worry.' She didn't want anything to spoil this moment, and the carpet had had much worse than half a glass of water on it over the years.

'Oh my, what's going on?' Rose's dad was standing in the doorway. 'I was just heading into my office. Are you okay, Rose?' Rose knew exactly why her dad was upstairs, and it had absolutely nothing to do with his office. Once Janet had known Rose was on her own with James in her bedroom, she would have been on tenterhooks and would have sent John up; her own presence would have been far too obvious.

'Everything's absolutely fine, sir.' Rose couldn't believe James still felt it necessary to call him sir. 'Rose said she was a bit fed up so I thought I'd carry her downstairs and she could sit in the garden for a little bit.'

'What a good idea.' John hurried back down the stairs. 'Janet! James is bringing Rose down to sit in the garden. We can all have a spot of tea outside.'

By the time James and Rose had made it to the back door, there was a makeshift bed on one of the sun loungers, ice-cold juice in a glass jug on the glass table and an array of cakes arranged neatly on a three-tiered stand. It always amazed Rose how her mum could rustle up a small feast at a moment's notice.

'Are you hungry, James?' Janet asked after he'd put Rose down on the lounger and her mum had covered her with a blanket. 'I bet you haven't had your tea. Did you come straight from work?'

'Blimey, Mum,' Rose said. 'Give him chance to answer one question before you ask another.'

'I have to confess to being a little peckish actually, because no, I haven't had dinner yet, and yes, I did come straight from work.' Rose was impressed by his ability to answer all three questions in one go and thoroughly please her mum in the process. Janet instantly stood up, went into the house and returned with steaming hot steak pie and mash.

'You can have Rose's portion.' She placed the tray of food on his lap, neatly laid with cutlery, salt and pepper and a small silver jug of gravy.

'Thank you.' Rose watched his eyes widen. 'Are you sure?' He looked at Rose and then to her mum.

'You eat up now while it's hot.' Janet waved his protests away. 'Rose isn't up to eating much just yet, but I'm so used to cooking for three that I made too much.' Rose could feel her stomach rumbling and would actually have liked the chance to eat at least the mash and some of the gravy-soaked steak.

'Is there any left, Mum?' she asked hopefully.

'Do you want this?' James held the tray out to her.

'No, no,' she replied. 'Just a bit of mash and gravy would be nice, Mum, but only if there's some left.'

'You know me, Rose.' Janet was up and back in no time, carrying another tray and a slightly smaller plate than the one she'd given James. Rose tucked in with gusto. 'It's so nice to see you eating again.'

'I'm so sorry for all of this,' James said between mouthfuls. 'If we hadn't stayed out in the rain, Rose wouldn't have got so ill.'

'It wasn't your fault.' John was helping himself to a third mini sponge cake under the scrutinizing gaze of Janet, who Rose knew was keeping count of how many he'd had for two reasons: the first was his health – he was under strict orders from the doctor to keep his cholesterol down – and the second, which Rose knew was most important to her mother, was to make sure he didn't eat too many of the same one and not leave enough choice for their guest. 'Dr Brown said she'd probably picked the bug up a couple of days beforehand. Just coincidence, that's all.'

'But surely the rain wouldn't have helped?' James remarked.

'It doesn't matter.' Rose had heard the same conversation over and over again and was fed up with it. 'I'm on the mend, and that's all that counts.'

'Hear, hear.' Her dad held up an éclair.

'No more, John.' Janet stood up and moved the table away from him.

'You won't be at the wedding fayre this weekend then?' James sat back in his chair, suitably stuffed. 'That was delicious, Janet.' Rose watched her mum beam from ear to ear.

'I couldn't get a place anyway,' Rose said. She forced down a final mouthful of mash. 'In fact, I haven't got another one booked till the one at Coombe Castle in June.' Rose couldn't help but feel uneasy at this lack of fayre spaces; after all, how could she get bookings if she was unable to advertise her business?

'The one at Coombe is amazing.' James poured himself a glass of juice and took a Viennese whirl. 'They have the rooms laid out for wedding breakfasts and receptions. They decorate the entire place as if a wedding were actually happening. You can see the bedrooms and honeymoon suite; they lay on entertainment; there's an array of food vans – and I don't mean burger bars.' He bit into the cake. 'This is scrumptious, Janet.' Janet beamed again. 'Oh, and they decorate the chapel as well. It's worth visiting even if you're not getting married.'

'Sounds delightful.' Janet looked at her husband expectantly. 'Can we go, dear?'

'I think we've got two weddings that day, my dear.' Rose breathed a sigh of relief. 'I can remember Rose telling me about it because it was the first one she'd booked. She was so excited.'

'Need a lift?' James asked. Rose smiled and nodded, shooting her mum a glare at the knowing look that was passing between her parents.

Rose yawned and received three anxious glances.

Her mum stood up. 'You'd best be getting back to bed, young lady.'

'I'll take her up and then get off home.' James scooped her up once more and carried her back to bed. There was no chance of a kiss, as her mum was fretting around her, tucking her in and tutting at the wet patch on the floor. 'I'll ring you tomorrow.' He blew her a kiss from the doorway when her mum wasn't looking.

'It's a date.'

'It's a promise.'

Millie: Are you feeling better, Rose?

Alice: You looked so poorly on Sunday.

Fanny: Oh no, what happened?

Rose: Caught a virus and then got soaked at the wedding fayre in one of Alice's beautiful gowns.

Alice: Don't you worry about the dress, as long as you are feeling better.

Millie: I hope James looked after you.

Natalie: Oooohhhh! What's been going on?

Lucy: Rose stayed over at James's house.

Fanny: Did she indeed? Is love in the air?

Rose: You lot are incorrigible. I was ill.

Millie: He looked so worried about you.

Natalie: Oh, bless him.

It took almost another two weeks for Rose to feel one hundred per cent better. Megan and James had been regular visitors, James even bringing his mum on one occasion, which had given them the chance to be alone while Janet and her old friend chatted and reminisced about their school days.

'I've not seen Mum this happy in years,' James had remarked as he and Rose watched from the dining room the two women laughing and joking in the garden. 'She's like a different woman. She even stood up to my dad the other day.'

'I take it she doesn't usually do that then?'

'No one stands up to Dad,' James answered. 'Except Grandma and Grandpa.'

'Well then,' Rose said, pouring tea for them both, 'perhaps it's time that somebody did.'

'Come on, sleepyhead.' Her mum was shaking her awake. 'Time to get up.'

'Why?' Rose asked, looking at the time on her phone. 'Its seven o'clock on a Friday morning, and I have absolutely nothing to do today.'

'On the contrary.' Her mum smiled knowingly. 'You need to be up, showered and ready for nine.'

'Do you and Dad need help in the church?' She shoved her feet into her slippers, stretched and yawned.

'No,' came the short reply.

'Nan and Grandad coming over?' Her mum shook her head. 'Then why do I need to be up? I'm just going to veg out in my trackies with a good book and go over my bookings again later.' She kicked off her slippers and got back into bed.

'I'll just tell James that when he arrives to take you out, then,' Janet said, heading out of the door.

It took a few seconds for her words to sink in, but when they did, Rose leapt out of bed and ran past her mum straight into the bathroom.

'James!' she screamed before shutting the door and then reopening it again. 'Why on earth didn't you tell me it was James?' She closed the door again and started rushing around, turning the shower on. 'Where's he taking me? What do I wear?' she asked her mum, opening the door once again.

'He just said to tell you to dress casual.'

'Casual? What does casual mean?' Rose closed the door for the final time, jumped in the shower and visualized every outfit she had in her wardrobe.

CHAPTER NINETEEN

After multiple exceedingly frustrating texts to and from Megan – frustrating because she was at work and couldn't answer straightaway – Rose found herself sitting in the living room, dressed in blue jeans, a pale yellow T-shirt with daisies on and her favourite navy-blue Converse.

'Have you got a jacket?' her mum asked.

'It's twenty degrees already, Mum,' Rose said. 'They've just said it could be the hottest day of the year so far.'

'You're just getting over a chill, my lady.' Her mum stood in front of her with her hands on her hips. 'Now go and get yourself a jumper.' Rose did as she was told, knowing full well that she'd take it off as soon as she was out of her mum's sight. 'And you'd better pack this in your bag, as well.' Janet handed her a bottle of factor thirty sun cream. 'You know how easily you burn.'

Rose loved her mum; she fussed way too much and seemed to forget that Rose was an adult now, but after seeing first-hand how some people's parents treated their children, she wouldn't have it any other way. A beeping horn announced James's arrival and she peeked out of the window expecting to see his black Audi. But the car that was currently parked on the driveway was a huge surprise.

'Is that . . .' Rose asked as James greeted her, holding the car door open, 'the one from the movie? The one that Jenny drives when she goes back to the Sixties?'

'Well, it's not the exact one.' Rose climbed into the British racing green Mini and James closed the door. She'd never been in a Mini before. 'The exact one is locked up in a Hollywood backlot somewhere.'

'Is this yours?' she asked as he sat down beside her and started the engine. It roared instantly to life, much louder than a modern-day engine but absolutely glorious.

'Sadly not.' He completed a swift and smooth three-point turn and headed off down the drive, turning left at the bottom. 'I've hired it for the day.'

'Why?' She was intrigued. 'Is your car broken?'

'My car is safe and sound at home.' He patted the steering wheel. 'We're having a very special day out and we needed a very special car to do it in.'

'Is that all the information I'm getting?'

'For the moment it is.' He shifted into third gear as they drove down the main street of Tointon. 'Now sit back and enjoy the ride.'

'Here we are then.' James had pulled up in the car park of the Pig and Whistle.

'Why are we here?' She stepped out of the car as James did the same. 'The Pig doesn't even open until half eleven.'

'We're meeting someone.'

Rose looked about her, suddenly suspicious. 'It's not the butcher, is it?' She wondered if James was hoping to get his own back.

'No.' He laughed. 'It's not the butcher, but thank you for putting that idea into my head for future reference.'

'Who are we meeting then?' But he refused to budge and leaned nonchalantly on the side of the Mini, his arms crossed against his chest. He was dressed in a white T-shirt and light blue jeans and black boots. The T-shirt had the same bee motif on it as the shirt he'd worn for their first date. 'Whose logo is this?' Rose pointed to the bee; she'd completely forgotten to look it up after their last trip to the pub.

'It's Gucci.' He grabbed her finger and pulled her against him. 'I haven't been able to kiss you for ages.' He tilted his head.

'And who says you can kiss me now?' She moved her head to one side and then the other as his mouth followed hers, almost touching each time. Just as she felt his lips on hers, she would move away.

'Please?' He looked at her with such longing that the next time his lips met hers she let them stay there. There was no gentle build up this time, just a pure need to feel each other's lips and explore each other's mouths.

'Mr Blume?' There was a cough behind them. 'Are you Mr Blume?'

They turned round sheepishly.

'Maisie?' James held out his hand and the new arrival shook it vigorously. 'James, Rose.' He indicated to Rose, and Maisie shook her hand with the same amount of enthusiasm.

'Maisie Johnson. Pleasure to meet you both.' She was around thirty, Rose would have said, and there was absolutely nothing unusual about her at all, except that she was dressed in a white and black mini dress and black thigh-high boots, and her brown hair was swept up into a beehive.

'That's the dress!' Rose was beginning to suspect a theme. 'That's the dress Jenny wears when she first meets Mitch in the movie.'

'A fan I see.' Maisie smiled.

'Can't fail to be when you live locally.' Rose had already watched the movie a few times. It was a wonderful romantic comedy with touching scenes, and she thoroughly enjoyed the time-slip aspect, but it was definitely the fact she recognized all the places that made her and most of the locals love it so much. If anyone ever asked where you were from, you always dropped in, 'You know, where *A Little in Love* was made.'

'I saw it ten times at the cinema,' Maisie admitted. 'And I was working at Coombe Castle when they were filming, so I got to meet all the stars.' She pulled out an A4-sized photo album from the white leather satchel that lay across her chest. 'Oh wow.' Maisie handed them the album then headed straight to the car. 'Will you take my photo, please?' She gave them her phone and Rose nodded, snapping a few photos in various positions. 'Can I sit inside?' She asked.

'Go ahead.' James, ever the gentleman, opened the door for her.

'My friend Lynne is going to go crazy when I send her this.' Maisie was back out of the car and, after taking back her phone and the album, she proceeded to text, and post to her social media too, judging by the amount of time it took her.

'The tour?' James prompted.

'Tour?' Rose looked at him. 'What tour?'

'Oh yes, the tour.' Maisie put her phone away, took out a leaflet and began her spiel. 'Welcome to the completely unofficial *A Little in Love* tour. I'm Maisie Johnson and I'll be your guide as we delve into the back stories and gossip of the fabulous Hollywood film *A Little in Love*. We'll be visiting some of the places from the film before stopping off for a very special treat at the end.' She turned around. 'Now, if you'd both like to follow me, we'll head off to where we first see Jenny Golding in the film.'

Maisie prattled on about the film, pointing out things and places as they walked through the streets of Weddington. Most of them Rose knew of, but James was in awe and asked questions as they went.

'Have you even seen the film?' Rose whispered to him

as they turned into the oldest part of Weddington. It had timber-clad buildings straight out of the Tudor period mixed with modern-day houses, which Rose knew had been built recently and straight off the back of the film.

'Watched it the other day for the first time,' he answered, hiding his mouth behind his hand as Maisie had turned to face them. 'Thought I'd better know a little about the film after I'd booked this. Then I watched it again last night.' He turned his attention to Maisie. 'Isn't this where Jenny, or Erin as she is in the film, first discovers the portal?'

'Well spotted, James.' Maisie applauded. 'Most people assume the building they can see is Weddington Hall, because that's where she is at the time, but the filming actually took place right outside this house.' She pointed to the lamp post. 'Of course, this was edited out in the film when she went back to Tudor times, and they cobbled the street, but the house stayed exactly as it is now.'

'Clever clogs.' Rose dug her shoulder into his arm.

'I just pay attention.' They followed Maisie as she announced they would be heading on to Weddington Hall next.

'Of course, as I'm sure you both know, the wedding scene in the film takes place in Coombe Castle where we'll be ending our tour, but did you know that . . .' Rose and James pretended to listen attentively to her never-ending facts and figures. Rose hadn't known anyone could talk so competently for so long; the woman knew everything there was to know.

'What made you book this?' Rose was curious. She could only remember mentioning the film to him a couple of times, and that was usually in relation to the increase in wedding fayres and guests.

'It was Megan's idea,' he said simply.

'Megan knew?' Rose was furious. 'She knew and she didn't tell me?'

'Wouldn't have been much of a surprise if she'd told you now, would it?' He chuckled. 'I realized the other day that we'd never been on a proper date, as such. Of course, we had that fantastic evening in the pub and our spur-of-the-moment picnics . . .'

'We had a breakfast date on the way to Haggerston Hall,' she reminded him.

'I know, but everything has always been at a fayre, on the way to a fayre or because of a fayre,' he said. 'I wanted to do something just for the fun of it.'

'Well' – she kissed him – 'thank you.' She kissed him again. 'It's really lovely, even if it was a complete surprise and I'm not keen on surprises.' She thought for a second. 'Did my mum know too?'

'Only that I was taking you out for the day. Megan told me not to tell her the full story – she said she isn't good at keeping secrets.'

'No, she's not.' Rose smirked. 'I'm surprised she didn't let slip that you were coming to pick me up until this morning.'

'I only asked her last night, and I made her promise not

to say a word.' They were walking up the road that led to Weddington Hall.

'Oh, look!' Rose cried out in mock surprise. 'It's where you drove past and soaked me.'

'Oh, look!' James retorted. 'It's where you stepped into the road without looking.' They both laughed, holding hands and walking close, their shoulders and arms touching as they went.

'And here we have the fabulous drive that leads up to Weddington Hall.' Maisie had stopped them by the gates. 'Now, being local you'll know that they actually used the gates from Moss Manor on the other side of the village, as Starburst Films thought they were grander than these, but in my humble opinion, I think these are beautiful.'

'I actually didn't know that,' James said. 'I only visited here for the first time a few weeks ago.' Maisie looked at him in horror. 'I'm not quite as local as Rose here. I work in the city.'

'You're not Blume as in Blume's Florist, are you?' Maisie almost squealed.

'The very same.' He mock-saluted. 'Third generation Blume at your service.'

'Then you'll know all about the bouquet and flowers that were used during the wedding scene!' Maisie looked fit to burst, but Rose was confused.

'Not personally, I'm afraid.' He put his hands in his pockets. 'It was my dad who made the bouquet and decorations.' Maisie looked crestfallen at this news. 'I did deliver them to Coombe Castle and help set them up though.'

This seemed to appease Maisie a little. 'Well, it's an honour to shake the hand of the son of the man who made such a beautiful bouquet.' She shook his hand once again, this time with even more vigour than the first, if that were indeed possible.

'You never told me that,' Rose said as they continued their walk up the drive, their feet crunching on the gravel while Maisie carried on about the driveway scene and the first shot of Weddington Hall on screen.

'Didn't think it was important, to be honest.' He shrugged. 'We're in the credits.'

'Who actually reads the credits?' Rose asked. 'I'm surprised your dad doesn't tell everyone he meets.' She stopped walking and puffed out her chest. 'Hello, I'm Geoffrey Blume and I made the bouquet for the Hollywood blockbuster *A Little in Love*.'

'Very good.' James laughed. 'There's stuff in the shop and on the website about it, but to be fair, everyone local to the business knew anyway. Dad made sure of that at the time.'

'Here we have the door to Weddington Hall.' Rose sighed in anticipation – she was getting a little fed up of Maisie's constant facts. 'This is the place where our star-crossed lovers share their first kiss.'

'It's where we first met!' Rose exclaimed, but this time James kissed her, replacing all her old memories about this place with a brand-new one.

*

A Little in Love

> **Natalie**: Well, well, well. Look what we
> have here?

A photo of Rose and James holding hands and walking down the street accompanied the message.

> **Millie**: Rose and James, sitting in a tree,
> K I S S I N G
> **Rose**: Dear God! Can I not go anywhere
> without one of you lot spying on me?
> **Natalie**: If you walk past my shop, holding
> hands with Mr Sexy Pants, then expect to be
> caught on camera.

CHAPTER TWENTY

'How much longer does this go on for?' Rose whispered to James after two hours of following Maisie around. 'I don't mean to sound ungrateful but I'm getting a bit bored now and my feet are killing me.'

'Don't worry, I know exactly what you mean.' James placed an arm round her shoulders. 'I think it's nearly over though – the tour finishes at Coombe Castle and, if I'm not mistaken . . .' – he paused – 'we are nearly there.'

'Please tell me she's not showing us round the castle as well though?' Rose asked hopefully.

'It's part of the package, I'm afraid,' he said despondently.

'Do you think we can lose her in the dungeon or something?' Rose looked at him expectantly. 'Or trap her in the priest hole?'

'That's not very Christian,' he said, pretending to be shocked. 'Don't you want to look round the castle?'

'Yes, but can we do it just the two of us?'

'She's already had her money so I'm sure she wouldn't

mind if we ended the tour a bit early.' He caught up to Maisie. 'Rose and I were just wondering if we could maybe go round the castle on our own.' Rose watched as Maisie stopped walking and a look of confusion crossed her face.

'On your own? But how will you know where all the scenes took place?'

'I'm sure we'll figure it out,' James said. 'And it's absolutely nothing personal,' he reassured her as her face fell. 'The tour has been brilliant. We will both highly recommend it.' He waved Rose towards them.

'Couldn't agree more,' Rose said, taking the hint. 'Your knowledge of the film is astounding.'

'It's just,' James went on, 'it's our first proper date, and we really wanted some alone time.'

'Don't you worry about it another minute,' Maisie said, instantly perking up. 'You should have told me sooner. Here's me prattling on when all you want to do is enjoy your date. Don't you just love love?' She clasped her hands together. 'I'll leave you both here then.' She shook their hands once more and Rose felt like she would shake her arm off. 'It's been an absolute pleasure to meet you both. Remember to be in the courtyard at one thirty, Mr Blume. That should give you enough time to look around first.' And with that, she was gone.

'Why do we need to be in the courtyard at one thirty?' Rose asked.

'You'll find out at one thirty, when we're in the courtyard.' He grabbed her hand. 'Now then, let's head to the castle.'

*

'Here we have the fireplace in the great hall,' James said, mimicking Maisie's voice. 'It's here that John Travolta and Olivia Newton-John did their famous hand jive scene.' Rose slapped him and laughed loudly, which drew funny looks from an older couple on the other side of the room. 'Why do you have to be quiet in these old places?' he whispered as the older couple turned away again.

'It's in case you wake up the ghosts,' Rose whispered back.

'So how long has it been since you came here last?' James asked as they climbed the wide wooden staircase with its bevelled handrail up to the first floor.

'Must be five or six years at least,' Rose answered.

'I think I remember Grandma and Mum bringing Peter, Elizabeth and me here one summer when we were about eight. They had an event going on and we got to dress up as knights, and Elizabeth dressed up as a princess. We ran around the grounds like lunatics.'

'Your childhood wasn't all bad then?' Rose asked tentatively. She could tell by his face that this was a fond memory and hoped he had many more of them to share with her in time.

'No, it wasn't all bad,' he admitted. 'To be fair, it was pretty decent till we left school.' Rose looked at him, eager for more. 'Dad was always a bit of an arsehole, but it wasn't till I started working for him that he became the absolute control freak that he is today. Grandpa just wanted his three grandchildren to work in the business so he was really disappointed when Peter showed absolutely no interest – other than in its profits, of course. Elizabeth worked there for a while but she kept getting upset when Dad shouted at her if she got something wrong. She was only fourteen, though, and she really doesn't have the Blume backbone that Peter and I have developed. Uncle Tony is her dad, so she had a much softer upbringing.'

'Well, I'm glad you have some nice memories.' Turning her attention to a nearby plaque, Rose said, 'This is the bedroom of Lady Olivia Philips, Countess of Coombe.'

'How little were people in the olden days?' James peered over the red rope that cordoned off the precious furniture. 'Look at the size of that bed. Our feet would stick out the end.'

'I think everything below the knee would stick out.' She looked at the four-poster bed with its ornate tapestry and plush velvet curtains. 'Do you think it's true that most rich people didn't actually share a bed? There's no way two people could sleep in that and be comfortable – it doesn't look much wider than a single.'

'It's bigger than it looks actually.' They hadn't noticed the uniformed man standing in the corner. 'And the average man was only around five foot seven in the eighteenth century, so over half a foot shorter than you, sir, if I'm guessing your height correctly.'

'Is this the actual bed that the Countess slept in?' Rose could never quite believe that things like this lasted for hundreds of years.

'It is indeed, and has been left untouched since the day she died in it.' Rose and James took an instinctive step back, but the man seemed not to notice. 'She died naturally in her sleep at the ripe old age of seventy-three,' he continued, 'which was considered ancient in those days.'

'Seventy-three?' Rose was amazed. 'My dad's parents never even reached their sixties.'

'She actually outlived all her children and three of her grandchildren and she lived to see her first great-great-grandchild born,' he said proudly. 'A major feat these days, I have to say, so you can imagine how big a deal it was back then when life expectancy was early forties.'

'She sounds amazing.' James nodded to a painting on the wall nearest the bed. 'Is that her?'

Rose looked up to see what appeared to be a life-sized portrait of Countess Olivia. She was dressed in a yellow ball-gown and had a diamond tiara placed perfectly on her head amidst a tumble of golden curls. She was holding a cream fan that had an oriental scene painted on it, and a gorgeous garden was blended beautifully behind her.

'It is indeed.' The man stepped closer. 'This was painted by her nephew Thomas. A fabulous but underrated portrait painter. Unfortunately, as happened with so many wealthy males in those days, he got caught up in gambling debts and was disowned by his father at the age of twenty-three. He was mugged and left for dead at twenty-five.'

'What a sad story.' James stepped behind her and placed his arms around her waist. 'So much heartache in those days. Parents losing children, no money, debts and, heaven forbid, the dreaded workhouse.'

'We've come so far in some ways, yet gone backwards in others,' the guide said. Rose wasn't quite sure what he was implying, but a distant clock chiming 1pm brought their attention back into the present.

'We'd best be getting a move on.' James looked at his watch as if to check the clock was telling the truth. 'We've got half an hour.'

'It was lovely talking to you,' Rose said over her shoulder as they moved on to the next room.

James didn't allow Rose to dawdle in any of the remaining rooms, and she felt quite rushed towards the end.

'We can come back another day,' he said, grabbing her hand and almost running down the stairs with her trailing behind him. 'We need to be in the courtyard.'

'Okay, okay, I'm coming as fast as I can.' She pulled back on his hand a little, hoping to slow him down before she tripped on the stairs.

'Will you hurry up?' They were by the door now, and James was almost stamping his feet in frustration. 'I can hear it coming.'

'Hear what coming?' Rose stopped and listened. She could hear wheels on the drive but no engine, just a jangling of metal. 'No, you haven't.' She ran past him, through the door and out onto the drive where a little crowd had gathered at the sound of the new arrival. 'Oh my God!' Rose screamed, and she knew this had definitely been Megan's idea. It had been a dream of hers from childhood.

A team of four matching bay horses was trotting up the

driveway pulling a beautiful claret carriage that currently had its top down. A woman dressed in red and black sat in the groomsman seat, an elegant long whip in her hand. Rose instantly recognized Lucy Greenfield.

'Surprise!' The horses pulled up slap bang in the middle of the cobbled courtyard, and Lucy beamed down at them.

'Hello there, Rose.' She swung down with little effort and weaved the end of the reins through a metal hook on the frame of the carriage. 'I didn't know it was you we were surprising.' She opened the carriage door and pulled down a metal step. 'Now, don't be disappointed. It's not Topsy and Tim – I know how much you liked them. I rest them during the week in wedding season.' She held out a hand and helped both Rose and James up into the carriage before folding the step back inside and closing the door. 'I've brought my finest team with me today though. Bertie and Bassett are at the front and Button and Bentley at the back.'

'This is turning into the best day ever.' Rose threw her arms around James and hugged him tight, jolting back into her seat with a scream of laughter as the carriage lurched forwards. 'I can't believe you've gone to all this trouble for me.' Rose could feel tears threatening to spill. She'd never been with anyone so thoughtful, so romantic. How could she have got him so wrong in the beginning?

'There's more to come yet.' He took her hand and held it to his lips. 'Now sit back and enjoy the ride.'

*

James hadn't lied about there being more to come. After half an hour's ride in the carriage through the country lanes of Weddington, they pulled up at Moss Manor.

'Here we are then.' Lucy pulled the horses to a stop. 'It's just over there, James, in the summer house.' She pointed towards an arched metal gate that stood between two pristine conifer hedges.

'Thank you, Lucy.' He shook her hand. 'It's been an absolute pleasure.'

'It's been fabulous, Lucy.' Rose hadn't stopped smiling from the moment she'd stepped into the carriage. 'Is this for you?' she asked as a huge horse trailer and van came up the drive.

'It is indeed.' Lucy started uncoupling the horses from the carriage. 'They can only pull the carriage for so long.' She patted each horse gently on the nose as she removed their bridles, giving each one a small treat from her pocket once their bits had been removed.

'We'll be off then.' James took Rose's hand. Rose was almost reluctant to leave the horses; she had always loved horses and had promised herself that one day she would learn to ride, and maybe even own one. 'Close your eyes.'

'Don't be silly.' She pushed his hands away as he tried to place them over her eyes.

'I'm not being silly,' he said, putting his hands back where they'd been. 'Close your eyes.'

She did as she was told, and in his arms stepped slowly through the gate, his steps guiding hers.

'Can I open them yet?' It had only been a few seconds, but in her anticipation, it already felt like they'd been walking for hours.

'Just a few more steps.' He turned her around just slightly. 'You can open them now.'

CHAPTER TWENTY-ONE

'Oh, James!' This time she did start crying, and this time he noticed.

'Hey.' He wiped her tears away with his thumbs and kissed her salty wet mouth. 'They'd better be happy tears.'

'They are.' More threatened to spill over as James led her inside a small metal summer house. It was painted a gorgeous sky blue and had a cream roof and glass windows along three sides. In the fourth side there was a glass door fitted with beautiful stained glass that depicted the house and gardens. 'Now I know this wasn't Megan's idea.' Megan hated eating outside. She wouldn't even sit and have a coffee in case a fly or wasp decided to land on her.

'All mine.' He pointed to a large hamper that was sitting on a tartan picnic rug. 'Well, my mum and grandma may have helped a bit.' He led her to the rug and indicated for her to sit down before undoing the buckles and taking out various Tupperware boxes filled with finger sandwiches, five different cheeses, grapes, crackers, pasta salad and the tiniest, poshest-looking sausage rolls Rose had ever seen. Instead of being entirely wrapped in puff pastry, the tiny sausage appeared to be wrapped in a slice of bread. 'Champagne?' He handed her a glass and held up a bottle. 'Non-alcoholic I'm afraid – I've got to drive later.'

'This is just ...' Rose was actually lost for words. James handed her a blue and white plate – not a plastic one, a real china one – and unbuckled some silver cutlery from the lid of the hamper.

'It's Grandma's.' He indicated the hamper and started to pile his plate with a variety of items. 'She told me it was a wedding gift from her sister, and she and Grandpa used to use it a lot. I think there's a picture somewhere of us all on Weymouth beach with it.' He bit into a cucumber sandwich. 'They still use it now when they go out in the Jag. Been relined a few times and the wicker has been repaired, but it's still going strong.'

'It sounds just like the old movies where the couple are driving down a country lane, the top down and a wicker basket strapped to the boot.' She loved watching those movies with her mum on a Sunday when her dad was still doing church stuff. 'The lady always loses her headscarf.'

'And it flies away behind them.' He laughed. 'Classic scene.'

'I can't remember ever having such a good time.' She placed her hands on the rug behind her and leaned back on them, shaking her head gently to free her hair from around her shoulders. 'You've thought of absolutely everything.'

'With help.' He placed his plate down on the rug.

'But I love that you cared enough to *ask* for help.' He crawled

186

over to her side of the rug, making sure he didn't put a hand, knee or foot in any of the food. 'Aren't you hungry?' she asked.

'Not anymore.' He placed one knee either side of her legs, his arms linking through hers. 'Well, at least not for food anyway.' His voice had taken on a husky tone, and when Rose looked into his eyes, she thought they had darkened.

'What are you hungry for?' she squeaked, her heart doing that flippy thing it liked to do when he was close to her.

'You.' His mouth came down on hers, his tongue prising her lips apart. She matched his force with the same passion, surprising herself at how fast she was falling for this man, how he had crept into her every waking thought and sometimes even her dreams. How he had managed to break down the wall she had so carefully built.

She reached up to run her fingers through his hair, pushing her body against his so her chest was pressed against his. He moaned and gently eased her down to the floor so he was lying on top of her. His hands caressed her thighs through her jeans but moved no further. She ran her fingers across his back, loving the feel of his taut muscles underneath his shirt.

'I could kiss you forever,' she said as they broke away, breathless but sated.

'Is that a date?'

'It's a promise.'

Rose didn't want to say goodbye to James at the end of the afternoon. He'd called them an Uber to take them back to the Pig and Whistle, and they'd now been sitting outside the vicarage for almost an hour, neither of them wanting the perfect day to end. Eventually, it was James that broke the spell.

'I have to get the Mini back before six.' He sighed. 'It's booked out again this evening for a stag do.'

'If you have to go, you have to go.' Still they lingered, neither moving.

'So, are we friends now?' he asked, looking deep into her eyes.

'I'd say we were much more than that.' She pulled him in for one last kiss, trying to fill it with every emotion she could, so he would be in absolutely no doubt of her feelings for him.

'I think I might be in very great danger of falling in love with you.' He caressed her cheek.

Then that makes two of us, she thought, reluctant to say it out loud. He kissed her again, gently this time. 'Off you go, Blume.' Rose knew he would never leave unless she made him. 'Some poor stag is waiting for this car to whisk him away for an evening of debauchery.' She opened the car door and stepped out.

'I'll speak to you tomorrow,' he said, before starting the engine and wheel spinning off the drive.

'That's odd.' The next evening Rose's phone beeped to signal an incoming email.

'What's odd, dear?' her mum asked.

'Remember that obnoxious girl I told you about a couple of weeks ago at the Haggerston Hall fayre?' Janet nodded.

'The group of sisters?' John asked, looking up from his newspaper. 'You said they were all terribly spoilt.'

'Yes, those ones.' Rose was still reading the email. 'The youngest one turned out to be quite nice in the end.'

'What's the problem?' her mum enquired. 'Does she want diamond-encrusted champagne flutes now?'

'No.' Rose put down her phone. 'She's cancelled.'

'Really?' Her dad was surprised. 'You said she seemed so keen.'

'She was, Dad, she was.' Rose racked her brain. 'Never mind. The youngest one did say she was prone to change her mind at the drop of a hat and told me to make sure I asked for a non-refundable deposit.'

'I wonder why she did change her mind, though,' her mum mused while her dad returned to his reading.

The next morning found another email sitting in Rose's inbox – this time it was a cancellation from the wedding she had booked in August – and a voicemail from a different lady who had provisionally booked her for September.

Well, this is just getting a little peculiar, she thought to herself as she headed down the stairs and into the kitchen for breakfast.

'Look who's here!' her mum said, meeting her at the kitchen door, delight etched across her face.

'James?' Rose couldn't believe it; she was sure he'd said he had a fayre today so she really wasn't expecting to see him.

But it wasn't James sitting at the breakfast bar, smiling from ear to ear.

'Hi, Rose.'

'Josh?' He stood and she threw her arms around him. 'Oh, it's so good to see you. When did you get back?' Josh had gone to America for a year out before starting university and had loved it so much he'd stayed there to study, eventually making it his forever home. This was the reason he and Rose had broken up – just the age old story of distance not making the heart grow fonder.

'A few days ago.' He hugged her tightly. 'You haven't changed a bit.' He sat back down at the breakfast bar.

'Well, I should think not – it's only been a few years, I'm not ancient yet.'

Janet had already dished out bacon and eggs to Josh and was now busy doing the same for Rose. 'I've missed your breakfasts, Mrs P,' Josh said as he tucked into his plate of food with gusto, his blond hair falling into his eye.

'Still got the floppy fringe, I see?' Rose flicked it.

'Leave my fringe alone,' he said through a mouthful of egg. 'It's my trademark.'

'You've had the same hairstyle since you were thirteen.' She picked up the teapot and poured everyone a cup. 'I think a decade is long enough don't you?'

They chatted for a while, reminiscing about school days. Rose had almost completely forgotten about her run of cancellations, but then Josh asked after the business.

'I saw your posts on Facebook about Pedals – it's such a fabulous idea. The Americans would go crazy for it. They'd think it quaint.' He and Rose were washing up, having insisted that her mum go and sit down.

'Don't think I'm ready to go global just yet. I haven't actually done a wedding or party yet, and based on the three cancellations I've had since last night, it's looking like I won't be doing any.'

'Cancellations?' he asked. 'Did they say why?'

'One just said they'd changed their mind. I was kind of expecting that one, to be fair – she was very flaky.' Josh nodded. 'The other two just said budget wouldn't allow for it.'

'There you go then.' He wiped the surfaces as if he'd lived in the house all his life. 'Seems perfectly plausible to me.' He helped her dry and put away the last of the things, remembering exactly where everything went. 'You just need to get more bookings. How are you advertising?'

'I'm just handing out cards at the fayres.'

Josh threw his hands up. 'Bloody lucky I'm here then.' Rose bristled slightly at this; she thought she'd been doing okay. Josh looked at his watch. 'I've got to get back to Mum and Dad's – they're having a big party for me this afternoon, all the family. You and Megan should come. I'm heading back to the States a week on Wednesday, but we need to talk strategy before I go.'

'And what would you know about strategy?' If she recalled correctly, Josh could never even win at Monopoly.

'I majored in business,' he said simply. Then he called goodbye to Janet and was gone.

'How lovely of Josh to pop by,' her mum said as Rose joined her in the living room. 'Is he back for good?'

'No, Mum, just a visit.' Seeing the look of disappointment on her mum's face, Rose continued, 'His life is in America now.'

'Such a shame.' Rose knew her mum had always seen Josh as a potential future son-in-law.

'He has a girlfriend,' Rose said as her mum sighed. 'In fact, I'm pretty sure they moved in together at Christmas and got engaged on Valentine's Day.'

'Living together is no commitment these days.' She patted Rose's hand, completely ignoring the part about getting engaged.

'Mum!' Rose looked at her in shock. 'I can't believe you just said that. And anyway, I'm with James now. I thought you liked James?'

'Oh, I do . . . we both do.' Her mum looked shiftily over her shoulder as if to check no one was listening, and then leaned in towards Rose. 'I really don't like his father, though. Some of the things Tabby has told me about him . . .'

'He's absolutely nothing like his father.' Rose felt she needed to defend him. 'Peter is, but not James.'

'They're identical twins, aren't they?' Rose could see her mum's mind working overtime.

'Only in looks, Mum, only in looks,' she said.

'In my experience the apple doesn't fall far from the tree.' Rose couldn't believe the sudden change in her mum's opinion of James, just because Josh was back, and wondered what on earth Tabby had been saying. 'Mark my words, there's trouble ahead.'

Rose: Can I ask if anyone has had any cancellations recently? I've had three overnight.

Fanny: Really? that's a little odd.

Lucy: Nothing here, very rarely get a cancellation though, sometimes a change of date or venue.

Natalie: A lady cancelled her cake last week, but she'd caught her fiancé in bed with her maid of honour.

Lucy: She never did?

Natalie: Right after they'd all been to see Reverend Timms it was.

Fanny: Well, I never. Who cancelled Rose?

Rose: One of them was that Petunia Carmichael, who I half-expected, but the other two seemed dead set. Said they didn't have the budget.

Fanny: Oh that happens all the time with the frivolous stuff, shall we say. No one ever realizes how much a wedding costs these days.

Lucy: I wouldn't worry about it, Rose, but we'll have a chat at our get together on Thursday.

Rose: So, looking forward to it.

Fanny: It's at mine, hun, I'll message you the address.

CHAPTER TWENTY-TWO

Rose: Guess who's back in the village?

Megan: Chris Hemsworth?

Rose: When has Chris Hemsworth ever been in Tointon?

Megan: Maybe if they do a sequel to *A Little in Love*, him and Chris Evans could be in it?

Rose: Why don't you petition Hollywood for the entire Avengers cast to make a film here?

Megan: Now you're just being silly.

Rose: I'm being silly?

Megan: Yes, as if they'd ever make an Avengers movie here. So ... what's the goss? Who's daft enough to come back to sleepy old Tointon?

Rose: Josh! He's asked if we want to go to a party at his later, one that his mum and dad are throwing for him.

Megan: Now ... do you mean a party or a PARTEEEEEE?

Rose: I think it's just a party.

Megan: Well, I've got nothing else to do and it would be nice to see Joshy again.

Rose: Come here first then and we'll walk together … bout 7?

Megan: Laters.

Rose checked her phone for the umpteenth time that day; she checked the WiFi, the signal, the battery, but everything was working perfectly. So why hadn't she heard from James all weekend? She'd heard nothing from him throughout Saturday and now it was Sunday evening and still not a peep. One part of her said she was being silly, that there was some perfectly legitimate reason that he wasn't messaging her all the time. But a nagging doubt at the back of her mind kept telling her that maybe he didn't like her as much as she thought, and she'd been taken for a ride yet again. Not to mention the comment her mum had made about James being trouble.

You could message him, a little voice inside her said, but she shook her head vigorously as if to rid her mind of the thought. *Why not? Why can't you just text him and say hi?* The little voice had a point. Why couldn't she? They'd expressed that they liked each other; though they hadn't had 'the conversation', they were more or less a couple. She fired off a quick text, nothing gushy, just a short, *How's things?*

There was no instant reply, no bubble to say he was typing, no notice to say the message had been read, just that it had been delivered. She crunched up her face in exasperation, then, hearing Megan arrive downstairs, vowed to forget all about James Blume and enjoy a night with her old school friends.

'Rose!' Megan screamed as she came down the stairs. 'I've found a bike.'

'What?'

'For Pedals.' Megan pushed the dirtiest-looking bike that Rose had ever seen into the hall. Its tyres were perished, its mudguards had more mud than guard, its frame was rusty and what little paint was left was flaking off.

'Where on earth did you find this?' Rose pushed it back outside before her mum saw it and went mental.

'Isn't it perfect?' Megan cocked a leg and sat on the seat only to jump up in pain when a huge spring shot up her bum cheek. 'Well, maybe not perfect, but it was a tenner in the charity shop next to work. Ten pounds!'

Rose had to admit that the price did make it slightly more appealing, but goodness it needed some work, not to mention the fact that she probably didn't even need a second bike – not if she got any more cancellations anyway.

'We'll put it in the garage.' The wheels squeaked, the chain wasn't even attached to the cogs and there were spokes missing, but with her dad's help, she was sure they could get it looking presentable. 'There's something I need to tell you as well, but you mustn't say anything to Mum and Dad.'

'My lips are sealed.' Megan pretended to zip her lips and placed the imaginary secret in her imaginary pocket.

'Not here, I'll tell you on the way to Josh's house.' They

shouted goodbye to Rose's parents, told them not to wait up and walked the ten minutes to Josh's parents' place on the opposite side of the village. They passed the war memorial cross in the centre, and said good evening to Mr Wagstaff, who was packing up the corner shop for the night and handed them a lollipop as he had done every time he'd seen them since the age of five. They'd tried to tell him they were too old, but really, you were never too old for a Chupa Chups. While they unwrapped their lollies, Rose filled Megan in on the emails she'd received and James's sudden absence.

'Okay, about the cancellations, I have to agree with Josh and the WOW ladies. Completely reasonable excuses. Money is tight for everyone. Perhaps the bride found a more expensive dress, or more guests came out of the woodwork.' She sucked on the cherry-flavoured lolly. It was always cherry for Megan and cola for Rose. 'James on the other hand . . .' She wagged the lolly as she thought. 'I'm afraid you've got me on that one. Absolutely nothing all weekend?'

'Not even a smiley emoji.' Rose was as confused as Megan. 'We had such an amazing time on Friday. Thanks for not telling me by the way.'

'You're very welcome,' Megan said sincerely, to which Rose shot her a look. 'What would have been the point of telling you? You'd have panicked about what to wear and how to do your hair. This way you had two hours to get ready and it was all a wonderfully romantic surprise.'

'Until today,' Rose reminded her.

'He hasn't even been AWOL for forty-eight hours – give

the man a chance.' They turned into Josh's road. 'Now this brings back memories.' The girls had been regular visitors to Josh's house in their teens. He had been the cool kid because his garage was a games room and his parents allowed him to have parties; they even allowed them to drink when they were sixteen, as long as they didn't get drunk, and because they respected Mr and Mrs Carter, no one ever did.

'Do you remember when Graham Clarke tried to grab your boobs under the mistletoe?' Rose laughed. 'You broke his nose.'

'Cheeky little fucker he was,' Megan replied. 'Can't believe I went out with him for two months.'

'And Matthew Hall kept asking me out even though everyone knew it was Josh I liked?' She sighed. 'What I wouldn't give to go back to school!'

'What? To exams and spots? No, thank you.' Megan crunched the last of her lolly as they walked up the drive to Josh's house. They could hear music coming from the back garden.

'I mean no worries about work or money, just hanging out with your mates.'

Her phone beeped.

'If that's James you'd best bloody ignore him,' Megan warned. Then, as the door in front of them opened, 'Hi, Mrs Carter. Remember us?'

The pair of them were ushered inside with warm welcomes and hugs.

'It wasn't James,' Rose lied to Megan, once they were in

the garden grabbing a bottle of cider each. 'Just an enquiry about Pedals. I'll answer them in a bit.' She didn't like lying to Megan – she'd never lied to Megan in her entire life – but she didn't want her advice either. She knew exactly what she would say: *Make him wait, he's made you wait long enough.* But Rose wasn't like that, and in his message, James seemed genuinely upset about something. She would sneak off to the bathroom in a minute and ring him.

'Joshy!' Megan screamed across the garden.

'Megsy!' Rose had never really understood why they had these pet names for each other; she had never been Rosey to either of them. 'I'm so glad you could both come.' Josh almost ran across the garden, grabbing Megan and hugging her. 'There's someone I want you to meet.' He pulled them both by the hands over to where he had been standing. 'Rose, Megan, this is Hannah. Hannah, this is Rose and Megan, two of my old friends from school.'

'It's an absolute pleasure to meet you,' Hannah said in a Southern drawl. 'I've just been dying to come here to England and see where my Josh grew up.' She was everything Rose had ever pictured a Southern belle to be: petite, glossy brown hair and red, rosebud lips.

'Pleasure to meet you too,' Rose and Megan said one after the other.

'This your first time here then?' Rose asked.

'I went to London when I was ten with Daddy once.' She sipped a glass of champagne. 'We saw Big Ben and went on a boat down the Thames but the best bit was seeing the

Crown Jewels.' She gasped at the memory. 'That crown looks so heavy. I don't know how the little old Queen keeps it on her head without falling over. I wore a tiara to homecoming once and it gave me a headache.'

'Hannah!' Mrs Carter called from the back door. 'Could you come here for a moment please? Auntie Pat and I want to show you some photos.' Josh groaned, but Hannah did as she was bid.

'Well, isn't she just a little cutie pie?' Megan said in her best sickly-sweet American accent.

Josh dug his elbow into her ribs. 'I like how happy she is. Makes a change from the miserable lot over here.'

'I'm joshing.' Megan looked at Josh, and then to Rose. 'No? Nothing? Joshing? Get it?'

'We get it,' Rose said. 'We just didn't think it was funny.'

'I've missed you two.' Josh hugged them both, and then his dad called him away.

'I'm just going to pop to the loo,' Rose said as her phone beeped again.

'Three sips of cider too much for the old bladder, eh?' Megan said, eyebrows raised. 'Just go and bloody phone him, will you?'

'I'll go over there.' She pointed to a huge apple tree in the bottom corner of the garden.

'Just promise me you won't be all gushy with him.' She pointed her bottle of cider at her. 'Remember to be a little bit pissed off with him at least.'

'I will,' Rose said, but she had absolutely no intention of

listening to a word of Megan's advice. She pulled out her phone and read the second message.

> **James**: Been in hospital with Mum, all very sudden, forgot to take phone with me in the panic. Still there now but Uncle Tony got my phone for me.

She phoned him right away, but it went straight to voicemail, so she fired off a message instead.

> **Rose**: That's awful, hope she is okay?
> **James**: She's sleeping now, and Uncle Tony is driving me home in a minute. It was gallstones. She woke up yesterday morning in agony. Dad and Uncle Tony were already on their way to the fayre with Peter, I was meant to follow on in the afternoon, but it never happened. Mum just got worse and worse and, in the end, Grandma phoned an ambulance. They operated this morning once they knew exactly what it was.
> **Rose**: James, I'm so sorry. That's a horrible thing to happen. Have you been at the hospital all this time?
> **James**: Yep, just me. Dad refused to come. Said she was in the best place and he was needed at the fayre yesterday and today.

> Peter popped his head in for five minutes this morning when she was in theatre, so that was of absolutely no use, and Tony and Maureen have just come now.
>
> **Rose**: Your dad hasn't been to see his wife?
>
> **James**: Nope. He phoned the ward this morning to ask how she was and sent a bunch of flowers in with Peter but that's it.

If it were possible, Rose's opinion of Geoffrey Blume sank even lower.

> **James**: I'd best go. Uncle Tony's just pulled up with the car. I'll ring you tomorrow. I'm just going to eat, shower and sleep when I get home xx.
>
> **Rose**: You make sure you do xx

Rose wasn't in the mood for socializing after her conversation with James, so she made her excuses and left. She spent the rest of the evening taking apart the 'new' bike and sanding down the frame and mudguards ready to be painted. She threw the seat away — it was beyond repair — and ordered a new one, along with a basket for the front. A trailer would have to wait, but at least they could start visiting shows together, and Rose could get Megan up to speed on how it all worked.

'You're up late, sweetheart.' Her dad stepped into the

garage, and Rose looked at her watch; it was past midnight. 'I saw the garage light on when I came down for some water.'

'Sorry, Dad, hadn't realized.' She stretched, her back aching from leaning over the bike.

'Where did this come from?' he asked, examining the bike.

'Megan found it in a charity shop,' she explained. 'I know it's in bad shape, but it was only a tenner.'

'Well, if it was only a tenner it was bloody worth it.' He looked at it more closely. 'I'm sure it's a Humber cycle.'

'Humber?' Rose asked. 'I presume that means something?'

'Very famous in their day, had factories in Coventry and Wolverhampton, if I'm not very much mistaken.' He placed his hand where the seat should be. 'Shame it's missing.'

'Oh, it's not.' Rose picked the seat out of the bin and handed it to him.

'I wonder if this can be restored; it'd be wonderful to have something local.' He passed Rose her phone from the side. 'Take a few photos of it for me and I'll have a look on the internet in the morning. And promise me you won't throw anything else away or do anything else at all to it until I've checked.'

Rose took some photos and sent them to her dad's email so he could access them from his office computer.

'Is it worth anything?' Rose asked as she turned off the light and locked the garage door.

'I have absolutely no idea, Rose. I just remember having a Humber bike as a kid – it was my dad's, and it's blooming lovely to see one again.'

CHAPTER TWENTY-THREE

The bike did in fact turn out to be an old Humber, and her dad spent the next week researching it and finding out how best to restore it. It was lovely to see him so excited, and he even managed to find a picture of his dad as a child with the bike he had remembered so vividly from his own childhood.

'Here's me and your grandad.' He beamed with pride as he handed her a black-and-white photograph the following Thursday evening, along with a whole box of old pictures he had dug out from the loft.

'Look at you in your little shorts.' She laughed. 'Are you about five or six here?'

'I'd say five.' He took the photograph back. 'It was taken in the garden at the old house before we moved to Tointon, and that was when I was six.'

'Do you think we can get the bike looking as good as that one?' she asked, pulling her hair up into a ponytail in front of the hall mirror.

'Don't see why not.' He looked at Rose's reflection. 'Where you off to tonight then?'

'I'm meeting some of the wedding fayre ladies.' She grabbed the car keys. 'Can I borrow the car?'

'Any other night, my dear, but I've got to drop your mum to her knitting club.' He smiled apologetically. 'I could drop you off too?'

'It's fine, Dad, thanks.' She kissed him on the cheek and picked up her phone. 'I'll order an Uber.'

'Rose!' She was greeted at the door by an extremely smiley Fanny. 'Welcome to my humble abode.' Fanny stepped aside and Rose walked past into a well-lit hallway adorned with flowery wallpaper and row upon row of smiling faces from various decades.

'Is this all your family?' Rose had never seen so many pictures in one place.

'Every single one of them.' She closed the door and pointed to a wedding photo that was slap bang in the middle of the wall. 'There's me and my Bert, God rest his soul. Happy as Larry we were.'

'I'm so sorry, Fanny.' Rose hadn't meant to bring up sad memories. 'I didn't know.'

'Well, how could you know?' She tapped her gently on the shoulder. 'Anyways, he's been gone ten years now.'

'Well, I'm sorry all the same.'

'Bless you, young Rose.' She ushered her through an open door, through which Rose could hear laughter. 'Rose is here, everyone.'

Seated around the room, which looked like it was stuck in a time warp from the Seventies, were Natalie, Lucy, Millie and a few other faces that Rose recognized from the fayres or from around the villages.

'Drink, Rose?' Millie was standing by a cocktail bar in the corner of the room, that could rival Pat Butcher's from *EastEnders*. 'I heartily recommend the rhubarb gin.'

'Sounds good to me.' Rose took a seat on the sofa in between Lucy and Natalie, and immediately sank into its softness. 'Can I have it with lemonade though, please – I find tonic a bit dry.'

'With Millie's measures, you'll have no chance of tasting anything but the gin.' Fanny laughed good-naturedly and sat on a garden chair in the bay window. 'I hope I've brought enough chairs in?' Rose watched as she scanned the room, taking in the mixture of garden and dining chairs, which stood out against the flowery sofa and chair that sat in the opposite corner. A huge carpet bag stood next to them, an array of wools and knitting needles poking out of the top.

'There's only Alice and Joyce left to come,' Natalie said, taking a sip of what looked like a pina colada.

'Aren't there any men?' Rose asked, suddenly noticing the absence of any males.

'James not enough for you?' Fanny quipped, laughing heartily when Rose blushed.

'Fanny frightens them off,' Lucy said.

'Do you remember when Joyce brought Ron that time?' Natalie reminisced. 'Poor man, couldn't get out of here quick enough.' The group erupted into laughter, which was only halted by the sound of an engine backfiring outside.

'Speak of the devil.' Fanny turned in her chair and Millie peeked through the net curtains.

'Oh, bloody hell,' Millie said. 'Who invited her?'

Rose followed suit as the others got up and went to the window, all of them leaning on each other to see who'd arrived.

There was Joyce, taking off her crash helmet and running her hands through her hair. She was dressed in full black leathers and was sat astride a motorbike. Attached to the motorbike was a sidecar, and inside was an extremely dishevelled Madison.

'She lives by Joyce, doesn't she?' Natalie said, sitting back down. 'Probably accosted her as she left.'

'Honestly.' Lucy shook her head. 'She's a bloody nightmare. Thinks she's so much better than everyone else. Just because she's the only wedding planner in the area. I wish someone else would give it a go, might knock some of the wind out of her sails.'

'Your James had a lucky escape, I'm telling you,' Fanny said to nods of agreement.

'But she keeps trying to get him back,' Natalie said. 'Look how she was at St Agatha's – all over him.'

'Such a shame she doesn't like Peter.' Fanny shook her head. 'Those two would be perfect for each other.'

'She can't stand him, Fanny,' Natalie answered. 'She's told me over and over again how much she hates him, how he doesn't compare to James, how . . .' She trailed off when she realized Rose was shuffling uncomfortably in her seat. The room had gone silent. 'All that's water under the bridge now anyway,' she said, nudging Rose's shoulder playfully. 'Anyone can see he's totally and utterly besotted with you.'

Rose smiled and nodded, but inside her thoughts were heading into turmoil. Could she really compete with Madison? She'd only known James a few weeks after all, and he had so much history with her. And even though Madison clearly annoyed him sometimes, it was also obvious that there had been affection between them. Was that affection still there? These ladies had known the Blumes for years, had seen James and Madison together. Her old insecurities threatened to resurface, but she pushed them away, reminding herself of James's smile and kisses.

'Evening ladies.' Joyce filled the room with her presence and a much quieter than normal Madison followed after her. 'Gave this reprobate a lift, although I don't think she was dressed appropriately for the journey.'

Madison sauntered towards the soft chair in the corner, darting a look at Rose as she did. She brushed her blue suit with her hands before sitting down, elegantly locking her ankles and placing them to one side. She pulled out a compact mirror from her matching bag, tucked the escaping tendrils of hair back into their chignon and tidied up her smeared lipstick and mascara. Within five minutes, she looked like she had just stepped out of the house, all traces of her journey wiped away.

'May I have a vodka Martini, please?' she asked Millie, who appeared to be the designated barmaid.

'Don't mind her and all this talk,' Lucy whispered to Rose. 'It's perfectly obvious that James is smitten with you and no one else.' This warmed Rose a little. 'He was like a kid in a sweet shop when he was telling me what he wanted for your date.' She smiled wistfully. 'Wish a man would do the same for me.'

'Are you not married then?' Rose said, keen to turn the talk away from James in case anyone else was listening.

'Goodness me, no.' Lucy laughed, although Rose thought it sounded a little sad. 'Given up on finding anyone decent. I'm closer to thirty than twenty-five with a string of failed relationships behind me.'

'You shouldn't give up though,' Rose said, trying to lift her spirits. 'No one knows what or who is just around the corner.'

'Very true, Rose.' She clinked her glass against Rose's. 'But I'm happy either way. I love my life, love the horses . . . it'd just be nice to have someone to share it with.'

'Am I too late for the party?' Alice had now arrived, peeking around the door. 'Door was open so I let myself in.'

'Well, we were just about to vote on whether or not you could still be part of the WOWs seeing as you no longer trade from Weddington.' Fanny stood up.

'Blimey, I've only been gone three months and already you're chucking me out,' Alice said, feigning shock with her hands on her hips. 'And me, the founding member.'

209

'Founding member?' Joyce stood up too. 'The Weddington and Tointon Society had been going ages before you came.' Rose could see that everyone was trying not to laugh.

'And isn't it a good job I came along when I did?' Alice crossed her arms. 'Imagine printing all those brochures with TWATS written along the top.' The room erupted again, and Rose was a little lost until Natalie explained that they had originally been called The Weddington And Tointon Society before Alice had pointed out that the acronym was TWATS, at which point, they had, on her suggestion, changed it to the WOWs: Weddings of Weddington.

'So now we're all finally here.' Fanny looked over at Alice, who stuck her tongue out. 'Let's raise a glass and welcome our newest WOW, Rose Pedal.' There were cheers from all but Madison. 'Now then, down to business.'

The three gins that Rose had partaken of – singles that she was sure had actually been triples – had gone straight through her and she found herself rushing off to the toilet within an hour.

When she came out of the bathroom, she found Madison barring her way. 'It won't last, you know,' she said. 'It's me he loves, not you. You're just like a sparkly new toy for him to play with. All the Blumes are like that, well, except for Tony maybe.'

Rose tried to step past her, but Madison wasn't budging.

'You mark my words, he'll be back in my arms before the end of the next fayre.' Madison's face looked ugly in the dim light of the landing.

'Is that a threat Madison?' Rose was taller, even in her flats, and she pulled her shoulders back to give herself even more height.

'Oh, sweet Rose.' She patted Rose's arm condescendingly. 'It's certainly not a threat.' She stepped out of the way to let Rose pass before heading into the bathroom herself. She stopped just before closing the door. 'It's a promise.'

CHAPTER TWENTY-FOUR

Rose made a decision when she woke up the morning after the WOWs meeting: although James had phoned every evening since his mum had been taken into hospital, he had seemed distant, so that afternoon she was going to surprise him. She borrowed her mum and dad's car and drove into the city, parking in the big multistorey, the one with the winding ramp that she loved driving back down. It had been a while since she'd visited, but she remembered exactly where Blume's Florist was located because it was opposite her favourite diner, Shakes!

She had no idea what time the florist closed so she headed into the diner, ordered a peanut butter milkshake and sat in a booth opposite the shop, ready to head out at a moment's notice.

Tony came out at about half past four, followed by Geoffrey and James about thirty minutes later. There was clearly tension between them; she could tell by the way James was standing and how angrily the pair of them were stacking buckets and taking in the stands from outside. At quarter past five, Geoffrey came out and stormed off, but there was no sign of James. At six o'clock, Rose decided enough was enough. She thanked the waitress and headed over to the florist.

She tried the door, not expecting it to be open, but it was, and a little bell rang overhead as she stepped in. It was delightfully cool inside; the air conditioning needed to be on, she supposed, to keep the flowers at their best for longer. But it wasn't the coolness of the shop that hit her the most; it was the heady aromas of all the different flowers merging together to give off the most delicious fragrance.

'We're closed, I'm afraid.' James's voice came first, followed by his footsteps coming down the stairs, and then he appeared through a door on the opposite side to her, from what Rose presumed was the flat above. 'Rose!' He crossed the shop towards her and hugged her so tightly she could hardly breathe. 'It's so good to see you. What are you doing here?' Each word in this sentence was punctuated by kisses.

'Have you been crying?' She noticed that his eyes were red and there were huge dark shadows under them. 'Is everything okay with your mum?'

'Mum's fine.' He rubbed his eyes. 'Touch of hay fever, and I'm still not caught up on my sleep from the weekend.' He walked over to the door and locked it. 'I thought Dad was locking up on his way out. Good job you came, or I might've left it open all night.'

'Why would you have left it open?' Rose was confused; wouldn't he have locked it on his way out?

'I'm pulling an all-nighter for the fayre at Coombe Castle tomorrow. Biggest one in the area, loads to do.' Rose had to admit he looked stressed, but she felt there was more to it than that.

'All on your own?' She looked around her. 'No one else helping? Just you?'

'Just me,' he confirmed. 'Dad and Uncle Tony have been upstairs all day while I've been in the shop. 'Been quite busy really for a Friday. A couple of bookings for weddings and, unfortunately, a funeral. Funerals are horrible to do. The family are so upset, the death is still quite fresh and raw and here they are picking out flowers to go on a coffin.' He shook his head sadly.

'I bet you do all you can to make it easier on them though.' Somehow she knew James would be extremely sensitive with his customers when it came to things like this.

'I do try.' He looked at his watch. 'Blimey, it's late. Have you had dinner yet?' She shook her head. 'Let me quickly tidy upstairs and then we'll go to the Italian on the corner – best spaghetti in the area.' He dashed upstairs and Rose found herself wandering around the shop floor.

It was stunningly decorated, and she had expected nothing less. Modern, light and airy, the decor suited the flowers and ornaments to perfection. There were a huge number of things on display, but it didn't seem cluttered in the slightest. You could tell that it had at one time been two shops, and she wondered whether it was Grandpa Blume or Geoffrey who had made the extension. She never seemed to think of Tony being involved in the business decisions; she doubted he ever got a word in with his dad and brother being so opinionated.

She walked over to the counter, where there was a book stand filled with what looked like photo albums. She took one out and placed it on the top of the stand, which had been specially designed on a slant to allow the viewer to flick through the pages with ease. Photo after photo of the most spectacular bridal bouquets passed before her eyes. She picked up another; this was filled with bridesmaids' bouquets and glorious baskets and posies for the younger girls. Another album was filled with table decorations; Rose marvelled at the exquisite use of colour to obtain depth. There were a few blank pages towards the end, and she went to close the book and put it away, but it was a little heavier than the others and it slipped out of her hand.

The book clattered to the ground, falling open on the very back page. Rose put her hand to her mouth.

'Are you ready then?' James looked at her face and then at the book on the floor. 'It's not what you think.'

'Tell me what I think,' she said, anger rising inside her. 'Tell me why there are photos of a bike that looks pretty much the same as mine in here?'

'It's a display I worked on.' He picked up the book and placed it back on the shelf. 'When I saw your bike that day at Weddington Hall I immediately saw a beautiful floral display in my head. So, I got a bike off eBay and decorated it with flowers. It's been very well received.'

'But it looks like my bike. It's even pink!' She wasn't

convinced. 'Hang on, did you say eBay? Have you bought more than one?'

'Why would I buy more than one?' he said. 'But I have been keeping my eye on the auctions in case something catches my eye for a future arrangement. And technically, it's not your bike.' He realized too late that this was completely the wrong thing to say.

'If by technically you mean it's not *physically* my bike, then you are quite correct, Mr Blume. But the very fact that you have bottles of Prosecco in there just proves that you have, in fact, stolen my idea!'

'But it's just a flower arrangement,' he said. 'I'm not going around selling flowers and serving Prosecco from the thing. Look!' He grabbed the book back off the shelf and pointed at the photos. 'It doesn't even have a chain on it – the bike is useless. It's purely for decoration and that's it.'

'I think I'll be heading home now.' She needed to leave; she needed time to think about what she had seen and heard, and to judge whether she was overreacting before she said or did something she regretted.

'No, Rose, don't leave like this.' He took her hand. 'Let's go and have dinner and we can talk some more.'

'If you would kindly unlock the door, please, so I can get out.' He sighed and pulled out a key, opening the door. 'I'm sure I will see you tomorrow at the fayre.' She walked past him, her head held high, fighting back the tears that were threatening to run down her cheeks.

*

'Well, I think it's a compliment really,' Megan said as they were driving to Coombe Castle the next morning. They were in the church minibus; Rose had finally asked her dad to put her on the insurance. They'd only brought the one bike this time – the other one wasn't quite ready yet – and besides they only needed the one to show off the business. They were running a little behind schedule thanks to Megan oversleeping, so Rose was driving a little faster than she normally would have.

'How is stealing my idea a compliment?' Rose said, swearing at a white car that had just pulled out in front of her.

'Road rage much?' Megan said. Rose shot her a look. 'He saw your bike, thought it was bloody fabulous and then went and made a decoration out of it. I really don't see why you're making such a big deal out of it.'

'Because it's a vintage bike.' Rose couldn't believe Megan didn't understand.

'You don't have the monopoly on vintage bikes, Rose.' Megan scrolled through her phone. 'Look.' She shoved it under Rose's nose.

'I'm driving, Megan, if you hadn't noticed.' Rose slammed on the brakes at a beeping horn. 'And the same to you with knobs on!'

'Rose, you need to calm down.' Megan looked out of the window. 'That guy had right of way.'

'Well, I'm bigger than he is,' Rose said. Then, realizing how ridiculous she was being, she laughed. 'Okay,' she said, 'I'm chilled.'

'There are hundreds of pictures on the internet of vintage bikes.' Megan scrolled and scrolled. 'Bikes with flowers, bikes with drinks, bikes with teddies, bikes with naked people.' Megan paused. 'Naked people? Oh, my eyes! I can never unsee that.'

'So, what you're saying is that I'm overreacting,' Rose said.

'That is exactly what I am saying, Miss Pedal.' Megan placed her feet up on the dashboard.

'When you put it that way . . .' Rose was beginning to see what an idiot she'd been. 'I suppose you're right.'

'Of course I am.' Megan smiled. 'And when we get to this bloody fayre, you'd best go right up to him and apologize.'

The rest of the drive passed in relative peace and calm, and they arrived at the castle with just a few minutes to spare. While Megan got the bike out, Rose headed inside to find the organizer.

'I am so sorry,' she said to the lady at the door, who'd introduced herself as June. 'We got stuck in a bit of traffic.'

'Well, it's almost time for the fayre to begin. It doesn't look very professional if you're still setting up while people are coming in, you know.' June spoke with what could only be described as a pretend posh accent; no one really spoke that way.

'Yes, I understand that, but it really doesn't take very long at all to set everything up.' She just wanted June to show her where to park the bike. She'd scanned the room already, and although the Blume's Florist stand was in the corner of the room, she hadn't spotted James. Only Tony and that bloody annoying Madison Michaels, who had managed to get the stall next to them – again.

'Name?' June held her clipboard out in front of her.

'Rose.'

'Of the business?' She could see June was getting annoyed with her.

'Pedals and Prosecco,' Rose said proudly. 'Vintage bike serving Prosecco to the guests.'

'Pedals and Prosecco ...' June shook her head. 'I don't recall seeing it before.'

'Could you just check?' Rose asked.

'I'm positive it's not there.' Rose wanted to yank the clipboard out of her hand and look at the list herself.

'Would you just mind checking again for me, please?' Rose smiled her sweetest smile.

'Oh, very well.' June scanned down the list with her pen. 'Pedals and Prosecco ... I'm very sorry but, like I said, you're not here.'

'What?' Rose pulled out her phone and showed June her booking confirmation email. 'I've paid fifty pounds to be here and I am most definitely on the list.'

'I did these lists myself last night and I know I would have remembered the name Pedals and Prosecco.' June called over a young man, who had been loitering a few feet away. 'Go and fetch Hugo, will you please, Mason.' Mason disappeared and returned in a flash with a middle-aged gentleman. 'Hugo, there seems to have been a mix-up with the bookings. Did you book a business called Pedals and Prosecco?'

'Oh yes, lovely sounding name.' He smiled at Rose.

'So where is it on the list?' June waved her clipboard in front of him.

'Oh, they phoned up last week to change the name. I much preferred Pedals and Prosecco, but each to their own.' He shrugged.

'Who phoned up and changed the name?' Rose couldn't believe what she was hearing. 'What have they changed the name to?'

'A man rang up last week and said could they change the name on the booking from Pedals and Prosecco to Cycles and Champagne.' Hugo looked suddenly scared.

'Well, you can bloody well change it back and show me to my space.' Rose tried to swallow her anger; it wasn't Hugo or June's fault.

'I can't, miss,' Hugo said, clearly flustered. 'Cycles and Champagne are already here.'

CHAPTER TWENTY-FIVE

'What do you mean they're already here?' Rose refrained from whacking the dumbstruck Hugo over the head with June's clipboard and instead tried to remain calm and professional. 'How can I already be here when I've only just arrived?'

'Clearly there has been some misunderstanding.' June waved away Hugo, who looked close to tears. 'If you want something doing you'd better do it yourself.' She pushed the pen through the hook on the clipboard and let it drop down by her side. 'Let's go outside and see what's going on, shall we?'

'The bike's all ready when you are.' Megan had arrived in the hall. 'Just let me know where to park it.'

'Just getting that sorted now,' Rose said, filling her in as they followed June out of the hall and into a long glass conservatory.

'There you go.' June pointed towards the end. 'The rest of your people are already here.'

Rose felt her knees go weak and almost buckle beneath her. There, stretched out along the bottom wall of the conservatory, were not one but four shiny gold and green bikes, complete with trailers and baskets. Bar the colours, they were almost exact replicas of Rose's. Except, instead of the words 'Pedals and Prosecco' on their signs, they had 'Cycles and Champagne'.

'What the fuck?' Megan's mouth had dropped open in shock and Rose was completely lost for words.

'I'll leave you to join them.' June went to walk away.

'That's not my business,' Rose said, finally finding her voice. 'I have one bike, my colours are pink and brown and I am called Pedals and Prosecco not Cycles and Champagne.' Her voice got louder with every word and she stormed over to the bikes to find out who they belonged to and why on earth they thought it was okay to steal her idea. 'Do you know who these belong to?' she asked a young couple who were exhibiting a photo booth and magic mirror. Rose had her suspicions. The green and gold was too much of a coincidence to be anyone else, but she had to be certain.

'He popped out a few minutes ago.' The woman looked a little scared. 'I'm not sure where.'

'Sorry.' Rose brought her voice down to a normal level. 'It's just ... I have a business just like this and I had the idea first so I really need to know who owns it.'

'Here he is now.' The young man nodded behind her and Rose turned around.

'I bloody knew it!' She wasn't shocked, not in the slightest.

As soon as she'd seen the gold and green, she'd known exactly who the bikes belonged to. 'Not content with your own business, you have to go and steal ideas from other people, do you? An idea, I might add, that you had absolutely no time for.'

'Cycles and Champagne is a far superior product to Pedals and Prosecco.' Geoffrey Blume stood before her with a smug smile, his hands folded across his chest. 'I have done nothing wrong.'

'Nothing wrong!' Rose was dying to wipe the pompous smile off his face. 'You've stolen my idea.' She stopped to think. 'And some of my clients, by the sound of it. Is this the first fayre you've been at?'

'We launched last week, not that it's any of your business.' He made to push past her.

'No, you bloody well don't.' She grabbed his arm, but Geoffrey reacted swiftly and flicked it back, his hand almost hitting her in the face. Rose gasped. 'How dare you!'

'Oh, calm down.' He was by the side of the bikes now. 'That was a bloody accident and you know it. I don't go around hitting women.'

'Did he hit you?' the woman from the photo booth stall asked. 'I saw him hit you. Do you want me to call the police?'

Rose was sorely tempted to let them, but she'd been brought up better than that. 'No, he didn't hit me,' she said, then turned back to Geoffrey. 'Does James know about this?' She hoped against hope that he didn't.

'Of course he does.' A sly smile spread across Geoffrey's

face. 'It was his idea – he told us all about your bike in the first place.'

Rose glared at Geoffrey, tears of hurt and anger welling up in her eyes. She couldn't look at him any longer and ran out of the conservatory, not stopping until she'd reached the relative sanctuary of the car park. Her bike stood next to the minibus in all its shiny pink glory and she flopped to the ground next to it with a sigh. All her hard work gone; how could she compete with the wealth and power of the Blumes? Had James been planning this all along? After all, thinking back, he had been overly interested in her business at that very first fayre. And then all those questions during their 'date' at The Pig.

'Rose?' No. It couldn't be him. 'Rose?' She looked up. 'What on earth is wrong?'

'Wrong?' she screamed, standing up to face James. He seemed startled by her outburst and stepped back. 'What on earth could be wrong?'

'I don't know.' He reached out a hand towards her, but it fell into thin air.

'Just a flower arrangement?' She placed her hands on her hips. 'How could I have been so bloody stupid?' She started pacing. 'I should have stuck with my gut. I knew you were no good from the moment I saw you. Running me off the road, soaking me from head to toe and then almost crushing my bike. Asking me on a date, spending time with me, saying you were falling for me. Getting me to trust you, when all you wanted to do was steal my idea.'

'Rose, it's not like that,' he begged. 'I didn't plan it this way.'

'Didn't plan on me getting feelings for you?' She laughed. 'Or didn't care? Mum was right, the apple doesn't fall far from the tree.'

'Don't you ever compare me to my father.' It was James's turn to get angry now. 'I am nothing like him and never will be.'

'I think you'd better go.' Megan had arrived and was standing behind him.

'I'm going.' He turned round quickly. 'You've got me so wrong,' he said over his shoulder as he stormed off down the cobbles.

'I don't think so!' Rose shouted after him before collapsing onto the ground again in a babbling, bubbling blob of snot and tears.

'Come on, you.' Megan helped her into the passenger side of the minibus, loaded the bike into the back and got into the driver's seat.

'You can't drive the bus.' Rose sniffed and hiccupped.

'Well, you bloody can't.' She pulled her seat belt on and Rose did the same. 'We're not staying here a minute longer and the alternative is to ring your parents.'

'No.' Rose shook her head. 'I mean, I know I'm going to have to tell them later, but just not now. I can't be doing with Mum's smothering and Dad's well-meaning kindness.'

'And that is exactly why I am driving us to my house.' She turned the key. 'Can't be any different to when I borrowed a van to move away for university.'

'Didn't you crash it into a wall?' Rose pulled her seat belt tighter.

'Details.' Megan waved her hand, pushed the gears into reverse and checked her blind spot. 'Hold on tight!'

'You need to fight fire with fire.' Megan and Rose were sitting under the parasol in Megan's garden. Rose was feeling a little better after a Megan special: hot chocolate laced with Baileys Irish Cream. 'I've messaged Josh and he's coming round for a powwow.'

'I can't believe I've been so stupid.' Rose put her head in her hands. 'I fell for his lies and his looks and his bloody kisses.'

'Speaking of kisses ...' Rose looked up expectantly. 'I'm not sure who it was, but when I went back into the main hall to look for you ...'

'Go on.'

'I saw James locked in the arms of some red-haired bint.' She said it quickly, as if this way it wouldn't hurt as much.

'Are you sure it was James?' Rose didn't know why she was asking; she knew it was him and she knew exactly who the redhead was ... Madison Michaels. Hadn't she promised Rose that he'd be back in her arms by the end of the next fayre?

'Tall, devilishly handsome and dressed like he's just stepped out of Vogue? Yes, it was James,' Megan said with certainty, placing a hand on her back as Rose started to cry again. 'Let it all out, my love, let it all out.'

'God, I've been a fool.' Rose wiped her nose on her sleeve.

'Bloody hell, Rose.' Megan handed her a tissue. 'Will you start carrying a packet of these?'

'James always had tissues.' Rose had never imagined that the sight of a packet of Kleenex would cause such a wealth of emotion. She sobbed once more. 'It might sound daft – I'd only known him a few weeks – but I was starting to really like him.'

'It doesn't sound daft at all,' Megan soothed. 'He sounds like a right bloody charmer, and fucking gorgeous to boot.'

'And I only ever seemed to see him in a suit.' Rose sniffed, the tears starting to subside. 'You know how much I love a man in a suit.'

'Nah,' Megan said. 'Give me a rough-and-ready, stubbled man in jeans and a T-shirt.' She lifted her eyebrows saucily.

'Like Chris Hemsworth?' Rose giggled at her friend's face.

'Oh yes please.' And they both laughed.

'Well, I wasn't expecting to walk into laughter.' Josh had arrived in the garden.

'Trust me,' Megan said. 'It's only just got here.'

'God, I'm such a failure at everything.' Rose threw her hands up in the air. 'I thought I'd finally got it right. Everything with Pedals was going so well, and it was all *me*, managing on my own. I didn't need anyone's help. But I guess I really can't do anything right.'

'Do you think . . .' Josh began, despite a warning look from Megan, who seemed to know exactly what he was about to say, 'that trying to do it alone was the biggest problem? No one can do anything alone.'

'I had to do it alone!' Rose straightened her shoulders. 'It was my chance to prove myself.'

'And you have,' Megan said. 'The fact that you've had your idea stolen is testament to that. But do you think all the WOW ladies go it alone?'

Rose thought back to all the times she'd seen a display of kindness at the wedding fayres, someone putting themselves out to help someone else. Even James had helped Alice with fresh flowers at the fashion show.

'I need help, don't I?'

Megan and Josh both nodded.

'Right, we need a plan and a strategy.' He sat down at the table, pulled his chair right up to it and took a laptop out of his backpack. 'Hannah and I are in agreement – we've postponed our flight for another week so we can both help you out.'

'I can't ask you to do that!' Rose said, shocked at such a kind gesture.

'It's done.' He started tapping away at the keys. 'This them?' He turned the screen towards them.

'Yes.' Rose held back tears as she saw 'the team' photo of Blume's Florist.

'And this?' He flicked onto another website; Cycles and Champagne glared out of the screen.

'They have a website already?' Rose grabbed the laptop, then shoved it back at Josh, but not before she briefly caught a glimpse of Geoffrey and a beaming James. 'I don't even want to see it.'

'Of course they have a website,' Josh said, taking the laptop back. 'Everyone has websites.'

'I tried to do it but all the talk about domain names and then paying for this level of service and that level of service, I just gave up.' She sniffed.

Josh shook his head. 'You act small fry, you'll stay small fry, and the big fish will gobble you up.'

'Talking of fish and fries,' Megan butted in. 'Anyone fancy a chippie lunch?'

Rose shook her head. 'I couldn't eat a thing.'

Megan ignored her. 'Shall I pop to Fishy Moores and get us three fish lunches dripping in salt and vinegar?'

'Sounds perfect.' Josh didn't even lift his head. 'Voila!' He showed them the screen. 'It needs photos and price lists, all those kinds of things, but here you go ... Pedals and Prosecco is ready to play with the big boys.'

Rose stared at the screen, and realized she was grinning. There was her business name in its beautiful pink and brown on display on the big wide web.

'If you want to get the bike out of the bus, Josh, you can take some photos now.' Megan threw him the bus keys. 'Rose and I have got aprons, so we'll be all ready to go.' She looked at Rose's face. 'Some of us may need a hairbrush and a touch-up on the make-up, but it's nothing that can't be fixed once we've had a spot of lunch. The rose arbour at the bottom of the garden would make a lovely backdrop and I'll get Mum to look out her Edinburgh Crystal champagne flutes from when they got married.'

'That would be brilliant.' Josh was still typing away as he spoke. Rose could see how excited he was; she knew that face well. She'd missed that face. If only he hadn't moved to America, maybe things would have been different. He looked at her with a reassuring smile. 'It's all going to be okay.' And it was then she realized that, as much as she had thought she'd loved Josh at the time, it wasn't anything compared to how she felt when she saw James's smile. And at the thought of his smile, she started to cry again.

'Will you turn that phone off?' Megan asked as Rose's phone bleeped for the tenth time that minute. The WhatsApp chat was going crazy with messages from all the ladies asking if she was okay. Lucy hadn't been at the fayre due to a wedding, but her mum, who Rose discovered was June, the event's organizer at the castle, had mentioned a mix-up with two businesses selling bubbly from bikes, and Lucy had known straightaway which the two businesses would be. The other ladies had been inside at their stalls and hadn't seen what happened, but they were all full of concern and messages of sympathy and offers of help. Rose fired off a quick thank you, said she would be okay and then muted the chat. She didn't want to read any more about it.

CHAPTER TWENTY-SIX

'I really can't thank you two enough.' It was early evening and Rose, Josh and Megan had spent the afternoon gorging themselves on delicious fish and chips, tubs of ice cream and pick 'n' mix sweets, all washed down with Coke. Josh had said no to the cocktails that Megan had wanted to make, insisting they needed clear heads and professional faces for the photographs. He didn't think blurry eyes and drunken smiles would make the best impression on the website.

'But it's called Pedals and Prosecco,' Megan had insisted, waving a bottle in front of his face.

'Yes.' He had taken the bottle from her hands and placed it in the front basket. 'But the Prosecco is for the guests, not the owners.' Megan had stuck her tongue out, but she'd accepted what he was saying and had turned out to be extremely helpful in the end. She had brought her old arts and crafts box down from her room and, using an ingenious concoction of pipe cleaners, cardboard hearts and superglue, had fashioned an almost perfect replica of the hearts spraying out from the neck of the bottle as they did on Rose's business cards.

'This is all well and good,' Megan stated, nicking the last fizzy cola bottle from the bag of sweets as she and Rose sat watching Josh furiously typing and uploading, 'but how exactly does it help Rose?'

'She has a website now,' Josh answered simply. 'An online presence means more traffic to the business and more traffic to the business means more bookings.'

'But how?' Megan's voice was almost a whine. 'How does having a website suddenly increase Rose's sales? It's not like everyone with the internet gets a message saying "new business, click here", is it?'

'A launch party will help,' he said distractedly, still flicking through the photos on his phone as he spoke.

'A what?' Rose looked over at him. 'Launch party?'

'Yep.' He unplugged the phone from the laptop. 'Saturday, we're having a launch party.'

'I don't understand. What launch party? How can we be having a launch party in a week's time that I know nothing about?'

'Hannah's sorting it.' He pressed the 'enter' button on his laptop with a flourish. 'And it's all done.' He turned the screen to face them again and there was Rose and her bike smiling up at them.

'Pedals and Prosecco,' she read. 'For the personal touch, contact Rose Pedal.'

'I thought we'd use your "smallness" as a selling point.' He made quotation marks with his fingers at the word smallness. 'Not everyone wants big businesses that are over commercialized. People like to know they are your priority. How are the Blumes going to do that with a florist to run and now the bikes as well? If you ask me, they won't last long.'

'They can afford to employ people,' Megan pointed out, then shrugged her shoulders at the look Josh shot her. 'It's true, though. They have money, and they've been running a hugely successful business for decades, while Rose is just starting out.'

'Doesn't mean she can't hold her own.' Josh smiled. 'As soon as I saw it on Facebook, I thought what a fabulous idea it was, and the fact that it's been effectively stolen shows that it's a good idea.'

Their conversation was interrupted by the sudden sound of Faith Hill singing 'This Kiss'.

'What is that?' Megan looked at Josh, who was trying to answer his phone as quickly as possible.

'Shush!' he said before getting up and heading to the bottom of the garden, returning a few minutes later.

'Please tell me that was Hannah,' Megan teased as Josh sat back down.

'Of course it was Hannah,' he said. 'We met at a line dancing club and that was our first dance.'

'Sweet,' Megan said sarcastically.

'Well, I think it's lovely,' Rose said. 'I'm glad you've found someone as sweet and special as Hannah.'

Megan shoved her fingers in her mouth and mimed being sick.

233

'Thank you, Rose,' Josh said, glaring at Megan. 'I'm glad some of my friends are not cynical, dried-up old prunes.'

'Dried-up old prune?' Megan blustered. 'I'm only twenty-three and I've no intention of settling down any time soon.'

'You have to have a boyfriend to be able to settle down anyway,' Josh teased, pulling a face, and Megan pulled one back.

'When you two have finished acting like five-year-olds.' Rose had always been a little jealous of the easy friendship between Megan and Josh. At one point, when they were around thirteen, she'd even thought they fancied each other, but both of them had said they were more like brother and sister, which was why they fought and teased each other so much.

'So, the launch party!' Josh said, clapping his hands. 'On Weddington village green, Saturday at two. It will be fabulous.'

'I'm so confused ... What launch party and how has Hannah managed to organize it in one afternoon while we've been out here eating fish and chips?'

'It's what she does,' Josh said with obvious pride. 'She's an events coordinator back home. She helps plan weddings, corporate stuff, all sorts.'

'But what do you mean by a launch party?' Rose asked. 'I haven't got money to pay for anything.' The thought of the almost-empty savings account, which was probably never going to be refilled now, made Rose sick to her stomach.

'Who said anything about money?' Josh waved his hands. 'Hannah's talked Weddington council into letting us have the green for free because it will bring people into the village. You've got your bike already.' Rose held up two fingers. 'Two bikes?' She nodded. 'Then all we have to do is get some bottles of fizz, Pimms maybe, and some strawberries and cream, make it a proper English affair. I'm sure your mum would make some cakes.'

'Yep, I'm sure she would . . .' Rose knew there wouldn't be a shortage of scones and shortbread if she could get her mum on the case. 'And maybe I could ask the WOWs too – they might be able to help?'

'That's settled then.' Josh snapped his laptop shut. 'Leave everything to me and Hannah.' He got up and kissed them both on the cheek. 'I'll ring you if we need anything, but if not, pick us up from mine on Saturday around ten with the bikes ready to go.'

'Thank you so much, Josh, and please say thank you to Hannah for me. I can't believe you've planned all this . . .' Rose felt so overwhelmed, she started to cry.

'It will all work out in the end,' he said, hugging her, and Megan joined in too.

> **Rose**: Hi ladies, just wanted to say thank you
> for all your kind messages and offers of help.
> Well, it seems I really could do with your help.
> My friend is organizing a launch party for me
> next Saturday on Weddington village green
> and it would be great if you could come and
> support me.

Fanny: Support you? We'll do more than
bloody support you, right, girls?
Natalie: Too right, Fanny. What's their name
and number, love?

Despite forecasts of heavy showers, Saturday dawned bright
and clear. Rose stepped out of bed with a mixture of excitement and trepidation. *What if no one comes? What if it's a
complete disaster?*

She walked into the kitchen to find her mum and dad
and grandparents busily icing cupcakes and sprinkling
sugar on shortbread rounds. There was already a moun-
tain of Tupperware boxes filled with scones, fruit cakes
and strawberry tarts on the breakfast bar. Her mum hadn't
stopped baking since the moment Rose had told them about
the launch.

'What a fabulous idea,' she'd said, immediately pulling
out her recipe book. 'Josh is just brilliant, isn't he?' Janet had
almost glossed over the part about James. 'Never mind, dear,
plenty more fish in the sea,' was all she'd said. Rose's dad,
however, was a different matter.

'I didn't think he was like that, you know,' he'd said as
they worked on getting the second bike ready. 'He didn't give
me that impression at all, and I'm usually a very good judge
of character.' He'd then held up the saddle he'd been working
on. 'Good as new,' he'd said with a smile of satisfaction before
reattaching it to the frame. 'I'm so glad you decided not to
paint this one pink. It would have been sacrilege.'

'I think your idea of keeping its original colour with pink signage is wonderful,' she'd said – although she'd debated the issue in her head for a long time before agreeing. 'It gives contrast to the other one and choice to the hirer. Not everyone likes pink.' Rose had never understood that; she loved pink.

'Are you sure it was definitely James?' Always one to want to see the good in people was her dad.

'He admitted in the shop that it was his design and idea,' Rose had said. 'I should imagine the driving force was his dad, but he could have stood up for me and told them no.' Rose had gone over and over the scenes in her head and always came to the same conclusion; there was no way James had not been a part of Cycles and Champagne. 'And then there's Megan seeing him kiss that bloody Madison.' She'd looked at her dad, suddenly contrite. 'Sorry, Dad.'

'I'll forgive you this time,' he'd said with a smile. 'Is she sure it was James? Couldn't it have been Peter?'

'No.' Rose shook her head; oh how she'd wished it was Peter. 'James told me that their grandpa had insisted that Peter was not to have anything to do with the business after the fiasco at Haggerston Hall; it cost the Blumes thousands. And, trust me, none of them go against Blume Senior. Plus, I know Madison hates Peter, and last time I saw her she promised me she'd get James back. So, no, Dad, unfortunately I am one hundred percent certain that it was James.'

'Morning, Rose,' her parents and grandparents said in unison.

'Grab that tub of pink iced flowers, will you, and start placing them on these cakes your nan has just iced.' Her mum loved to have a mission.

'Thank you so much for this.' Rose could feel her eyes welling with tears, but she'd done too much crying this past week, and she wiped them away quickly and did as she was asked.

'It's going to be a wonderful afternoon,' her nan said. 'Everyone in the area is buzzing about it. I've told my bridge club, knitting club and bingo club and your grandad has told everyone at the allotments.'

'Got a little something for you here, too.' Her grandad handed her a cheque for two hundred pounds. 'Your nan had a little win at bingo, so we thought you could add this to your house fund.'

'Thank you,' Rose said with more enthusiasm than she felt and a false smile on her lips. 'That's so kind of you. You really shouldn't have.' How could she ever tell them the money was almost gone? *Please let this launch party be a success.*

'We passed the village green on the way here – it looks amazing.' Her grandad was packing the shortbread rounds into another plastic container as he spoke.

'That's brilliant,' Rose said, smiling fondly. Trust her grandad to try and big up the excitement of a few stalls on the village green.

'What time are you leaving?' her dad asked; he had pink icing on the end of his nose, clearly having stolen a cupcake.

'Megan is getting here just before ten, and then we've got to pick up Josh and Hannah.'

He nodded. 'Well, I'll drive you all over and take some of these boxes when we go.' He dolloped more icing into the cloth icing bag. 'Then I'll come back and fetch you three,' he said to Janet and Rose's grandparents, 'and the rest of the things.' He squeezed the icing down the bag a little too hard and the nozzle flew off the end, pink icing spurting all over the table.

'John!' her mum scolded. 'Really?' He grinned like a naughty child and started scooping the icing up. 'I'll have to make more now.' She turned to her mixing bowl. 'Honestly.'

'Morning, Pedals and non-Pedals,' Megan announced from the kitchen doorway. 'Front door was open.' She surveyed the organized chaos. 'Wow, cupcake central in here.' She headed over to the sink and washed her hands. 'Thought I'd get here early and help out.' She rolled up her sleeves. 'Lead me to the cupcakes, Mrs P.'

Two hours later, Rose, Megan and Josh were squashed in the back of the minibus with the two bikes, trailers, mountains of boxes filled with cakes, bottles of Prosecco and Pimm's, which Josh was leaning against in case they fell, and rolls of plastic champagne flutes. Rose had wanted to use glass, but Josh had insisted that it wasn't practical, or indeed safe since the village green was used for recreational purposes; the last thing they wanted was a child or dog to cut themselves on a piece of smashed glass.

Rose had been absolutely amazed by the generosity of the WOWs and various businesses from Weddington and

Tointon. Bottles of Prosecco and Pimm's had been arriving almost hourly at the vicarage over the past week, and a case had even been sent from Mr Booth, her old employer.

They'd all agreed that Hannah should sit up front so she could see the village and its sights as they passed. In reality, she was so little that Rose had been worried she'd end up in A&E or something after getting squashed on the way; there really wasn't very much room in the back of the bus at all.

'Here we are then,' her dad announced, pulling on the handbrake and turning off the engine.

Rose stretched her legs and clambered out the back door after Josh and Megan.

'I'm so glad that's over,' she said, reaching in and grabbing the nearest boxes to her. 'Where are we setting this lot up, Josh?'

Shifting the box's weight in her arms, Rose turned around and her mouth fell open. If Megan hadn't caught the boxes as they slipped out of her arms, they'd have been very short on fruit cake.

'You have got to be kidding me!'

CHAPTER TWENTY-SEVEN

'How have you done all this in a week?' Rose stared, absolutely flabbergasted at the sight before her. She hadn't known what to expect – maybe some bunting and a tent – but this went far beyond any of her imaginings.

A white marquee was pitched to one side of the green, tastefully decorated with pink ribbons to match the Pedals and Prosecco colours. People were coming in and out, faces she recognized from the fayres, and she waved enthusiastically as she saw Fanny heading inside. On the other side of the green were fairground stalls, games like hook-a-duck and the coconut shy. Then, to Rose's great pleasure, was a big wheel; granted, it wasn't London Eye big, but it reached a good twenty feet into the air.

'Do you like it?' Hannah asked, joining them at the back of the bus.

'Like it?' she cried. 'Hannah, it's absolutely unbelievable.' She hugged her tightly. 'Thank you so much for everything you've done.'

'That's not even the half of it,' Josh said. 'Wait till you see inside the tent.'

'Hey up, Josh,' a male voice called, and they all turned. 'Did you want popcorn, candyfloss, chocolate fountain or all three?'

'Graham?' Megan's mouth dropped open at the sight of her old flame. 'Graham Clarke?'

'Megan Broad, as I live and breathe.' He clamped his arms round her and lifted her off the ground; he was much taller and broader than Rose remembered.

'What on earth are you doing here?' Megan asked, slightly flustered and red-faced. Rose hid a knowing smile.

'These are all Graham's.' Josh threw his hands around. 'He owns Clarke's Amusements.'

'When Josh told me what he was doing for Rose's business, I offered my services.' He grinned. 'It's nice to come back home once in a while.'

'That's so kind of you.' Rose hugged him; Megan seemed to have lost the ability to speak. 'Where are you living now then?'

'We haven't got time for reunions, I'm afraid, Rose,' Josh said abruptly. 'We can all catch up later on this evening.' He clapped his hands and everyone stood to attention. 'Popcorn and candyfloss, I think, Gray.' Graham saluted and marched off, Megan watching him as he went. 'Megan, Rose – you start unloading the boxes. Hannah will show you where to put them. And Mr Pedal, sir, would you mind helping me with the bikes? I've got the perfect spot set up that will show them off to perfection.'

'No problem at all, Josh,' Rose's dad said with a smile, hopping into the back of the bus and starting to hand the boxes down.

'Please tell me there aren't any more cakes left at home, Dad,' Rose said, after taking what must have been her twentieth box into the tent.

'You know what your mum's like,' he said, huffing and puffing a little as he pulled at a sack trolley loaded with bottles of Pimm's. 'And it's all raising money for local charities.' It had been Hannah's idea to, rather than give all the cakes and drinks away for free, charge a small amount and donate the profits to charity. She'd managed to get a fair few bottles donated this way too, in return for a mention.

Rose placed the last box down, and finally managed to have a proper look around. There was Fanny setting up her favours towards the back. Buttercup Bridals had a small rack of dresses and a couple of mannequins on the right-hand side as you walked in, and Natalie and her cakes were near to the front. Rose's heart fell to her stomach when she saw a flower stall, but it turned out to be Weddington's own florist, Val.

'Everyone here is small and local,' Hannah said while setting up tiered cake trays on a nearby stall. 'No room for the big boys today.' She started to line up the glasses and cups for drinks. 'All the stallholders have paid a small fee or donated something to the day. Fanny made all of the bunting and ribbons, and Natalie got the ingredients for your mom's cakes from the wholesalers.' She giggled to herself. 'Josh has explained to me why Fanny is a funny name over here.'

'I'm astounded by everyone's generosity.' Rose looked around, responding to waves and smiles from the friends and stallholders in the marquee.

'It's the community spirit,' her dad said. 'We always come together for one of our own.'

'But we're from Tointon, not Weddington,' Rose said.

'That only makes a difference during cricket matches. All other times, we live together in perfect peace and harmony.'

'Reverend Pedal?' Rose turned to see Reverend Timms approaching and she made a quick getaway, knowing that the two of them would talk for hours once they got going.

She headed over to Alice's stall. On one of her mannequins was the very dress Rose had worn at the fashion show. 'You got it clean!' Rose exclaimed. 'It looks as good as new.'

'It took me a while,' Alice said. 'Managed to get James's suit up to scratch too.' At this, she pulled another mannequin out of her oversized trunk. It was wearing the same suit James had worn at the fashion show, and Rose had to bite back tears when Alice placed it next to the mannequin wearing her own dress. 'Where is the handsome devil, anyway? Thought he'd be here to support you.'

Rose swallowed. 'Would you excuse me a moment?' Suddenly overwhelmed, she made her excuses and rushed out of the tent in the most dignified manner she could muster.

She ran along the side of the marquee and came to a halt at the end, slumping down in a heap at the corner, hoping she was out of sight. She knew it had only been a week, that the feelings she had for James were going to take longer than a few days to heal, but she hadn't expected to feel quite so emotional at the sight of a suit he'd once worn.

But it's not just a suit! she said to herself; it was memories of kisses in the rain and falling asleep in his arms, not wanting to move from his side. It was daft, really, to have fallen so hard and so fast for him, especially after such a dreadful start, but she had really thought that she meant something to him, that maybe he was feeling the same way for her.

When she sat and thought about it, she didn't know which part hurt most: the fact that he'd stolen her business idea, or that he'd lied to her about Madison Michaels.

'Here you are.' It was Josh. 'Everyone's looking for you.' He sat down on the grass and put an arm around her, pulling her in for a cuddle. 'I know it hurts, Rose.' He placed his chin on top of her head as she nestled into his chest, tears falling down her cheeks and wetting his shirt. 'It's a bloody evil thing to do to someone, and I don't know how that family live with themselves.' He tutted. 'Megan has told me all about how authoritarian his father and grandfather are – perhaps he just doesn't know how to be anyone else.'

'But he was never like them,' Rose mumbled against his shirt. 'Only at the beginning, and I just thought that was a front he put up because we got off to such a shaky start.'

'I wouldn't have given him the time of day if he'd tried to run me off the road and then squash my bike.' Megan had clearly filled Josh in on the rest of the story. 'And then to set up his stall right outside next to yours?' He whistled through his teeth. 'The nerve of the man.'

'He's a bloody good actor, I'll give him that.' Rose sniffed, her tears starting to subside. 'Because I fell for his lies hook, line and bloody sinker.'

'Haven't we all fallen for a pretty face before?' She looked up into his face and could see a tinge of sadness behind his eyes.

'You're a good friend, Josh.' She found herself wanting to reach up and kiss him, even got as far as putting her hand up to touch his face, but Josh drawing away pulled her back to her senses. 'God, I'm sorry.' She shook her head. 'I don't know what's wrong with me.'

'It's okay, you're missing James,' he said simply. 'You've gone from having this attentive man around, making you feel good, taking you out on dates to being utterly flat on the floor with no hope of ever finding love again.' She slapped him on the chest. 'And me being so irresistible.' He earned another slap. 'Ow! That one hurt.'

'Good.'

'No, in all seriousness,' he went on. 'It just shows how strong your feelings were for him, and how much he meant to you.'

'Fat lot of good that's done me.' She blew her nose into his sleeve.

'Dear God, woman.' He pushed her away and wiped his sleeve on hers. 'When will you learn to carry bloody tissues around?'

'I don't need to.' She looked over at him. 'There's usually someone around who has one.'

'Here you go.' He pulled a small packet out of his pocket and handed her a clean tissue.

'You see.' Rose smiled at him before crying again. 'James always carried tissues.' Here she was again, crying over the sight of a tissue.

'Come here, you daft mare.' Josh put an arm around her and she rested her head on his shoulder.

'Well, this is all very touching.' They both stopped what they were doing immediately and looked up. The sun was directly behind the new arrival and Rose couldn't make out their face. 'Didn't take you long, did it?' She might not have been able to see the face, but the voice she knew, and it filled her with dread.

CHAPTER TWENTY-EIGHT

'It isn't what you think,' Rose started to explain. Then, 'No, actually, it doesn't matter what you bloody think. It's got fuck all to do with you.' Rose even surprised herself with the force with which she spoke. 'You turn up here, on *my* day to do what exactly? See what other ideas you can steal? See what other businesses look like they need a Blume makeover?' She stood up. 'Well, matey Jim, you can just crawl back into the hole you came from.'

'Well, aren't we little Miss Gobby all of a sudden.'

'You heard her mate.' Josh had stood up now as well. 'Do one!' He grabbed Rose's hand. 'Come on, you. We've got a launch party to go to.'

'My dad was right about you,' he called after them. 'You were never going to be good enough to be a Blume.'

Josh had to stop her from turning around and lamping him one.

'He's not worth it, Rose.' He kept her looking forward, but by the time she reached the tent she was shaking with anger. Luckily, her dad had left to go and fetch her mum and grandparents, but Hannah and Megan were there looking frantic.

'Thank goodness.' Megan hugged her then stepped back to look at her properly. 'Alice said you went all weird on her and ran out of the tent. What on earth has happened?'

'I believe I've just had the pleasure of meeting the not-so-charming James Blume,' Josh said.

'He's here?' Megan rolled up her sleeves. 'Where is the bastard? Wait till I get my hands on him.' She made to step outside, but Rose pulled her back.

'It wasn't James.' She spoke through deep breaths as she tried to calm herself down. 'It was Peter.'

'Who the fuck is Peter?' Megan looked at her as if she was speaking French.

'That was definitely James,' Josh said. 'I saw his photo on your Facebook page.'

'Trust me, it was Peter. James's twin brother.'

'He has a twin?' Megan's stared at Rose. 'And you didn't think to tell your best friend that?'

'I did tell you.' Rose could distinctly remember telling Megan about the incident with the window at Haggerston Hall. 'He got into a fight and went through the sash window.'

'You just said it was his brother – you didn't say it was his twin.' Megan was clearly trying to digest this new information. 'Crucial piece of evidence that is.'

'What do you mean?'

'What if it was this Peter I saw kissing that Madison woman?'

Rose shook her head. 'James was there,' she said. 'You saw him.'

'But now I think about it . . .' Megan hesitated. 'He was coming from the car park and I'd just come from the hall.'

'No!' Rose was adamant. 'I saw how she was with him at that second fayre: she was all over him, and he didn't seem to be doing much resisting.'

'But he told you afterwards what happened.'

Rose's head was a whirl. 'Are we sticking up for him now?' She put her hands on her hips. 'Is he bloody God's gift again because he possibly didn't kiss Madison fucking Michaels? Are we forgetting that he stole my business idea, that he's the reason we're here with enough bloody cakes to feed the five thousand?'

'Rose Amelia Pedal!' She cringed at the sound of her mum's voice, and turned around to find her parents and grandparents standing behind her, boxes of even more cakes in their arms and horrified looks on their faces – well, on all but her grandad's. He was just trying his very best not to laugh, and gave Rose a wink.

'I'm really sorry, Mum.' Rose took the boxes from her. 'I've just seen Peter, that's all, and it shook me up a bit.'

'Well, I understand, but there's still no excuse for that kind of language, nor for sounding ungrateful. Everyone has gone to a lot of trouble to help you out.' She kissed her cheek and went to stand behind the table next to Hannah, who had been incredibly quiet. Rose wondered if she was shocked by Rose's use of language. 'Mind you, Tabby has told me about

that boy – rotten to the core he is. You're much better off
out of that family.' Turning away from Rose, she said, 'You
must be Hannah. Rose and Josh used to date, did you know?'

Rose groaned and shot Hannah an apologetic look. 'Yes,
Mum. Hannah knows and it was years ago. Show my mum
your engagement ring.'

Hannah held out her hand. 'Well, isn't that just beautiful,'
Janet gushed. Engagements were a serious commitment to
Rose's mum; in her eyes, it was almost as serious as actually
being married. And even though Rose had already told her
mum they were engaged, actually seeing the ring in person
made it real. Thankfully, from then on, there were no further
mentions of Rose and Josh.

'Blimey,' Josh said as the village clock chimed two. 'It's
time to open. Positions everyone.' A band started to play
outside, and a town crier could be heard ringing his bell and
announcing that they were open.

The party went on long into the evening and it seemed
like the whole of Weddington, Tointon and the other sur-
rounding villages had come out to enjoy themselves on what
turned out to be a beautifully warm June day. Amazingly,
the cakes and biscuits had sold out within a few hours,
everyone rushing to get their hands on Mrs Pedal's famous
home baking, which usually only went on sale at St Michael's
summer and winter fetes.

Natalie had raffled off a two-tiered lemon sponge creation, raising three hundred pounds. Fanny's white elephant

stall with knitted and crocheted animals proved extremely popular, and at the end of the day she handed Rose an over-flowing jar of pound coins. The children of the villages had run around with their prizes from the fairground stalls, their fingers sticky from candyfloss and toffee apples.

But the most successful draw of the day had been the bikes. People had lined up to be served ice-cold Prosecco by Rose and Megan. Josh and Hannah had even helped out at one point when the queue got too long. The pop and elderflower cordial had proved surprisingly popular, and Rose made a mental note to add a variety of different drinks to her price list for the future. Her diary was now overflowing with parties and weddings, and she couldn't stop smiling.

Josh had even made a speech, dragging a red-faced Rose beside him.

'Now, I'm sure many of you will know me and Rose here,' he'd begun. 'Tointon through and through.' There had been good-natured booing at this. 'We just wanted to say the biggest thank you to all of you for coming out and supporting Rose with her new business, Pedals and Prosecco.' Cheers and clapping followed. 'We've raised a couple of thousand pounds, which we're donating to some local charities and clubs, including the children's play area, which is badly in need of new swings and slides.' More clapping. 'And all that is left for me to say is, please go and enjoy yourselves some more.'

The green had come to life as dusk started to fall and Graham had switched on the fairground lights. They gleamed and shone, filling the sky with a warm glow.

'We're all going on the big wheel,' her dad said after the bikes and boxes were stowed safely away in the minibus. 'It's been a few years since I've been on one and your nan and grandad have already been on three times. Did you see your grandad won a giant teddy on the hook-a-duck?'

Rose was enjoying seeing her parents and grandparents acting like kids again. It wasn't very often that they got the chance to let their hair down and just enjoy themselves. Her dad especially was always on duty, come day or night. Rain or shine, he could be called on to attend one of his parishioners and, without fail, he went.

They reached the wheel just as a ride was starting. Her parents and grandparents went on as pairs, Hannah and Josh went together and that left Megan and Rose.

'Come on, you.' Rose went to link arms with Megan, but just as she did, Graham appeared behind her and invited her into the waiting carriage. Rose was about to protest, but when she saw the look of happiness on Megan's face, she didn't have the heart. She stepped into the next carriage alone.

She leaned back into the seat and closed her eyes, breathing in the smell of popcorn and burgers as she thought over the day's events. The wheel moved slowly at first as each carriage filled, and then it started to spin a little faster. Rose opened her eyes just as she reached the top, looking out over the village. She could see church spires and the turrets of Coombe Castle. She hadn't realized how high up she actually was.

She looked down and saw a man standing by the clock

in the middle of the green. Was it James? Had he come to apologize?

She was sure it was him; she would have recognized him anywhere, even if he was dressed in blue jeans and a black shirt rather than his usual green suit. His hands were in his pockets and he was leaning on the lamp post that lit the clock at night. Should she wave? Should she smile? In the end, she did nothing but watch him. He wasn't looking at her, just staring into space. She fidgeted in her seat, eager for the ride to be over, but as she neared the ground, the ride continued spinning and she lost sight of him as the wheel took her round again.

This time when she got to the top he was no longer there. She twisted in the seat, looking for him. Desperate to find him, to see what he had to say for himself. But there was no sign, and she was beginning to think she'd imagined the whole thing. Then, as she reached the top of the wheel for the third time, she saw a black Audi with the registration BL19 UME spinning off into the distance.

The highs of Saturday faded quickly for Rose, and even her bulging diary full of bookings did little to lift her spirits. She moped around on Sunday, snapped at her parents on Monday and hid in her room on Tuesday, watching sad romance films and eating ice cream. It was only when Josh came by on the Wednesday morning to say goodbye that she actually forced herself to be civil.

'You have got to stop this,' Josh told her. They were sitting at the dining room table, the best place in the house for not being overheard as it was the only room in the house that had no other room attached to it and sat in relative privacy under the stairs.

'I know I do.' She hung her head. 'I'm just finding it so hard.'

'Once you've done a couple of weddings, you'll be fine.' Her diary was on the table and he pulled it towards him. 'You've got so many booked now, even into next year.' He flicked through the pages. 'Jesus, Rose!' He shoved the book under her nose. 'Have you forgotten something?' He tapped today's date.

'Oh, bloody hell!' Her first event was tonight and she'd completely forgotten. It was Ruth Whittaker's garden party, fifty guests and she hadn't done a thing for it. 'I need to shower, shop, clean the bike.' She picked up her phone, flicking to her emails. 'Thank God! She doesn't need me to supply the glasses.' She ran out of the door, coming back moments later to kiss Josh on the cheek. 'Thank you so much for everything. Have a safe flight back and say thank you and goodbye to Hannah for me.' She blew him another kiss as she left the kitchen again, taking the stairs two at a time.

How could she have been so stupid? Her first proper event and she'd nearly forgotten all about it because she'd been moping about after James. He clearly wasn't thinking about her, hadn't even tried to contact her since their meeting in the car park at Coombe Castle. Yet something niggled at her, something that made her think everything wasn't quite as it seemed. Why would James have turned up to the launch party? And why had Peter come for that matter? But she had little time to worry about that now, and vowed to put James Blume and his blasted family out of her mind for good – well for the foreseeable future at least.

She messaged Megan to tell her what a twat she'd been in forgetting her first booking, and then got in the shower. She washed her hair as quickly as she could, wrapping it in a towel before throwing on jeans and a top and shouting to her parents that she was popping out.

Borrowing her parents' car, she drove to the cash and carry on the outskirts of Weddington, grabbed a trolley and dashed straight to the alcohol aisle, ignoring the funny looks she was getting from the other customers. Luckily, there was plenty of Prosecco in stock, and she grabbed the required number of cases, dragged them onto the trolley and headed to the till. Suddenly remembering that Ruth had asked for a few bottles of non-alcoholic wine as well, she swiftly turned the trolley and knocked a gentleman right off his feet.

'I am so sorry,' she exclaimed. She went to help him to his feet, and found herself staring right into the face of Tony Blume.

CHAPTER TWENTY-NINE

'I'm not my brother, you know.' Tony chuckled, pulling himself up on his trolley.

'Trust me, if you were, I'd have done it deliberately.' She brushed his jacket where he'd managed to collect some dust and dirt from the floor. 'Sorry.'

'It's me that should be saying sorry,' Tony said. He sounded so genuine, but she wasn't going to let herself be fooled by a Blume again.

'Business is business,' she said nonchalantly. It didn't matter how nice Tony was or had been; he was still a Blume and the Blumes were now the competition and the enemy.

'I didn't know.' He grabbed her arm as she went to walk on down the aisle.

'How could you not have known? They're your family; you work with them; you were even there at the fayre with a fleet of bikes. How can you not have known?

'They did it in secret,' he said, moving out of the way of another shopper. 'Even my father didn't know.'

'What?' Rose's mind was spinning.

'I mean, obviously I'd seen your bike and James's floral design,' he admitted. 'But the rest was done in secret.' He moved again as a couple pushing two trollies headed their way. 'Have you got time for a coffee?'

She shook her head, suddenly wishing that she did. 'I haven't, I'm afraid. I've got my first event tonight.'

'Another night this week?' he asked, then he shook his head. 'No, that's no good.' He reached into his pocket and pulled out a business card. 'Text me your number and we'll arrange to meet up.' She took the card and placed it in her jeans. 'Good luck for tonight.' He started to walk down the aisle, but turned back. 'By the way, you've got a towel on your head.' Then he rounded the corner and was out of sight.

Rose instantly reached up to her hair where, sure enough, her favourite Bratz towel, which she'd had since she was eight, was wrapped around her head. No wonder people had been giving her funny looks. She pulled the towel off and started to finger-comb her hair as best she could. But it was almost dry now, and as it had been wrapped around her head for the best part of an hour, it was a lost cause so she resigned herself to more funny stares thanks to her 'dragged through a hedge backwards' look.

Picking up the non-alcoholic wine and elderflower cordial she'd almost forgotten, she paid for her purchases, loaded up the car then blasted out the latest Charlie Puth CD, singing along badly to distract her brain from going into overdrive. In fact, for the rest of that day, any time even the tiniest thought of James and his family popped into her head, she shoved it quickly away and concentrated on the task in hand, focusing only on getting everything ready for the event.

She had arranged to be at Ruth's house at bang on five o'clock. With guests arriving from six, this gave her ample time to set everything up. Rose had spent an hour straightening her hair, thirty minutes cleaning the bike and two hours talking to Megan, who had got out of work early on the pretence that she was feeling sick and turned up on Rose's doorstep.

'Tell me everything,' she demanded as they loaded the minibus with the boxes of bottles and wedged the bike and trailer in between the seats, before laying the parasol in the back.

'Like I said in my text,' Rose explained, 'there isn't really anything to tell, except it looks like James and his dad did it all on their own. Even the grandad didn't know.'

'Sneaky little bastards.' Megan shook her head. 'So, do you think the whole "my dad doesn't love me routine" was an act as well?'

'Possibly.' Rose sat down on one of the seats in the minibus. 'Or maybe it was his way of getting into daddy's good books.'

'I'd never thought of that.' Megan inclined her head towards Rose in a nod of approval. 'You were always saying he could never do anything right and that he got the blame for things that weren't even his fault.'

'I've experienced it first-hand.' Rose recalled the car ride home after Peter had been sent to the hospital.

'It seems you've hit the nail right on the head then.' She patted Rose on the arm. 'Well done, Detective Pedal.' She smiled. 'So, are you still going to meet up with the uncle?'

'Yeah, I think so.' Rose checked the card was still in her pocket. 'He was always so nice, nothing like his brother, and perhaps having it confirmed properly will help me come to terms with everything and move on.'

'Speaking of moving on ...' Megan began hesitantly. 'I didn't want to tell you before but Graham has asked me out on a date this Friday.'

'Really?' Rose was ecstatic. 'I'm so pleased for you.' She got up and hugged her friend. 'Just promise me one thing.'

'What?' Megan asked.

'You won't break his nose this time when he grabs your boobs.' Megan went to swipe at Rose but she was too quick and had leapt out of the minibus and onto the drive, Megan chasing after her. They fell into a heap of giggles under the willow tree in the front garden.

Megan grabbed Rose's hand. 'I don't know what I'd do without you, Miss Pedal.'

'The feeling is mutual, Miss Broad.'

The party was a huge success and Rose thoroughly enjoyed every minute of it. She'd judged the amount of drink needed almost to perfection, running out of non-alcoholic wine a little too early, but having only three bottles of Prosecco left at the end of the night, which she left with the host.

Everyone had loved the bike, even taking selfies and posting them on Instagram using the hashtag, #PedalsandProsecco. This gave Rose an idea: maybe she could host a monthly giveaway for anyone who posted a picture of themselves with the bike and used the hashtag. She could draw a random name to win a bottle of Prosecco if local, or a gift voucher if not.

Her parents agreed it was a brilliant idea as they sat in the kitchen, having waited up to hear all about the night's events.

'Anything you can do like that, that doesn't really cost you anything, is always a good idea,' her dad had said. 'The word "free" goes a long way these days.'

'I'm so glad it went well,' her mum said through a yawn. 'It's nice to see you smiling again.' She headed to the washing machine and started pressing buttons.

'Is that a coloured wash by any chance, Mum?' Rose asked hopefully. 'I've had these jeans on all day. I managed to spill elderflower cordial down them and my apron and now they're all sticky.'

'Go and get them off and I'll put them in with mine and your dad's stuff.' Rose dashed upstairs, returning a few minutes later, dressed in pyjamas and holding her jeans and apron. 'How many times?' Her mum tutted and took the jeans. 'You always turn the clothes inside out.'

'Sorry, Mum.' Rose headed into the living room, switched on the TV and curled up on the sofa. Her mum and dad wished her goodnight as she flicked through the channels before settling on an episode of *Pride and Prejudice* starring Jennifer Ehle and the one and only Mr Darcy, Colin Firth.

Rose had seen the series so many times she'd actually lost count. She knew the scenes off by heart, but was still trans-fixed by the romance of Darcy and Elizabeth. The episode playing was the one in which Elizabeth has just discovered that Darcy wasn't quite the arrogant arsehole he'd appeared to be and that whatever he had done he had only the very best intentions at heart.

'But he didn't steal your business idea, did he?' Rose mut-tered at the TV, grabbing the box of chocolates her mum hid in her sewing box thinking that no one knew about them. She proceeded to shovel the entire top layer into her mouth – apart from the strawberry creams – and then sobbed into a cushion until she fell asleep.

She awoke a little while later, a chocolate wrapper stuck to her face, to Elizabeth and Darcy sharing their first kiss as they rode off in a carriage. She threw the cushion at the TV before turning everything off and climbing wearily up to bed.

'Rose!' She tried to ignore her mum's voice, but admitted defeat when Janet started shaking her.

'What's the matter?' She looked over at her bedside table for her phone, but her mum was holding it and was thrusting it under Rose's nose. 'Bloody hell, Mum. What time is it?' She took the phone and with bleary eyes saw it was six thirty in the morning.

'You need to watch your language, young lady.' Janet made that tutting sound again. 'Ever since you fell in with that boy.' She shook her head. 'Anyway, he's gone now so hopefully you'll stop with the swearing.'

'Yes, Mum.' Rose placed her phone next to her bed and lay back down on the pillow. 'Did you wake me up to tell me to stop swearing?'

'Of course not.'

'Well?' Rose asked. 'Why did you wake me up?'

'You left your phone downstairs last night,' she told her, 'and ate half my box of chocolates.' She wagged her finger at Rose. 'How did you know they were there?'

'Dad and I have known about your hiding place for the past fifteen years.' She laughed. 'We normally just take one or two so you won't notice, or we buy a new box and replace the ones we've eaten.'

'Well, that explains many conversations I've had with myself about eating too many chocolates.' She sat down on the bed. 'I'll have to find another hiding place now.'

'Sorry, Mum.' She hugged her. 'I'll get you a new box when I'm next at the shops.' She lay back down. 'Is that why you woke me up?'

'No, I don't think so . . .' Her mum thought for a second. 'It's gone clean out of my head.' Rose's phone pinged. 'That's it!' Janet picked up the phone and gave it back to Rose. 'You left your phone downstairs last night and it just pinged. I thought it might be important so I came and woke you up.'

Rose looked at her phone; there were no missed calls or notifications on the lock screen, so she knew the ping must have been heralding the arrival of a new email. She unlocked her phone and, sure enough, there were a couple of emails waiting for her. Two were spam but one . . .

'Daisy Carmichael?' Rose read out loud. 'Rings a bell.' She clicked on the email.

> Dear Rose,
>   Was wondering if Pedals was free on August 21st next year?
>   Daisy Carmichael

'Who is Daisy Carmichael?' Her mum was trying to peek over the screen to read the email.

'She was the youngest of those three sisters – you know the ones you saw practically fighting over me at Haggerston Hall? The older sister cancelled me for her wedding next year.' Rose clicked the reply button.

'They were horrid young girls – so undignified.' Her mum pulled a face. 'You don't need the business of that kind of people.'

'Actually, Mum, I need the business of every person I can get right now.' And although she'd had more than enough of spoilt children, warring siblings and overbearing fathers, she flicked open her diary and sent over an email to say, yes, she was free and would call to discuss further arrangements.

CHAPTER THIRTY

'Rose, could you pop into Weddington for me?' her dad called down the stairs later that day. 'The printer's run out of ink. I need to print the summer fete tickets and I've got a meeting at the church at four.'

'No problem, Dad.' She grabbed the car keys and drove the few miles into Weddington, parking in the Pig and Whistle car park as most people did and trying very hard not to remember the last time she had parked there. Had it really been only three weeks since she and James had their official first date?

She took the shortcut through the village green to the high street. Dog walkers were out in force this afternoon, and she nodded to familiar faces, stopping to stroke a rather enthusiastic English setter called Roni and a gorgeous greyhound called Olive.

It was just as she was nearing the edge of the green that she saw a familiar figure sitting on a bench, staring into space.

'Daisy?' Rose said. The woman turned at the sound of her

name, and it was obvious that she'd been crying. 'What on earth are you doing here?'

'Rose?' Tears started falling from Daisy's eyes again. 'Oh, Rose. It's all gone so terribly wrong.' Rose sat down on the bench next to her. 'I don't even know where to start. Everything was just perfect, but ... oh, it's just awful.' She started to sob.

'First of all,' Rose said in a soothing voice, 'calm down and tell me what's happened.'

'I'm sorry.' Daisy took a deep breath. 'I desperately need to find a wedding planner.'

'Have you tried Madison Michaels?' Rose suggested. 'She's local.' Rose might not like Madison, but Madison really was the only wedding planner she knew in this area, and Daisy was so upset.

'That stuck-up cow wouldn't know how to plan a wedding if it whacked her in the face with a "how to plan a wedding for dummies" book.' Daisy sniffled. 'No, I'm being mean. She's apparently too busy due to her new business venture.'

Rose raised her eyebrows. 'Please don't tell me you mean designing bridal gowns?'

'How did you know?' Daisy said. 'She made me believe it was all very hush-hush.'

'Let's just say I've seen one of her creations and I don't think M and M Bridal will be taking off anytime soon.' Rose shuddered at the memory of 'that dress'.

'The thing is, she *was* my wedding planner, but we've had a little change of plans and now she says she can't do it.' Daisy started crying again. 'I've just been to see her and now I'm sitting here wondering what on earth we're going to do.'

'So, what do you need?' Rose couldn't believe Madison could drop a client so easily. 'I'm not a wedding planner but I could put you in touch with a few people from Weddings of Weddington who could help?'

'Thank you.' The relief in Daisy's voice was clear. 'And of course, I really want to book you for my reception if you can still do it? I'm fuming with Petunia over what she did to you.'

'Water off a duck's back,' Rose lied. 'You warned me she'd change her mind.'

'It was only because of that new one she saw the other week – Cycles and Champagne is it?' Rose's heart froze. 'They promised her twin bikes and twin male servers, so of course Petunia almost bit their hands off.'

'When did she see them?' Rose was racking her brain. Geoffrey had said they'd launched the weekend that Tabby was in hospital, but she'd only seen the Blumes' bikes at Coombe Castle, and Petunia's and the other two cancellations had come through the week before. They must have launched at the wedding fayre Rose had missed. She'd just assumed they'd launched online or something. She tried not to think about the promise of twin male servers – unless Oliver and William were being roped in at the age of four, that could only mean James and Peter.

'They rang her up,' Daisy said. 'Invited her to come and see them at an event they were doing a couple of weeks back, I think it was.'

267

Rose wasn't sure she'd heard correctly. 'They rang her up?' she repeated.

'Yes,' Daisy confirmed. 'Said they'd found her number from the local list of upcoming weddings and would she be interested in a new business they were starting.'

Rose sighed. 'There isn't such a list. It would be totally against the GDPR rules, unless she'd signed up to some website or something?'

'Who knows with Petunia?' Daisy sounded annoyed. 'All I know is that Dad drove her off somewhere and she came back like the cat that got the cream.'

'Well, they're welcome to her,' Rose said bravely. So, not only had the Blumes stolen her idea, it now seemed that somehow they had managed to steal her clients as well. 'Do you want to pop over to the vicarage later and I can make some calls for you?' Maybe she'd be able to find out more about the Blumes if they continued to chat in person.

Daisy checked her watch. 'I could come now.'

'I've just got to run an errand for my dad and then I'll be home.' She gave Daisy the address, which Daisy tapped into Google Maps on her phone. 'See you in about an hour?' Daisy nodded and remained seated while Rose headed off. *At least she's stopped crying*, Rose thought.

'So, first of all, in your email you said the wedding is on August twenty-first?' Rose and Daisy were sitting in the dining room of the vicarage.

'June twenty-seventh or twenty-eighth,' Daisy said.

Rose thought back to Daisy's email. 'I thought it was August,' she said. 'So, it's not confirmed yet? Are you waiting to hear back from a few venues? June is such a popular month to get married. After all, didn't they sing about being a June bride in *Seven Brides for Seven Brothers*?' Rose loved that film; she watched it with her parents every Christmas.

'Never seen it,' Daisy said, and Rose couldn't help but feel a little disappointed. 'We just need to find something that's available.'

'That's not normally how weddings work.' Rose didn't know a lot but she knew this at least. 'You normally visit the venues you like most, find out when they're available and the costs, then choose one and pick a suitable date. You could always get married in a different month next year or even wait till the following year if your preferred venue is fully booked.'

'Oh, the wedding isn't next year.' Rose looked at Daisy. 'It's this week.'

Rose wasn't sure she had heard correctly. 'This week?' Daisy nodded. 'You can't organize a wedding in two days!'

'But we have to,' Daisy begged. 'My fiancé goes back to America in two weeks and straight into a six-month tour. He's in the navy, you see. They only told him this morning. We were originally getting married after Petunia in August next year, like I said in the email. Everything was booked and sorted. We've done all the paperwork, visited the minister, but we want to do it now, you know, just in case.' She burst into tears. 'Petunia has thrown an absolute tantrum and Dad

269

has totally taken her side and threatened to disown me. He says the eldest always gets married first, but I know that's an excuse. He just doesn't want me marrying an American.'

'It's just like *Pride and Prejudice* when Darcy defies his aunt to marry Lizzie.' Rose got up and put her arm round Daisy. 'Okay, it's a challenge, I won't lie, but I'm sure, with the help of the WOWs, we can get something sorted,' she said with a confidence she didn't feel. 'Can we at least push it to the following weekend though? Even that is cutting it fine, but it might give us a fighting chance.' Rose knew that the legalities of a marriage would be covered – people often changed dates – but arranging a whole wedding, reception and all, in such a short space of time was another thing. She kept her thoughts to herself though and she smiled at Daisy in what she hoped was a reassuring way.

Daisy seemed to perk up a little. 'I said to myself on the way over here that you'd be able to help me. I knew when I met you at Haggerston you were a kind soul. And yes, the following weekend would be fine, as long as it's before he leaves.'

'Don't count your chickens just yet,' Rose said, grabbing her notebook and pen. 'First things first: venue.' She started jotting down a list of things including dress, flowers, cake and food.

'Don't forget horse,' Daisy butted in as Rose paused for a second. 'I want to arrive on a horse.'

'We need to think simply,' Rose said. She needed to keep Daisy's feet on the ground; she'd already mentioned releasing doves and having circus entertainers. 'Remember, we've only got ten or eleven days.' Daisy looked downcast, and Rose relented, writing the word 'horse' on the list. 'I'll see what I can do,' she said. 'You do have your licence, don't you?'

Daisy nodded. 'Yes, sorted that ages ago.'

'And because Clive is American . . .' Rose trailed off. 'Back in a minute.' She shot out of the room and up the stairs to her dad's study. 'Are you and the church free next Saturday or Sunday for a wedding?'

Her dad looked up from his computer. 'I beg your pardon? Who on earth for?'

Rose explained the situation quickly and handed her dad the big church diary.

'It would mean so much to her, Dad,' she pleaded as he flicked to next week's dates.

'I could do late Saturday afternoon, I suppose, but what about the banns?'

Rose leapt up and kissed him. 'He's American and they've got their licence already, so I think I'm right in saying that they don't technically need to be read?' She could remember a similar wedding a few years ago. The groom had been local, but the bride was Swedish. 'If one of the couple isn't British, then the licence rules apply and the banns don't have to be read. That's right, isn't it?'

'It is indeed.' Her dad looked at her, clearly a little surprised by her knowledge. 'Shall I pop them in for five o'clock then?' Rose nodded and was down the stairs in a heartbeat, rushing past her mother, who was just opening the door to an elegantly dressed lady. Rose didn't recognize her; she must have been someone moving to the area or enquiring about the church.

'Good news,' she almost squealed as she sat back down in the dining room with Daisy. 'My dad will marry you here in the church.' Daisy really did squeal at this. 'That's the first hurdle sorted.' Rose ticked 'wedding venue' off the list. 'Now, on to the reception.'

After putting in calls to everywhere they could think of, it quickly became apparent that a reception venue was going to be much harder to pull off than the wedding venue.

'Honestly,' Daisy said, putting the phone down after her tenth refusal, 'if we can't have a reception, it isn't such a big deal. None of my family will come anyway, and all of Clive's family are in America. The main thing is that Clive and I are married.'

'I'm not giving up hope yet, but let's move on to the other bits, shall we?' Rose was formulating a plan to ask her parents if they could put a gazebo up in the garden, but she didn't want to share this with Daisy in case it didn't happen. 'Flowers,' she said instead, looking at her list. 'I'll call Val first. You head on home now and tell Clive the good news.' She handed Daisy a list of things she needed to do, one of which was getting a dress.

'Where will I get one at such short notice?' she cried out. 'We've only got five thousand pounds to pay for the whole thing. The dress I wanted was fifteen.'

'Two seconds.' Rose wrote down Alice Buttercup's number. 'Ring Alice, tell her I've sent you. Even if it's one on loan, I'm sure you'll find a wedding dress that you love.' Daisy's bottom lip started to stick out; Rose was getting the distinct impression that Daisy was used to getting everything she wanted. 'What's the ultimate goal here?' Rose said.

'That Clive and I are married.' Daisy cheered up at this, and repeated the statement to herself. 'I'll ring her as soon as I get home.' She hugged Rose. 'I'll let myself out. Thank you so much for everything! I'll ring you later, if that's okay, in case I can't find a dress?'

Once she'd gone Rose gave herself a few minutes to digest everything, then cursed herself for not having asked Daisy if she knew any more about Cycles and Champagne. She picked up her phone and rang Val, who unfortunately was already booked, but did say Rose could use the artificial bouquet she normally had in her window display if she was unable to acquire fresh flowers anywhere else.

Rose put the phone down and thought what her next step would be. Surely with all her contacts her mum would know someone able to help. Even if they could only make a simple posy, at least Daisy would have a fresh wedding bouquet on the day.

Taking her pen and pad, she walked into the kitchen.

'Mum . . .' she began, not realizing that Janet was talking to someone.

'Say hello, Rose,' her mum said, sounding insistent.

'Hello,' Rose said, still not looking up from her pad. 'Mum, do you know anyone who could make flowers for a wedding next week and isn't already fully booked?'

'Lovely to see you again, dear,' said a familiar voice, and Rose looked up.

'It's lovely to see you too . . .' She took in the expensively cut pale-blue tailored jacket and skirt, the grey hair that was neatly twisted into a soft bun at the nape of the neck and the face that belonged to none other than . . . 'Mrs Blume!'

CHAPTER THIRTY-ONE

'We do miss seeing you at the house,' Tabitha said. Rose was a little surprised by this, seeing as she'd only ever visited the house twice, albeit overnight on both occasions.

'Tabby was just telling me all about the holiday she's going on in November,' Janet said. Rose continued to study James's mum. Was this really the same frail old woman Rose had seen on her last visit to the Blume mansion?

'I'm off to Edinburgh for a few days on the train, and I've just popped in to ask your mum if she'd like to come with me.'

Janet looked at Rose. 'What do you think?'

'I think you should blood—er . . . blooming well go,' Rose said, correcting the swear word just in time. 'You've always wanted to see Edinburgh Castle, and Dad is always too busy to go. It would be nice for you.'

'I'll come then,' Rose's mum said, a huge smile creeping onto her face. Mrs Blume grinned too. 'Right, you were asking about flowers for a wedding?'

Rose explained the situation, telling them both that the

wedding was being held at the church, and she also slipped in her idea of holding a small reception in the vicarage garden.

'That's no problem at all; we can have the party here,' Janet said. Rose had known her mum would be instantly on board once she'd heard the story. She was such an old romantic. 'And you said you've phoned all the local florists?'

'Every single one, Mum.' Rose looked down in despair.

Mrs Blume looked up from her cup of tea; Rose noticed her mum had got the best china out. 'Can't James help?' Tabitha said.

'Erm . . . I don't know,' Rose stuttered, 'but I'm not really comfortable asking him, to be honest.'

'Why ever not?' Mrs Blume asked.

'You have heard what's happened?'

'Oh, of course I have.' Mrs Blume shook her head. 'Terrible business. Honestly, my poor boy. I've never known such a kind-hearted soul. He's always so willing to help others, and people take advantage of it. It was such a betrayal.' A phone pinged. Rose looked at hers but there was nothing. 'Oh, that's mine.' Mrs Blume pulled a brand-new iPhone out of her bag. 'Be a dear, Rose, would you look at what it says, please? I can't get the hang of this newfangled technology, but James insisted I have one, now I'm out and about on my own.'

'It's from James.' Despite herself, Rose's heart flipped at the sight of his name. 'He says he's waiting for you at the end of the drive.' *He's here.* He was outside the house and obviously too ashamed to come in.

'I don't know why he couldn't come to the door,' Tabitha said, climbing off the stool. She took her phone from Rose and placed it back in her bag. 'It's been lovely, Janet. I'll get that hotel and the train booked and ring you later.'

'What do you make of all that?' Rose's mum asked after Mrs Blume had left.

Rose shrugged. 'I honestly don't know. She's clearly been told some sob story that paints James as the victim. And what about her hair and clothes?'

'I almost didn't recognize her when she came to the door.' Her mum was busying herself with washing the cups. 'She said she'd had a revelation recently and made the decision to look after herself better – hence the clothes, hair and holiday.'

'I'm pleased about that,' Rose said honestly. 'She's such a nice lady. She deserves to be happy. How she ended up with such an overbearing husband, I'll never know.'

'For that exact reason.' Her mum carefully dried the two cups and placed them back on the Welsh dresser. 'She's too nice and she's allowed him to walk all over her. Now, don't get me wrong, I'm sure he was lovely to begin with, but men like Geoffrey Blume know exactly how to drag people down.'

'Apart from the uncle, I think all the Blume men are the same.' Speaking of Tony, Rose suddenly remembered their conversation. 'Actually, I bumped into him at the cash-and-carry the other day. He said he had something to tell me and asked if I could meet him for a drink.'

'You don't want anything to do with any of the men in that family,' her mum warned.

277

'It sounded important.' Rose ran upstairs to grab the card out of her jeans, searching her room to no avail. 'Oh no!' Her hand flew to her mouth as she remembered. She ran back down the stairs and stuck her head in the washing machine, which was now empty.

'I hung the washing out this morning,' Janet said. Rose shot out into the garden and yanked her dry jeans off the line.

'Oh, bloody hell,' she said, knowing her mum couldn't hear, as she pulled out a mass of mushed card, now unrecognizable.

'Was that important?' her mum asked, looking at the paper mush in Rose's hand as she walked back inside.

'It had Tony's number on it.' She threw it in the bin and folded her jeans.

'Surely they have their numbers on the website.'

Rose kissed her mum. 'Of course they do.' Grabbing her phone, she scrolled through Google. 'Only a main number and email I'm afraid.' She put her phone back down. 'And there's no way I'm ringing that. I don't know who'll pick it up.'

'What are you doing about the flowers for Daisy?' Janet asked, clearly trying to change the subject.

Rose sighed. 'We'll just have to use that artificial ones Val offered, won't we?'

Thankfully, Rose didn't have a wedding fayre booked this weekend, or the weekend after. In fact, most of the local fayres had already been and gone. There was just one left at the end of July, which was held in Weddington town hall, and then the season ended back where it began at Weddington Hall in September.

The majority of her bookings had now been confirmed with deposits and she was excited for her future, even if it wasn't going to involve James. She'd managed to squirrel away the profit she'd made from Ruth's party into her savings account, but she had a long way to go to replace all the money she'd withdrawn to set up Pedals in the first place. Even with all the bookings she'd taken, it still wasn't enough to live on if she ever decided to move out of her parents' house.

She'd managed to rope Megan into helping with Daisy's wedding, and was actually starting to enjoy the planning. On the Saturday afternoon, they both met Daisy at Buttercup Bridals to pick out her dress. Daisy had insisted Rose meet her there once she'd arranged the appointment.

'So, what are we looking for?' Alice said. Rose had briefly explained the situation to her when they arrived, and Alice had kindly said that Daisy could borrow one of the shop samples if she couldn't find one in her budget.

'I always fancied getting married in red and cream, you know,' Daisy said. Rose, Megan and Alice all looked at her in shock. 'What?' She laughed when she saw their faces. 'You were expecting me to be all traditional, weren't you?'

'To be honest,' Rose said, 'yes. The fact that you want a horse kind of pulled me in that direction.'

'I've got the perfect dress if you're arriving on horseback.'

Alice dashed off to the back room. Daisy looked so excited, Rose couldn't bear to dampen her joy by pointing out how very unlikely it was they'd be able to get horses for the wedding. 'It's ivory and red rather than cream,' she said as she appeared back on the shop floor with a huge bridal bag. 'Let's pop you into the changing room and see how it looks.'

Daisy practically ran behind the velvet curtain, unbuttoning her jeans before it was even closed. Rose and Megan exchanged knowing smiles as squeals of delight came from behind the curtain.

'I just have to have this dress!' Alice pulled back the curtain and Daisy stepped out.

The dress was mainly ivory, but with a deep red embellishment down the middle, which started in a small inverted v in the middle of the chest and gradually grew larger as it travelled down to the bottom of the skirt. This was mirrored on the back, which fell into a three-foot-long train. The bottom of the gown and the sweetheart neckline were both red, and the back was decorated with tiny red-cushioned buttons and the corset was tied with red ribbons.

'It's stunning,' Megan admitted, wiping a tear from her eye.

'Why are you crying?' Rose whispered as Daisy twirled in front of the mirror. 'You've only just met the girl.'

'It's just such a sad but beautiful story.' She dabbed at her eye again. 'And she just looks amazing in that dress.'

'I don't mean to burst your bubble,' Rose said, standing up. 'But you know you won't be getting the horse, don't you? We can't even get real flowers. We're slap bang in the middle of wedding season, so I'm sure all wedding horses in the area will have been booked up a long time ago.'

Daisy sighed. 'I know. But I still want this dress.'

Alice smiled. 'Then it's yours.'

'What do you mean it's mine?' Daisy looked at her. 'To borrow?'

'No, to keep.'

Daisy gasped. 'Oh, no.' She started to twist her body, looking for the tag. 'It's eighteen hundred pounds. I couldn't take that for free.'

'Honestly, you'd be doing me a favour.' Alice took Daisy's hands. 'This dress has been sitting in my storeroom for three years now. A lady bought it, paid for it and then about a week before the wedding completely changed her mind and went somewhere else. She never asked for a refund and she never came back for the dress.'

'I can't believe it.' Daisy started walking up and down the shop.

'Is that true?' Rose asked Alice, as Megan and Daisy started trying on tiaras near the front of the shop.

'Every single word of it,' Alice said, a knowing smile on her lips. 'Come on, Miss Daisy, let's get a few pins in. The other lady was a little larger than you.'

Once Alice had taken her measurements, Daisy bought a tiara and some jewellery, and left her purchases with Alice to be delivered to the vicarage on Friday along with the dress. Daisy bought some shoes as well, and wanted to leave them at the shop too, but Alice insisted she take them and wear them a few times to make sure they wouldn't hurt her feet on the day.

'Thank you so much for a lovely afternoon.' Daisy hugged the three women all at once before heading off.

'Right ... the horse?' Alice asked once Daisy had gone.

'She's desperate to arrive on horseback, but the only stables I know of are Lucy Greenfield's and there's absolutely no way any of hers are going to be available at such short notice,' Rose explained.

'She's getting married at your dad's church, isn't she?' Alice asked and Rose nodded. 'And getting ready with you at the vicarage?' She nodded again. Alice seemed to be mulling something over.

'She's had to leave home over all this.' Rose was still in shock that a family could be so cruel. 'Her dad hates the fact that she's marrying an American. Daisy had hoped he'd come to terms with it over time, but the eldest sister is outraged that she's daring to marry before her. Daisy and Clive are staying in a hotel, but Mum said she could come to us the night before the wedding. I don't know who's more excited about all of this: Mum or Daisy.'

'Your mum's just getting in practice for your big day,' Megan said, nudging Rose with her shoulder.

Rose raised her eyebrows. 'Like that's ever going to happen.'

'What's happened with you and James, then?' Alice asked. 'You seemed so loved-up at the fashion show, and he couldn't stop talking about you when he dropped the suit back to me.'

'It's an awfully long story.' Rose really wasn't in the mood to go over it again.

'I've got time.' Alice sat down on one of the chairs at the front of the shop and patted the one next to her. 'My next appointment isn't for half an hour. So, come on, tell Auntie Alice and let's see what we can do about it.'

Rose told her all about Cycles and Champagne and the kiss with Madison. It seemed to get slightly easier each time she told the story.

'So, you see, there isn't anything to be done about it.' Rose had managed not to cry. 'He lied to me about Madison and then to add insult to injury he stole my business idea.'

'Well, the business idea I can't help you with,' Alice said, squeezing Rose's hand reassuringly. 'But I think I can shed some light on him kissing Madison.'

'How can you?' Megan asked.

'Because I was there,' Alice said. 'And I saw the whole thing.'

CHAPTER THIRTY-TWO

'I was there too,' Megan said. 'I saw him kiss her.'

Alice shook her head. 'It was Peter. I don't think James had even arrived when you got there.'

Rose's brain was going into overdrive. 'She'd done her usual trick of moving business names around to ensure she was next to the Blumes' table,' Alice went on. 'The look of disappointment when she saw it was Tony and not James though . . .' She laughed as she remembered. 'She pulled out that hideous creation she'd designed and stood it in front of her stall. That's when Peter came in, but I don't think she knew it was Peter. I heard her call him James. He went to answer, but she never gave him a chance. She just grabbed him by the tie, pulled him in and kissed him.'

Rose still wasn't convinced. 'How do you know it wasn't James? They're identical twins.'

'Jesus, Rose.' Alice tapped her gently on the cheek as if trying to get her to see sense. 'I've been doing these fayres a lot longer than you. Peter has a much harsher-looking face than

James, and besides, the real reason I know it wasn't James was because a), he would have pulled away instantly and b), he came storming into the room two minutes later. Madison's face was a picture. Peter tried to kiss her again and got a right slap.'

'It still doesn't change the fact that James stole Rose's business idea,' Megan said, taking Rose's hand. 'Did you see the bikes outside?'

'No, I was inside the whole time. And I didn't see James again either,' she admitted.

'He was probably helping his dad steal all of Rose's clients,' Megan scoffed.

'It just doesn't seem like something he would do.' Alice sounded very certain of this. 'He's always seemed so nice on the few occasions I've spoken to him. Could you not talk to Tony about it? Everyone says how lovely he is.'

'I don't have his number,' Rose said quietly. She felt suddenly numb.

'I'll try and speak to Tony on Monday,' Alice told her. 'Take her home, Megan. Take her home and feed her chocolate and wine.'

Megan did just that, and by eight o'clock, Rose was feeling more than a little tipsy.

'So . . .' Rose poured herself another glass, spilling more than she caught. 'How was your date with Graham?'

'Which one?' Megan giggled. 'We've been on three.'

'You brazen hussy.' Rose glugged her wine. 'Whatever happened to playing hard to get?'

'I give advice.' Megan wagged a drunken finger in Rose's face. 'I don't take it.'

'Give me some then.' Rose tried to sit up straight in her chair. 'Give me some advice, oh wise one.' But Megan didn't answer, she'd fallen asleep, her head on the table, and when Rose prodded her, she let out a loud snore. 'Fat lot of good you are.' Rose tipped the last remaining dregs of wine into her glass. 'I'm going to phone him,' she said to herself. 'I'm going to phone him and ask him outright why he's been such an arsehole.' She flicked through her contacts, pressed James and held the phone to her ear. 'It's ringing,' she whispered to the sleeping Megan, and then shushed herself, giggling.

'Hello?' someone answered.

'Why are you such an arsehole?' she asked.

'Rose? Is that you, Rose? Are you drunk?'

And that was all she heard, for within seconds she too was face down on the table fast asleep. It was only when she woke up to tuts from her mum and a banging headache that she realized, thankfully, she'd actually phoned Josh.

The day of the wedding dawned bright and clear. It wasn't too hot – around twenty degrees, as Des, the local weatherman, had predicted – but it was dry; perfect for a wedding. Even though the ceremony wasn't until five, Daisy had been awake since six that morning, and was helping Rose's dad with the church and the flowers for the two weddings he had that day before hers.

'She is such a lovely girl,' John said when he came back to

the vicarage to shower and change. 'I really can't believe her father won't be there to give her away.'

'It's a sorry state of affairs, and that's for sure,' Janet said, offering her husband a cup of tea.

Declining the tea, John said, 'I've just got to pop out.' He grabbed the car keys and was gone, leaving Rose and Janet looking bewildered.

'What on earth was all that about?' Rose looked over to her mum.

'I have absolutely no idea. But he'd best not be long – the first wedding is at twelve.' They both looked up as there came a knock on the door. 'I wonder who that can be?' Janet said, looking at Rose – her not-very-subtle way of asking her daughter to answer the door.

'I'll go then.' Rose didn't have a problem answering the door, but ninety-nine per cent of the time, it was either for her mum or dad, and she had so much still to do for the wedding that she needed every spare second.

'Here comes the bride,' Megan said as Rose opened the door.

Megan walked into the hallway singing the bridal march and dragging a bewildered-looking Graham behind her. 'We've come to help,' she announced loudly. 'Graham has kindly volunteered to put up the gazebo.'

'Volunteered isn't the word I would have used,' he said, earning himself a smack from Megan. 'I'm only joking – anything to help. And I've brought my sweet cart. Thought we could set it up. I know Megan said there aren't really going to be many guests, but it still looks nice at a wedding and, well, me and Megan will be there and you and your parents of course.'

'Alice said she'd pop in for a couple of drinks too, after the shop closes.' Rose felt so sorry for Daisy, only having a handful of people at her reception, most of them virtual strangers, but at least she would be granted her wish of being married, having a first dance and cutting a cake. 'You should see the cake Natalie has made,' Rose said.

She ushered them into the dining room where a small but beautifully decorated two-tiered chocolate cake sat at the back of the table, out of the way of anyone who might walk past. The artificial bouquet, tiara and jewellery were also on the table, Daisy's dress was hanging up on the door and Fanny had sent some favours for the tables. Again, Rose had been in awe of everyone's kindness.

'Where is the bride anyway?' Megan asked as they walked through the kitchen into the back garden, saying hello to Rose's mum as they went.

'She's just gone upstairs to have a soak and a chill,' Rose said. 'I don't think she's slept all night, and she's been in the church with Dad since the early hours helping him put out the hymn books and order of service for the first wedding.'

'She must be so nervous.' Megan, Rose and Graham started to unwrap the large gazebo, which had been used for many a summer garden party in the Pedal household. 'It must be nerve-wracking enough for any bride, but without her parents and family and friends around, it must be doubly so.'

'Their mum died when Daisy was small.' Rose pulled out

the long metal poles while Graham started laying out the bases for them. 'I think that's why the dad has spoilt them so much. And I've never heard her mention friends at all. I mean, how can you not have friends?'

'Some people aren't as lucky as you and me, kid.' Megan placed an arm around Rose's shoulders and hugged her hard. 'Things like this make me realize just how fortunate we actually are.' She gave her a huge kiss on the cheek, exaggerating the noise from her lips. Turning back to the gazebo, she shouted at Graham, 'It doesn't go that way!' He was currently trying to slot the pole that was for the roof into the round base. 'Honestly, I don't know how he's managed all these years without me.' She sauntered over to him and grabbed the pole, pretending to hit him with it, but he grabbed it first and pulled Megan towards him to kiss her.

'There's someone here,' Rose's mum called from the back door, 'asking for you, Rose.'

Rose headed back into the house to find Tony Blume holding the most glorious wedding bouquet Rose had ever seen. 'But how?' was all she managed to say.

'Alice popped in to see me in the shop.' He handed her the flowers and Rose just stared at them; not only were they beautiful in every way, but their colours matched the red and ivory of Daisy's gown. 'She told me you'd lost my number, so I thought I'd deliver these myself.' He handed her a box. 'There's a buttonhole for the groom as well, and I've got a couple of table decorations in the van.'

'Daisy will be thrilled.' Rose held the blooms to her

nose as Tony popped out to the van, and she was suddenly swept back to the times James had brought her flowers when she was ill. 'They smell of summer gardens and promises,' she murmured.

'Beg pardon?' Tony had come back into the hallway carrying a box of matching table decorations. 'We weren't sure how many you needed. Or even if you needed any at all. Alice just said you needed flowers for a wedding and explained Daisy's situation.'

'We're just having a very small party in the garden after the ceremony,' Rose explained. 'Wait, what do you mean by we?'

'Is that for me?' Rose hadn't heard Daisy come down the stairs. She was now standing in the hallway, dressed in Rose's dressing gown, her hair wrapped in a towel and a smile on her face as wide as the Cheshire cat's.

Tony nodded. 'Freshly made this morning. Alice sent us a picture of the dress, so we knew exactly what colours to use.' There was that 'we' word again, and an 'us' thrown in for good measure.

Rose was in a daze; surely Geoffrey Blume wouldn't have allowed such a grand gesture. Yet, who else could it have been? He was the boss, and there was no way Tony could have made these and snuck them out of the shop without Geoffrey knowing.

'Can I hold them?' Daisy said, pulling Rose away from her thoughts.

Rose handed her the bouquet. 'Sorry, I was miles away.'

It was the perfect size for Daisy: wide enough that it covered her hands when clasped together, with a little bit of length to elongate the body.

'I really don't know what to say.' Daisy started to cry. 'Everyone has been so wonderful and kind. I'm just lost for words.'

'We love a good wedding round here.' Tony handed her a tissue. Did all the Blumes carry tissues with them at all times? Maybe it was working with flowers on a daily basis, or perhaps there were just a lot of tears, both happy and sad, in the flower industry.

'Is your mum in the kitchen?' Daisy asked. 'Has she seen this?' Rose shook her head and Daisy sped down the hallway calling, 'Mrs Pedal?'

'I'd best be off then.' Tony gave her the other box. 'We'll have that chat another day. I can see you're busy.' He stepped out onto the drive.

'What did you mean by we?' she asked again.

'What do you think I meant?' he replied, looking her straight in the eye. 'Just call him, Rose. Speak to him.'

'You mean James?'

'Of course I mean James.' He closed the back door of his van and walked around to the driver's side. 'Give him a chance to explain. I think you'll be pleasantly surprised.'

It was only as the van drove away that Rose realized it wasn't green and gold. It was just a hire van from the local rental firm. *Why on earth isn't he driving a Blume's van?*

CHAPTER THIRTY-THREE

Rose didn't have time to think any more about what Tony had said, or the mystery of the blank hire van. Her dad had returned and was rushing around, grabbing a quick sandwich that he would eat on his walk to the church. Rose had seen the first wedding guests of the day starting to arrive. She could only see the cars from the vicarage, because there was a long line of oak trees separating the church from the house, but from the looks of it, the groom had arrived in a blue Porsche and the guests in an old-fashioned double-decker bus. At ten to twelve, the bridal car had driven by: a vintage Rolls-Royce with lilac ribbons on the handles and tied to the silver lady at the front.

Megan and Janet were doing their best to get Daisy to eat and drink something, while Rose and Graham put the finishing touches to the mini marquee. What would normally have been the top table for the bride and groom's families was now for the cake and one of the floral decorations. Next to this was the Pedals and Prosecco trailer, only because there hadn't been quite enough room for the bike as well. Glasses and bottles of Prosecco and soft drinks were ready to be served.

Rather than ordering any catering, Daisy and Clive had decided on a fish and chip supper delivered from the local chip shop. Apparently, they had first met in Whitby when a seagull had pinched Daisy's fish as she walked along the harbour. Clive had been visiting family and offered to buy her another, which they ate together before continuing along the harbour with an ice cream.

'He proposed to me there as well,' Daisy had told Rose and her parents the night before. 'We'd climbed the steps to St Mary's Church and were looking out over the sea when he got down on one knee and proposed.'

'How long had you been together?' John had asked.

'About four hours,' Daisy had said, laughing at the shocked looks on their faces. 'He said he knew I was the one for him the minute he saw my face after the gull stole my fish. He said I looked so sad that he just wanted to protect me for ever.'

'I think that's the best we can do,' Graham said now, standing next to Rose at the entrance and surveying their hard work.

'Looks fab,' Megan said from behind them. 'We've all done a cracking job and I think we should go into wedding and party planning next.'

'I have to say, I've enjoyed helping Daisy much more than I thought I would.' Rose had been thinking about this very thing the night before. 'Has Daisy eaten anything?'

'Two tiny bites of a sandwich and a banana.' Megan

looked at her watch. 'We need to start thinking about her hair and make-up.'

'What time is it?' Rose had been so busy inside the tent, she'd completely lost track.

'Three-thirty.'

'Oh shit!' Rose ran out of the tent, leaving Megan and Graham behind.

'I'm so sorry, Dad,' she panted as she arrived at the church, out of breath and red-faced. 'I said I'd help you clear up and get ready for Daisy. I just got side-tracked with everything else.'

'That's okay,' John said. 'I've had some help.'

'Where shall I put the confetti, sir?' Rose froze at the sound of James's voice behind her. Her heart beat faster, her stomach flipped and her mouth went dry.

'I'll take it from you.' John winked at Rose, walked past her and took a dustbin bag full of the previous wedding's confetti from James, before making some excuse about new candles and disappearing into the vestry.

Rose turned to face James, unprepared for how her body was reacting at the sight of him. He looked cool and calm, not dressed in his usual green today but a deep blue suit that reminded Rose of the ocean.

'Why are you here?' she said.

'I heard there was a wedding that needed flowers.' He walked up the aisle towards her.

'But your uncle brought those earlier.' He continued to come closer, slowly and surely. Rose was rooted to the spot.

'These ones are for the church.' He was just a step away from her now; she could smell his aftershave and her senses were overwhelmed by his closeness. 'It wasn't my fault, Rose.'

'I can't talk about that now.' She gathered all her strength and stepped past him, not ready for the bolt of electricity that shot up her arm as he tenderly reached for her hand.

'Later?' His eyes searched hers, looking so intently she felt he could see her very soul.

'Later.' She reluctantly let go of his hand.

'Promise?'

'Promise,' she said, and smiled at him before rushing out of the church and running straight back to the house to find Megan.

'The nerve of the man!' It took all of Graham's and Rose's strength to stop Megan from running out of the house and into the church.

'I don't think we know the full story,' Rose said, trying to calm her down. 'Remember what Alice told us, and then the things Tony and Mrs Blume have said. They're people who have known him for years.'

'Exactly,' Megan said, while Graham tentatively let go of her arms. 'You can't trust a word they say. Of course they're going to stick up for him.'

'So, you're saying,' Rose said, 'that if I'd done something really wrong to someone, you'd lie for me, would you?'

'Yes!' Megan was very matter-of-fact. 'To everyone else, but I'd damn well give you a right rollicking.'

'Maybe that's what they've done then,' Graham suggested. 'Maybe his mum and uncle have been covering for him to save face, but have read him the riot act and so he's trying to make amends.' Rose knew that Megan had already filled Graham in on the ins and outs of Rose and James's situation. 'Let's face it, he didn't have to do the bouquet, and he certainly didn't have to come and decorate the church. Seems like he's going to a lot of trouble to impress a certain someone, and I can guarantee you that it's not Daisy.'

'I honestly don't know what to think anymore.' Rose was in absolute turmoil. She wanted to believe James was innocent of all charges, but how could she when all the evidence seemed to be stacked against him?

'Maybe if you just listened to him,' Graham suggested, receiving a scathing look from Megan.

'I suppose I owe him that.' It was Rose's turn for a look from Megan.

'Owe him?' she screeched. 'You don't owe him a bloody thing. He stole your idea and broke your bloody heart. Okay, he may not have kissed another woman right under your nose, but that's beside the point. He played you for a fool, Rose Pedal.'

'But like Graham said' ... Rose suddenly felt the need to try and defend him; he had looked so honest and true just now in the church ... 'he's spent all that money and time on the flowers for a complete stranger's wedding. He didn't have to do any of that.'

'Fetch me my bag would you, Graham.' Graham did as

he was told, bringing in Megan's bag from the living room. 'I'll write the arsehole a cheque, and then it won't have cost him a thing.' She pulled out a chequebook and pen. 'Five hundred should more than cover it.'

Rose shook her head. 'That won't work.'

'And why the hell not?' She had already written 'James Blume' on the payee line.

'Because that chequebook is for the Abbey National, and they don't even exist anymore.' She picked up the cheque-book. 'I knew it!' She laughed. 'This was your nan's – we used to play shops with it. What else have you got in here?' Rose pulled out an old credit card in Megan's nan's name from 2005 and some Monopoly money. 'Why is all this still in here?'

Megan took everything back from Rose and shoved it in her bag. 'I found it a few weeks ago. I put in there to show you and then completely forgot about it.' Rose wasn't sure she quite believed her; Megan had always been a hoarder.

Rose's mum came into the room, looking slightly pan-icked. 'Do you lot know what time it is? Daisy's upstairs waiting to get her dress on.'

'Jeez, we forgot about Daisy!' Megan and Rose rushed up the stairs, leaving Graham with Rose's mum as she tutted after them.

'I'll grab the dress, you get the tiara.' Rose looked at the time on the grandfather clock in the hall. 'Bloody hell, Megan, we've got less than an hour.'

'It's not as if the vicar is going to turn us away if we're late, is it?' Megan laughed.

'We don't want to leave Clive on his own in the church, though, do we?' She had hold of the bridal bag. 'Bugger! Who's going to give her away?'

'I could ask Graham?' Rose nodded and headed upstairs while Megan went back into the kitchen.

'I thought you'd forgotten about me.' Daisy was sitting in the guest room at the dressing table. Her hair was already curled, falling in soft waves around her face and waiting for the tiara to be pinned. Megan had applied a small amount of make-up to give Daisy a natural and even complexion.

'As if we would.' Rose came up behind her and placed her hands on her shoulders, meeting her eyes in the mirror. 'You look beautiful.'

'Graham says he'll play father of the bride,' Megan said from the doorway. Daisy looked confused. 'Rose thought you needed someone to walk you down the aisle.'

Daisy stood up. 'That's so kind of him.'

'Right then, lady, time to get you into this dress.' Rose unzipped the bag; the dress was even more beautiful than the three of them remembered. Within ten minutes, Daisy was zipped in, the decorative buttons hiding the zip, the red ribbons pulled and tied in a neat bow.

Daisy did a little twirl. 'How do I look?'

'Like a princess.' Megan's eyes started to glisten with tears again.

'What's that noise?' Rose headed over to the window. 'Is that hooves?'

Daisy screamed and dashed out of the room, down the

stairs and out of the front door, Megan and Rose close behind. Standing in the driveway was a black mare in full tack with a side saddle. In front of her stood Millie and Alice.

'Did somebody need a ride to the church?' Millie asked, smiling. 'Alice told me there was a bride in need of a horse. This is my mare, Maggie, and she'll be more than happy to carry you to church.'

Daisy was almost jumping up and down with joy.

'Shoes?' Rose's mum came rushing out onto the drive with Daisy's shoes dangling from her hand. 'And are you two getting changed or wearing jeans to the wedding?' Rose and Megan ran back inside, leaving Daisy to acquaint herself with Maggie, while Alice took a few photos on her camera.

Rose and Megan had decided to surprise Daisy with matching dresses. They'd found red cocktail dresses in the sale at Next, and Alice had made them an ivory sash each, which tied in a bow and flowed down the back of the dress. She'd even added some embroidery to the necklines to match the detail on Daisy's dress.

Megan looked out of the window at the sound of a car approaching followed by brief silence and then doors slamming.

'Who the bloody hell is that?' she asked, and Rose looked out of the window too. A silver Daimler was now parked up on the drive. 'Don't tell me someone's hired her a car as well. She's only got to go next door.'

'Well, that there is Daisy's middle sister, so I'm presuming the gentleman dressed in the suit is her father. No sign of the eldest sister though.' Both girls took a last look in the mirror. 'Isn't this turning into an interesting day?'

CHAPTER THIRTY-FOUR

Rose and Megan watched from the window as the man they assumed was Mr Carmichael walked over to Daisy with his arms open wide. She ran into them, and they were sure they heard an apology from her father.

'Now, isn't that a lovely sight.' Rose and Megan turned round, a little startled; they hadn't noticed Rose's dad behind them.

'Did you have something to do with this?' Rose asked, remembering his sudden errand this morning.

'I may have done.' He looked like the cat that got the cream. 'I asked Daisy where she lived and paid Mr Carmichael a visit.'

'What did you say?' Megan asked.

'I just told him that nothing and nobody would stop me from giving my daughter away on her wedding day.' He looked over at Rose as he spoke. 'And I also told him that God saw and judged everything and asked did he really want this on his conscience for the rest of his life.'

'How did you know he was religious?' Rose couldn't believe this had worked; from the little she knew of Daisy's dad, she didn't think he'd be scared of God.

'Trust me,' her dad said, 'in full vicar mode and dress, even the most hardened atheist would rather not anger God, just in case.'

'Well, it definitely did the trick.' They watched as Alice started taking photos of Daisy and her father and then the other sister too. 'Looks like Petunia isn't bothered about God's wrath though?'

Her dad shook his head. 'I've never met such a spoilt child in all my life.'

'John?' Rose's mum called up the stairs. 'You need to be at the church. The groom has arrived. And will someone please explain to me why James bloody Blume was just at my front door telling me this?'

Megan, Rose and her dad all looked at each other before bursting out laughing.

'And on that note,' John straightened his collar, 'let's get this wedding started.'

Alice had been right, of course: the dress was perfect for arriving by horse, and it was clear she and Millie had been in cahoots. The skirt and train fell into soft folds over Maggie's side and the red and ivory contrasted perfectly against the horse's black coat.

Daisy's sister Lily was in tears as they walked behind the bride on the way to the church. 'She looks like a queen,' she said. 'I can't believe I was going to miss my baby sister getting married.'

'But you didn't,' Rose reassured her. 'And that's all that matters.'

Rose's dad was waiting by the church door, resplendent in his wedding ceremony regalia, and he welcomed everyone formally into the church, before leaving Daisy and her father in the apex that led to the aisle.

The rest of the party said goodbye to Millie and Maggie, issuing invitations to join them back at the vicarage afterwards, and then walked up the aisle. Rose gasped at the simple but stylish decorations that James had provided. Tall jars with red and cream roses stood at the end of alternate pews, and a beautiful spray had been placed on the altar table between the two huge wax candles in gold candlesticks.

'Is that why James Blume was here?' her mum whispered as they shuffled along the first pew, giving a thumbs up to Clive, who looked extremely nervous standing there on his own.

'You can call him James, you know,' Rose whispered back. 'And yes, he provided these flowers as well as the bouquet and the other things Tony brought this morning.'

'I bet that was Tabby's doing.' Janet sat down at the end of the pew with Rose, and Megan and Graham filed in next to them. Alice and Lily sat on the opposite side; it wouldn't have made sense to have the traditional bride side and groom side, seeing as everyone here was here for Daisy. 'Doesn't he look handsome in his uniform?' Forever one to change a subject was Janet, but Rose had to agree that the full dress uniform, complete with white gloves and white cap, suited him. He also had two gold stripes around his sleeve and wore two medals above his left breast.

The opening bars of the wedding march began, played by the organist, Mr Young, and everyone stood up to watch Daisy walk serenely down the aisle on her father's arm.

'Dearly beloved . . .' John began, and all were seated.

'I've never seen a more beautiful bride,' Janet said for approximately the twentieth time since Daisy had arrived in the tent on Clive's arm, Graham introducing them as Lieutenant and Mrs Miller. Right now, Clive and Daisy were taking to the makeshift dance floor for their first dance to 'I Will Always Love You' by Whitney Houston, played through Megan's phone linked up to a Bluetooth speaker. Rose's parents joined them as the next slow song came on, followed by Megan and Graham, and then Mr Carmichael and Lily.

'Might I have this dance?' Alice bowed in front of Rose, who knelt into a deep curtsy.

'Actually, I was wondering if I might have the pleasure.' Rose turned to find herself looking up into James's green eyes, and nodded, her voice lost. Oh, how she wished he didn't have such an effect on her.

He held his hand out to her, and she took it, feeling that familiar skip of her heart as he pulled her in close against his chest. It felt so good to be in his arms again, and for just the length of the song, she forgot about everything but that feeling. He sang along with Ed Sheeran's 'Thinking Out Loud'; he had a sweet voice. When Ed sang about falling in love and kissing under the stars, James whispered the words directly into her ear.

They didn't even notice when the song ended, and they continued swaying together until Dua Lipa's 'New Rules' blasted out of the speaker.

'Join me outside?' He had such an earnest look on his face, and she couldn't refuse him. They stepped out of the tent; had Rose looked back, she would have seen Graham physically restraining Megan, and Rose's dad talking her mum out of going after them.

'Thank you again for the flowers,' Rose said. It was getting dark now and the solar fairy lights that lit the garden were sparkling in the dusk. 'You really didn't have to.'

'When Mum told me, I wanted to help.' They were walking down the path towards the bottom of the garden, towards the kissing seat that sat under a metal arch of honeysuckle.

'Speaking of your mum ...' They were walking so close together that their hands brushed with each step, but neither made the move to actually hold hands. 'What brought about the wonderful change in her? She was so ...' Rose searched for the right word. She wanted to say dowdy, but that sounded too rude.

'Downtrodden?' James suggested. 'Under the thumb? As though she'd lost all sense of herself?' Rose nodded slightly in agreement. 'She finally saw the light, and I think you and your mum had something to do with that.'

'Me?' Rose asked as she sat down on one side of the bench, James sitting on the other. As was the nature of a kissing seat, they were each facing in opposite directions, but they needed only to turn their heads to the right to face each other. 'How did I help?'

'Indirectly.' He took her hand. 'You helped me to see a great many things that were wrong in my life, one of them being my father, and through that my mother saw it too.' He took the other hand in his. 'It really wasn't my fault,' he pleaded. 'I asked them to stop but they wouldn't.'

'Start from the beginning,' she said, dropping his hands as the spell broke. 'Explain to me what happened.'

'Hand on heart, I never ever stole your idea. Like I said back in Blume's that day, I just thought it would make a beautiful arrangement, and it did. I wanted to show you, but when my father saw it and I told him about your business, he went all secretive and took the bike from me saying it was rubbish.' He looked down at his hands. 'Never one for a compliment my father.'

'Well, it wasn't rubbish from what I could see.' Rose had to admit the display had looked amazing.

'I didn't think any more of it until a couple of nights before the fayre at Coombe Castle.' He swallowed hard as if the memory was painful for him. 'Grandpa had asked me to fetch him his pipe from the conservatory, and that's when I saw my father and Peter acting strangely. They were out by the old stable block. That thing's not been used since Grandma was a young girl. I took Grandpa his pipe then sneaked back out into the garden and hid behind one of the open stable doors. That was when I saw them.'

'Saw what?' Rose was entranced by the story.

'The bikes.' He spoke matter-of-factly. 'A whole bloody fleet of them, even the one I'd spent days making into a floral arrangement had been stripped bare and painted green and gold.'

'What did you do?' Rose knew exactly what she would have done.

'I didn't know what to do to start with,' he said. 'I sort of just sat there, knelt on the floor. It was only when I heard Peter saying how they'd well and truly pulled the wool over your eyes that I saw red. I leapt up and started shouting. Next thing I knew, everyone else in the house was there too, including Mum. My grandpa went mad at them, told them they'd sully the Blume name, that they didn't need to go around stealing young girls' ideas.'

'I'd like to have seen that.' Rose smiled wryly. 'The great Geoffrey Blume brought down a peg.'

'You haven't heard the rest of it.' Rose wasn't sure she wanted to. 'It turns out, the time Dad took the wrong van home "accidentally" wasn't an accident at all. He and Peter spent the day poring over the bike and trailer to see how it all worked. And I'm really sorry about this, but . . .'

'What?' She didn't like the sound of that 'but'.

'You'd left your diary in the basket,' he admitted. 'So Peter took down the names and numbers of your bookings and tried to steal your clients.'

'He succeeded,' Rose told him. 'I lost three over a weekend.'

'I'm so sorry.' He hung his head. 'They'd officially launched Cycles and Champagne the previous weekend when Mum was in hospital; that's why he never came to visit her.'

'So, if that happened before Coombe Castle . . .' Rose was trying to think. 'How come all the bikes were still at the fayre? Did your grandpa change his mind?'

'Grandpa didn't know. I didn't know.'

'How could you not have known?' This was where his highly believable story started to fall apart. 'You live under the same roof, albeit a rather large one, but still the same roof.'

'Not anymore.' Rose shot him a look. 'I moved out that night.'

CHAPTER THIRTY-FIVE

'What do you mean you moved out?' Was this the reason he'd seemed a little distant that Friday evening in the florist?

'I was so angry at them both, not only for taking your idea but for all the hurt it would cause you. I knew I had to tell you, but I just didn't know how.' He took her hands again, and this time she let him. 'I went and stayed in the flat above the shop and then when you turned up, I decided that I'd tell you that night over dinner.'

'But you were on the website. Your dad promised twin servers to Daisy's sister.' Rose shook her head in despair, trying to sort out the truth from the lies.

'Website?' He looked at her with a blank expression. 'I don't know anything about a website.'

'Have you got your phone?' He nodded and pulled it out of his pocket. 'Google Cycles and Champagne.' There was no way he was wriggling out of this one.

'You did actually look at this, didn't you?'

She shook her head. 'Not properly – I couldn't bear to.' He laughed suddenly, throwing Rose completely off guard. 'I really don't think any of this is in the least bit funny.'

'It's just that' – he handed her the phone – 'I'd have been pretty upset if you'd looked at it and thought that was me.'

She stared at the photo. 'It's Peter with your dad. But you said your Grandpa banned Peter from the business after the window incident.'

'Yes, he did, from the floristry business. I suppose they thought they were being clever by starting a new one.' He took back the phone. 'And as for the twin server thing, I think my father thought I'd eventually come round like the good little son I've always been.'

'How did the fayre at Coombe still happen then?' This was the final question.

'Grandpa told my father and Peter to get rid of the bikes and stop all the nonsense, but obviously they didn't listen.' He was searching her face. 'When I saw you in the car park at Coombe, I'd only just arrived. The traffic had been a nightmare from the shop, so I was running late. I didn't know anything about the bikes, and I discovered later that Uncle Tony didn't either.'

'So, they just went behind everyone's backs?' Knowing the Blume family as she did, Rose found this astounding. Didn't everyone know what everyone else was doing?

'They did indeed.' He nodded. 'When I saw you, I thought you were still mad at me about the previous evening, I didn't have a clue that the bikes were there and that Megan had thought she'd seen me with Madison.' He reached a hand up against her cheek. 'I'd never have done that to you.'

'I should have known that.' She rested her head into his palm. 'My dad said it didn't sound like you, but I was so hurt and angry. I've not had much luck in the past with boyfriends, and then with all the other things that happened and Peter turning up at my launch party . . .'

'He probably came to spy on you, see what trouble he could cause.' He started to caress her cheek with his thumb. 'I came that day too, but I didn't have the courage to speak to you.'

'I saw you from the big wheel.' At least now she knew she hadn't been dreaming of him that night.

'Grandpa threatened to disown Peter and my father if they didn't immediately cease everything they were doing, and you'll never guess what my mum did.' James looked shocked even as he was recounting it.

'What?' Rose was enjoying the feeling of his touch on her skin again; how could she have got him so wrong?

'Uncle Tony said she slapped him, threw her wedding ring at him and moved in with her sister.' He was beaming with pride. 'I'd love to have seen that. We've all allowed my father far too much power over us all, but now it's all changed, and I've never been happier.' He placed his other hand on her other cheek. 'Well, that's a little lie, there was a time when I was happier.' He bridged the gap between them in an instant and she felt the soft touch of his lips on hers. 'I'm so sorry, Rose. Can you forgive me?'

She kissed him back. 'From the looks of it, there isn't anything to forgive. I should be the one apologizing to you.' He kissed her again, wrapping his hands into her hair and holding her so tightly she could feel the wood of the arm in her stomach. 'Ouch.' She laughed, and they broke away.

'Will you meet me tomorrow in Weddington?' he asked as she rubbed her stomach. 'There's something I want to show you.'

'Of course I will.' She kissed him again. 'It's a date.'

'It's a promise.'

It took more than a little convincing to get Rose's mum and Megan to believe that James was entirely innocent. Luckily, James had told the story to Rose's father in the church before-hand, so at least she had a little help.

'All this could have been avoided if you'd told me he had a twin brother, you know.' Megan still wasn't happy about the situation. 'And don't you go jumping into his knickers as soon as he looks at you with those green eyes and perfect smile.'

'Well, I'm not convinced, but whatever makes you happy,' Rose's mum said, tutting as she made tea for everyone. The wedding party was over, and Clive and Daisy had left for the hotel, Alice hitching a ride back with Millie, who had turned up with her husband later on once she'd returned Maggie to her stable in Tointon.

'Give him a second chance, eh, love?' Rose's dad came up behind Janet and hugged her. 'After all, you gave me one.' He kissed her neck and Rose's mum swiped at him playfully.

He grabbed her by the hand and twirled her around the kitchen humming 'I Could Have Danced All Night' from *My Fair Lady*.

'Get off with you now, John,' she protested, but he continued to spin her round, while she giggled like a teenager.

'If you hadn't agreed to meet me that second time after I'd stood you up on our first date,' he said, 'goodness knows where we'd be now.'

'You'd be married to Trinny Shaw. That's who you stood me up for in the first place.'

'And I regretted it as soon as I did.' He kissed her hand. 'My ladybug.' She giggled again and Rose, Megan and Graham made a tactful withdrawal to the living room.

'They are so cute,' Megan squealed. 'I hope we'll be like them after twenty-five years of marriage.' She pinched Graham's cheek and he just shook his head.

'I promise that on our twenty-fifth anniversary I will spin you around the kitchen and sing songs from *My Fair Lady* to you.' He rolled his eyes at Rose, who laughed. Most men would have done a runner at Megan's words, but Graham took it all in his stride and even joined in when Megan started singing as well.

'I am off to bed, lovebirds.' Rose retreated to the doorway. 'Feel free to pull out the sofa bed if you want to crash, or let yourselves out. Just tell Mum and Dad what you're doing.'

'Night, Rose,' they said in unison as she headed up the stairs. About half an hour later, she heard a car and guessed they'd called an Uber.

She didn't even know why she'd come to bed; sleep was the last thing on her mind, but she wanted some alone time to process everything she had discovered that day.

She went over and over the past few weeks in her mind, all the things she'd accused James of; she'd been wrong the whole time. She felt slightly ashamed, if she was honest with herself. But then, if this hadn't happened, maybe he'd never have stood up to his father. Maybe his mother might never have realized she could be happier without Geoffrey Blume.

Reaching for her phone she googled Cycles and Champagne, wanting to see once more how Megan and Josh had managed to mistake James for Peter. She supposed it was an easy mistake to make if you didn't know them, but to her, James's face was so much softer and kinder than Peter's.

'That's odd.' She searched again after Google came back with zero results, and then again for a second and third time. She typed in 'Blume's' and was startled to see just a picture of Geoffrey and Tony. She read the 'about us' section and found a small mention about James leaving the business to start his own adventure. *What on earth does that mean?* she wondered.

The next day she found out.

'Where am I meeting you?' She was standing in the car park of the Pig and Whistle, speaking into her phone.

'Just walk down the high street, you'll see me.' Rose said goodbye and started walking. She went past Tucker's butchers and Brown's greengrocers, past the bookshop and tea rooms, and then she saw it.

Most of the shops on the high street had originally been houses. Some were bigger than others, some had moved into two or even three frontages, but here at the end was what used to be Val's old florist shop before she semi-retired and started to work from home.

It was still set up exactly as it would have been a century ago. There were fresh flowers on display in the large bay window, and a modern shop door had been put in. The outer walls had been given a fresh lick of paint, and the old Flower Shop sign had been replaced with a new one that read 'Petals'. A stunning window box was hanging outside the upstairs window, and was that – Rose did a double take – Mrs Blume leaning out of the window watering it?

'Hello, Rose love.' Rose still wasn't used to Tabitha's immense transformation, and although it was more than welcome, it was still a little disconcerting. 'You found us okay then?' She bobbed her head back inside.

'You're here.' James stepped out onto the street; dressed in a white shirt and jeans, he looked younger and far more relaxed than she had ever seen him. 'What do you think?'

'Is this yours?' *What a stupid question*, she said to herself.

'Yep,' he said with pride. 'Only renting it at the moment, but who knows in the future.' He grabbed her hand and she felt suddenly shy in his company. 'Let me show you inside.' She followed him through the door. 'Of course, it's not a patch on Blume's, but it's mine.'

Rose looked at the highly polished wooden shelves and at the neatly stacked buckets of flowers in stands. There was a book open on the counter. She stepped over and started flicking through; it was full of the most imaginative and modern-looking arrangements she'd ever seen.

'I think it's the loveliest shop in Weddington.' She turned to him. 'Are these your creations?'

'I'm trying something a little different.' He took hold of her hand. 'I have you to thank, Rose, for giving me the courage to step out of my family's shadow and stand on my own two feet. You made me see how much I relied on them for everything, even food and clothes. I'd already been thinking about setting up on my own and had enquired about leasing Val's old place, but I was still unsure until that debacle with my father and the bikes.'

'Speaking of which, their website has disappeared,' she told him.

'I told Grandpa and he made them take it down straight-away.' He pulled her behind the counter and into a hallway that led to a small lounge, which in turn led to the kitchen. 'Can you keep an eye on the shop a minute please, Mum?' he asked Mrs Blume as she emerged from upstairs.

'It would be my pleasure.' She walked out into the shop, grabbing an apron from a hook on the wall.

'How is your mum?' Rose asked as she followed James out through the back door and into a surprisingly large garden. 'Is she coping okay? It's rather a sudden change, isn't it?

'She has her moments,' he said sadly. 'In fact, this morning she was so disorientated it took an hour just to coax her out of bed. I had to ring my Auntie Jan, her sister, to come over. I think being with Jan really helps her, and the time she spends with your mum. It reminds her of how she used to be. Don't get me wrong, my father wasn't always like this, apparently he was a model husband and father, but mum had a bit of a health scare when we were about ten and although she physically recovered, it really affected her mental health.'

'So, your dad took advantage of her weakness?' Surely, that was even worse, Rose thought.

'No, not like that,' he replied quickly. 'We've chatted a bit since all this happened. Mum said she sank into depression and Dad tried the soft route, the not-caring route and then the harsh route, but nothing seemed to work. She said she couldn't find the strength to bring herself out of it, until that day she saw your mum. Something clicked, she said, like a light had been switched on.'

'But why did your dad treat her so appallingly?' Rose was disgusted that a husband could treat his wife that way. 'She was ill.'

'He said he didn't really understand it. None of us did, if I'm honest with you.' Rose noticed how sad he looked. 'He didn't know how to deal with it. He felt like he'd lost his wife and threw himself into the business instead.'

'It's all change in the Blume household then.' They were at the bottom of the garden now, next to a large brick shed.

'I'll say,' he agreed. 'My father and Uncle Tony are now joint partners in Blume's with fifty per cent each. Elizabeth has decided to do teacher training and, well, Peter is Peter, but he's a little softer than he used to be.'

'I'm glad some good came out of it in the end.' She watched as he unlocked the door.

'I've got a present for you.' Rose frowned, unsure what sort of present you would keep in a shed. 'In you go.' He flicked on a light switch and ushered her inside. 'These are for you.'

Rose gasped; before her stood the bikes that had once belonged to Cycles and Champagne, but now they were painted in pink and brown with Pedals and Prosecco signs, all except one that had been transformed back into the floral arrangement James had been so proud of.

'I can't take these.' Rose was flabbergasted. 'Besides, there's only me and Megan.'

'For the moment,' he said. 'But you'll get bigger and bigger, I know you will.' He pointed to the one covered in flowers. 'Do you mind if I place this outside the shop? I want to change it every week with the different seasonal flowers. I think it's really eye-catching.'

'I don't know what to say,' Rose said. James looked so excited, like a little boy on Christmas morning.

'Then don't say anything. Just kiss me.' And kiss him she did.

EPILOGUE

It was Halloween, and the first frost of the season. Rose was wrapped up against the chill as she prepared three bikes for what was to be the biggest event she'd attended yet. Pedals had been booked to serve the drinks at Weddington's annual Halloween ball, and so the bikes needed spooking up. Both Megan and James would be helping her that evening, each serving from their own bikes, and Graham would be around to lend a hand as well.

'I'm going to bloody smack you in a minute,' Rose said to Megan, who was fidgeting instead of helping to wrap pumpkin tinsel around the bike frames.

'It's just so exciting.' She was stepping from one foot to the other, almost as if she needed a wee.

'You've been saying that all day.' Rose sighed. 'It's getting rather annoying.'

'James wants to ask you something,' she blurted out and then slapped her hand across her mouth. 'I'm sorry, I wasn't meant to say anything.'

'What do you mean he wants to ask me something?' Rose stepped in front of her. 'And why do you know about it?'

'He wanted my advice.' She removed her hand just long enough to speak those four words. 'That's all I'm saying.' She covered her mouth with her hand once more.

'Tell me.' Megan shook her head. 'Megan? Tell me.'

'Shan't.' She sounded like she had when they were eight and Megan had tried to keep a secret from Rose about her getting roller skates for a Christmas present.

'Well, if you won't tell me, will you at least help me with these bikes?'

Megan nodded and grabbed the ghost lights Rose had purchased. 'It's just so romantic.' Rose shot Megan a look. 'I'll shut up about it now.' She threaded the ghost lights along the handlebars. 'How's my amazing wedding planning idea going?'

'Brilliant.' Rose was glad of the subject change; she knew a lost cause when she saw one. 'I've had lots of interest. Daisy has spread the word, and even Petunia has come back begging with her tail between her legs. I've almost managed to get my savings account back to where it was.' She had confided in Megan about her financial situation a few days after Daisy's wedding and together they'd hatched a new business idea that would run alongside and complement Pedals and Prosecco. 'And Josh and Hannah are setting up Pedals and Prosecco over in America – they said the brides are going mad for it over there.'

'That's amazing! And I told you wedding planning was a

good idea. A few more bookings and I'll be able to tell my boss where to shove his job.' Megan wagged a finger at her. 'If bloody Madison Michaels can do it then you can.'

'Speaking of Madison Michaels ...' Rose leaned in as if the gossip needed to be whispered. 'Natalie told me she's moving away.'

'Really?' Megan was intrigued.

'Yep,' Rose said, thoroughly enjoying herself. 'Natalie said she took great pleasure in delivering the new WOW brochure to her with the information about the new wedding planner service. She apparently took one look at it and ripped it into tiny pieces. Then Natalie topped it off by telling her how happy James and I are.'

'Well, I'd love to have seen her face.' Megan flicked the switch for the lights and each ghost face glowed yellow from the eyes and mouth. 'Wish I could see your face later too.' She shot a hand to cover her mouth. 'Sorry.'

A few hours later, Rose was sitting next to James as he drove them through Weddington.

'We haven't got time for this, James.' She was panicking; although they'd already dropped the bikes off at the venue, they still had to get dressed up and do their make-up. And if truth were told, she didn't want to know what it was James had to ask her. It could only be one thing and even though they'd grown close and spent virtually every day together over the past few months, marriage was completely different. Of course, she'd fantasized about marrying him, even practised writing 'Rose Blume', the very name James had found so funny on their first meeting, but she was thinking a few years down the line yet. Surely Megan had it wrong.

'It won't take long.' He pulled over in a part of Weddington that Rose rarely visited. It was a much newer than the old high street, and the only stores were bridal shops, suit hires and – Rose's heart stopped – jewellers. 'Here we are.'

They were outside one of the older jewellery shops called Thompson and Son. Rose knew it well; it was where her parents and many of Tointon's residents had bought their engagement and wedding rings from.

'Why are we here?' Her mouth went dry. She loved him – she had admitted that to herself and to him many weeks before – but marriage? At twenty-three?

'I've got something to ask you.' He switched off the engine and turned to face her.

'But it can wait surely.' She looked at her watch and started faffing about in her seat. 'I mean, there's no rush, we're perfectly happy as we are, aren't we?'

'Rose!' He took hold of her hand. 'Will you sit still for five minutes?' She did as she was told, her mind racing with possible ways to say no without hurting his feelings. 'Now, you know I love you. I've loved you from the first moment we met, the moment you stood up to me. No one had ever stood up to me like that and I found that I rather liked it. I love being with you, spending time with you. I even quite like arguing with you, and I especially like making up with you.' She smiled at this, remembering their first argument,

which had led to their very first time making love. 'I want
to spend my whole life with you, and so I've been thinking.' He reached into his pocket. 'Rose Pedal.' He paused.
'Will you—'

'I can't,' she blurted out before he had time to finish. 'Oh
God, James, I can't.' He looked sad and confused. 'I love you
with all my heart, and one day I can see us getting married,
but we've only been together a few months and—'

He put a finger on her lips and laughed. 'I wasn't asking
you to marry me.'

She sighed in relief. 'Thank God for that.'

He feigned heartbreak. 'I'm hurt.'

'You know what I mean.' She shook her head at him. 'I
want to enjoy just being us. Now your mum's so much better
and going out more, we can start spending more nights alone
together in the shop.'

'Well, that's what I wanted to ask you about.' He reached
into his pocket again and handed her a small golden envelope. 'Don't open it yet, just hear me out.' Now she was
intrigued; there definitely wasn't a ring inside. In fact, she
couldn't really feel anything, just a piece of card. Perhaps it
was an invitation to something? 'You are doing so well, and
my business has taken off so quickly I've had to employ staff,
so I was thinking of expanding.'

'That's a brilliant idea.' Rose clapped her hands together,
and it was then that she noticed the 'sold' sign above the shop
next to the jewellers, and realized that it was empty. 'Here?
You're setting up here?'

He nodded. 'Mum is looking to buy the shop on the high street from Val. She and Auntie Jan are going to turn it into a coffee shop, a place where people can come and chat or just sit and not be alone. She says it's really helped her, talking to all the people that come into the shop.' Rose watched his face light up as he talked about his mum.

'I think that's a fabulous idea,' Rose said with a smile. 'She is such a natural with the customers. What has your dad said?' Rose was still a little dubious about Geoffrey Blume. She'd only seen him the once since the debacle of Cycles and Champagne. He'd offered her a stilted apology under the watchful eye of his father, but according to James he had been trying extremely hard with him and his mother.

'He's giving her the money.' Rose raised her eyebrows in surprise. 'Least he can do really. He turned up at the shop last night and took the pair of us out for dinner. He even paid.'

'I'm glad he's trying,' she said honestly.

'It's early days yet, and he's got a fair few years to make up for. Let's face it, I'm never going to have the relationship you have with your dad, but you never know, maybe one day.' He shrugged. 'Anyway, do you want to look around?' He jangled some keys in front of her.

She got out of the van – the new one he'd just purchased the previous week to replace the one he'd been renting – and followed him to the door. 'Now before we go in . . . I want to ask you something.' This time she stood in front of him in silence, waiting, but James said nothing.

'Come on, James, I'm freezing to death out here.' Not

expecting to spend any part of this evening outside, she'd left her coat at home, and the early evening was beginning to grow cold.

'Open the envelope.'

She did as he asked and pulled out one of her business cards.

'What's this?' she asked holding it out towards him. 'Oh, are these new ones with the new business on?'

'Sort of,' he said, pushing it back towards her. 'Look again.'

'Oh!' This time she examined the card properly. Although it was her colours and what appeared to be her business name written in gold, on closer inspection it read Petals and Prosecco, listing the proprietors' names as James Blume and Rose Pedal.

'Will you be my business partner?' When she looked away from the card, she realized that he had gotten down on one knee and was holding a key out towards her. She knelt down beside him, took the key out of his hand and kissed him with all the love she could put into one kiss.

'I will.'

ACKNOWLEDGEMENTS

Although this is not my first published novel, it certainly feels that way. I have been on such a steep learning curve since September and cannot thank the team at Books and the City enough.

To Anna, whose faith in the idea of this story gave me the courage to write it. I just wish she was as good at picking lottery numbers.

To Kim, thank you for all of your advice and numerous chats. You truly are an inspiration.

To the Chick Lit and Prosecco Facebook group. A wonderful group full of incredibly supportive people who always have your back.

I am extremely lucky to have strong women as role models in my life. My ninety-seven-year-old grandmother who continues to cook and clean every day and care for my aunt with special needs. And my mother who cares for them both and up until a few years ago cared for my father as he fought dementia. Although neither of them will go down in the history books, they are truly inspirational and remarkable women.

My wonderful dad, who never knew that I became a published author but I know he's up there in heaven, telling everyone he meets how proud he is of me.

Being a mother is a truly amazing and terrifying thing. My children are almost independent and following their dreams in their chosen career paths. I wish them long and happy lives.

Not many people meet their future husbands at their christening but at the age of four months, this is what happened to me. Of course neither of us knew it then, but I love that we have such a story to share.

Friendship means the world to me, like it does to Rose and Megan. I'm still friends with three girls I went to school with; two of them I've known for forty years. We've shared love and heartbreak, happiness and grief, and there's very rarely a day when I don't speak to them.

Thank you to the RNA for organising one-to-one sessions and to Rhea Kurien, Becky Slorach and Hannah Bond, whose feedback gave me the faith and courage I needed to enter the open submission day at Simon & Schuster. Can I also say thank you to Radhika Sonagra, who wrote the best rejection email ever.

My incredibly patient editor, Alice, who has taught me so much in these past few months, but I'm still rubbish at getting a plot out of my head and on to a piece of paper. For this, I apologise.

And last but by no means least, to the absolute powerhouse that is Sara-Jade Virtue. Who saw something in this story when it was just a few chapters long and incredibly still liked it when it was finished. I'm still pinching myself to check that it is real.

Dear Reader, I hope that you have enjoyed the story of Rose and James as much as I enjoyed writing it.

Until we meet again.
Florence xx